Murder in Bloom

Also by Rosie Sandler

Murder in Bloom

Rosie Sandler

embla
books

First published in Great Britain in 2025 by

embla books

Bonnier Books UK Limited
HYLO, 5th Floor, 103-105 Bunhill Row, London, EC1Y 8LZ
Owned by Bonnier Books
Sveavägen 56, Stockholm, Sweden

A CIP catalogue record for this book is available from the British Library.

ISBN: 9781471416378

This book is typeset using Atomik ePublisher.

Printed and bound in Great Britain by Clays Ltd, Elcograf S.p.A.

Embla Books is an imprint of Bonnier Books UK.
www.bonnierbooks.co.uk

MIX
Paper | Supporting
responsible forestry
FSC
www.fsc.org
FSC® C018072

For my family.

Cast list

The Garden Designers

Steph: human companion to our canine hero, Mouse.

Anil Ahmad: an internationally sought-after garden designer, specialising in commercial commissions. Trained at Writtle College at the same time as Toby Butcher.

Delilah Deville: in her mid-twenties, she is the youngest competitor and something of a rising star.

Koko Yamada: known for her expertise in British wildflowers, Koko is looking for a change of career and location.

Toby Butcher: forty-something booming TV presenter of *Force of Nature*, a garden transformation show. Married to Sarah Cartwright.

The Others

Addie Adebayo: front-of-house manager at the National Trust property of Coleton Fishacre, she is spearheading the flower show.

Gertrude Jones: fifty-two-year-old tattooed and enthusiastic volunteer at the flower show, she is shortly to begin training as a garden designer.

Mike: in his thirties. Under-gardener at Coleton Fishacre, he is helping out with the builds and other jobs during the competition.

Sarah Cartwright: producer of Sonny's TV show. Filming the build progress and behind-the-scenes interactions around the show gardens. Married to Toby Butcher.

Sonny Carden: fluffy-pink-haired celebrity garden show presenter and garden designer. Mentor and one of three judges for the competition.

Extras

Chaplin: Toby and Sarah's Miniature Schnauzer. Takes his duties seriously.
The Judges: Frank O'Connor and Gillie Goudge.
The Police: Detective Sergeant (DS) Jasmine Bhatti; Detective Constable (DC) Rob Bridges.
The Volunteers: Alex and Jay, a pair of young non-binary volunteers.

1

My beloved dog Mouse is fast asleep on the passenger seat of the van, his legs twitching. I'm sure the dream rabbits he's chasing are easier prey than those he encounters on our daily runs. With a sigh of relief, I pull the van into a shady space at the service station and turn off the engine. After taking a long swig from my water bottle, I rub my stiff shoulders and stretch my cramping fingers. We're on our way from Derbyshire to Devon and the roads are busy, making progress slow. It's only early June but the whole country is suffering a heatwave. Even with the windows open, the van is as hot as the inside of a Cornish pasty.

I'm intending to climb out and wake Mouse for a drink and a walk in the shade, but my hand has other ideas. Instead of reaching for the door handle, it picks up the envelope that's sitting unopened on the dashboard.

I stare down at the insignificant-looking rectangle in my lap. This is the first solid object I've received from my birth mother since she gave me up for adoption as a baby. I take a few calming breaths, steeling myself to open it. I can't work out why I'm so nervous.

At last, I slide a shaky forefinger under the flap and manoeuvre until the glued triangle comes unstuck.

Inside, I find a sheet of blue writing paper, folded around a photograph. I read the short note first, which is written in black ink, in neat lines of curly script:

Dear Steph,

I am so glad we've found each other. I can't wait to see you again! In my head, you are still the baby girl with the big grin and the mop of curly hair, and it is hard for me to imagine you all grown up, however many times I look at that photograph of you on your website!

By the way, thank you for sending me the link to your website. I keep gazing at all of the beautiful spaces you have created. You are very talented.

I thought you might like to have this photograph of us together, when you were little.

Only a couple of weeks now before we don't have to make do with photographs, but can see one another in the flesh! I can't wait!

With love,

Verity Joseph, your birth mum x

I pick up the photograph. It shows a young woman with Afro hair, light brown skin, a neat shirt dress and a big smile as she holds a baby up to the camera.

There must be a mistake. Surely this woman can't be my biological mother? Pulling down the visor, I stare at my own reflection: dark eyes and dark curls, contrasting with pale skin.

Turning my attention back to the photograph, I study the baby in the woman's arms. And, as I stare at that baby, any doubt I have that the woman in the photograph could be my birth mother vanishes. This child, with her light skin, dark curls and surprised baby eyes, is identical to the little girl in the photographs Mum has of me at home.

I let out a slow breath, trying to process what this discovery means for my identity. After thirty-two years of believing myself to be white, I am no longer sure. My mum and dad only told me I had an African great-grandparent on my father's side. Were they misinformed?

I snap a picture on my phone and send it to my brother Danny with the message:

This is Verity with me as a baby.

Mouse stirs and I fold the note back around the photograph, slipping them inside the envelope and returning it to the dashboard.

'Hey, sleepy boy,' I say to Mouse. 'Do you fancy a walk?'

He's immediately wide awake. Laughing, I grab his lead and climb down from the van, walking around to let him out. I pour some water into his bowl on the ground, and he laps it up in seconds, before tugging on his lead to tell me he's ready to go, Mr Rabbit, his favourite toy, held gently in his big jaws.

The service station is set in large, wooded grounds, where he's able to stretch his long legs as we pick up our pace and go from jogging to running, matching our strides, our breath rhythmical in the welcome shade. It occurs to me, not for the first time, that family is not just the person who birthed you or the people who raised you. It's also this: a companion who matches your strides, who understands your moods and who offers you nothing but love.

2

A couple of hours later, we're finally pulling in at the gates of Coleton Fishacre.

'Look, Mouse, it's the sea!' I say. He regards me with a questioning face, and I realise we're going to have to spend time on the beach before he starts to recognise the word 'sea'.

The National Trust property was built in the 1920s for the wealthy D'Oyly Carte family. The grey stone house hunkers down in the valley, as if seeking shade from the blazing sun.

I pull up the battered old van in the car park and turn off the engine. After letting Mouse down from the passenger seat, I give the vehicle's warm bonnet a pat. It's done us proud once again. Fishing out a cap with a wide brim and pulling it down firmly over my thick curls, I take Mouse through to the gardens, but stop abruptly at the sight before me, of a spectacular, fully grown tulip tree. Part of the magnolia family and even more dramatic than its relatives, the large, cup-shape flowers of *Liriodendron tulipifera* boast curious, greenish-yellow petals with an internal flush of sunset orange. Poor Mouse has to nudge me out of my reverie.

'Sorry, boy. Come on, we'll do a short walk now, and maybe we can go for a longer one later, before dark.'

He offers me an approving rumble in his throat as we begin to stroll through the thirty-acre gardens. Birds are singing and fluttering in the many trees and a squirrel runs across the path ahead of us. Mouse is in his element, letting out whines and barks to show his excitement.

The garden itself is stunning. Beside the house, swathes of the purple ice plant, *Lampranthus spectabilis*, drape themselves over the lower terrace walls like carpets laid out to dry. The purple theme continues with masses of the giant globes of *Allium cristophii* punctuating the flower beds almost everywhere I look.

We follow a path along the far side of the house and up through trees, until we reach a spot known as Scout Point according to the Coleton Fishacre website. Here, I take in a sharp breath at the vista before us, of curving sea and a series of black rocks grouped like a tiny island, called Blackstone Rocks. Even Mouse pauses, making tiny yaps of excitement at the water spread out below, as if talking to Mr Rabbit, whom he's placed at his feet.

'That's the sea,' I tell him. He looks up at me and gives a single bark before picking up his toy and turning both their gazes to the view.

After half an hour, I take us back to the van to fetch Mouse's bed before heading to the house. There are now a couple of other vehicles in the car park, including a gleaming white Volvo XC60 and a well-tended vintage Mini in racing green.

We cross the circular paved courtyard to where the house stands, and I note that the building offers more than a nod to its Arts and Crafts influence. Built from stone quarried from its own grounds, it both forms a part of its landscape and blends almost seamlessly into it. I open the wooden front door and we step into a deliciously cool interior. Here, we find a tall, tanned white man in his thirties with a name badge, a clipboard and a neat, dark beard. He immediately crouches to greet Mouse and I see that his forearms are lean and muscled.

'Hello! Who's this, then?' His voice is deep, with a strong Devonian accent.

Mouse promptly licks his hand.

'This is Mouse,' I say.

'Well, hello, Mouse. Aren't you a gorgeous boy?' Mouse rumbles his assent and presents himself for stroking.

Accustomed to being the less interesting member of our partnership, I leave them to bond for a few minutes, and take a walk along the corridor that leads from the hall, admiring the honeycomb ceiling lights, carpet runner with zebra-stripe edging over polished floorboards and ceramic vases on the sills of the large, square windows. At last, the man stands up and runs a hand over his already ruffled brown hair.

'Sorry about that! I'm a sucker for a friendly dog. Anyway, welcome to Coleton Fishacre. I'm Mike Lassiter, one of the under-gardeners. I'm here to meet and greet, to give Addie a bit of extra time to prepare.' He has a pleasant, open face and dark brown eyes with crinkles at the corners.

'No worries,' I say, smiling at him. 'I'm Steph Williams. I'm here for the garden design competition.'

'Excellent!' He ticks off my name on his clipboard.

'Remind me,' I say, 'Addie is . . . ?'

'Oh, sorry! Adwoa Adebayo is our wonderful front-of-house manager here at Coleton Fishacre.' There's no sarcasm in Mike's tone, so I take it she really does score highly with her staff. 'She deals with everything to do with visitor experience, though her second-in-command has taken over the day-to-day for the foreseeable, so that Addie can focus on the flower show and competition.'

He hands me a square of folded paper bearing the National Trust logo alongside an Art Deco floral design. 'Here's your map of the house and grounds. Now, let's see . . .' He consults his clipboard. 'Ah! You're in the bedroom which was once the dressing room of Rupert D'Oyly Carte!' He grins. 'You've got great views of the garden from there. Turn right at the top of the stairs, then it's the first door on your left. Would you like me to show you?'

'No, that's all right, thanks. I'm sure we'll find it.'

He nods. 'Well, I'm here if you need me. Oh! And we're all meeting around six, for pre-dinner drinks in the Saloon. It's this room right here.' He points to a partially open door, opposite the stairs and next to the front door. I catch a glimpse of more polished floorboards and cream rugs. I accept the proffered key and take Mouse up to inspect our lodgings.

At the top of the cream-carpeted staircase, I take in the view to my left, where a long corridor boasts a curved ceiling reminiscent of a cave or chapel. This house is fascinating. Following Mike's directions, I turn right and twist the doorknob on the limed oak door immediately on my left, leading Mouse inside.

I like the idea of staying in the room that was once frequented by Rupert D'Oyly Carte, whose renowned theatre company produced Gilbert and Sullivan's operettas. Although the room is modest – a single bed with a wooden headboard and matching wardrobe and drawers – the curved lines of the furniture are beautiful in their craftsmanship and simplicity, allowing the natural shading of the wood to come to the fore.

I place Mouse's bed in a cool corner, along with his blanket and Mr Rabbit, and pause for a moment at the mullioned windows. Mike wasn't overselling this view, which extends over the stunning gardens to the hills beyond. I could stand here for a long time, but I need to get on.

Turning my attention back to the room, I see I have a washbasin with a splashback made from small, rectangular glass tiles in a striking shade of aqua, plus a little curtain underneath the basin, concealing its plinth. I remember reading that all of the bedrooms are outfitted with these washbasins and tiles, made to the same specifications as those in the luxurious Savoy Hotel, also owned by the D'Oyly Cartes. The entire house is about pared-down luxury: the best quality, without flounces or frills, to illuminate the clean lines of the building and its contents.

While Mouse sniffs his way around the space that will be our quarters for the next week and a half, I make a couple more trips to the van. Bedding and towels are provided, so I don't have a lot to bring in.

Once I've stowed my clothes in the drawers and wardrobe, I set out food and water for Mouse and have a wash at the basin, keen to remove all trace of the sticky journey before my pre-dinner appointment with my hosts and the other garden designers.

Out of more than three hundred entrants, six of us have been selected for the garden design challenge, and I'm eager to meet my fellow competitors. I check my reflection in the mirror above the basin. My curls are escaping their ponytail, so I remove the elastic and shake them loose. They spring out, as if delighted to be freed from their constraints. I'm in a white t-shirt and jeans, but I figure this is a gardening convention, so everyone's bound to be casually dressed.

My phone rings with a video call and I perch on the edge of my bed to answer as soon as I see it's Danny.

'Wow, so your birth mum is maybe mixed heritage,' says my brother. 'Does that change anything?'

'I'm not sure. I'm still processing,' I tell him.

'I'm not surprised. It's a lot. I don't understand why Mum and Dad didn't tell you from the start.'

'What? You think they knew?'

It's his turn to pause. At last, he says, 'I guess *maybe* not.' He sounds unconvinced. 'Have you spoken to them?' he asks. 'About this, I mean.'

'Not yet. I've not really had a chance.'

We chat for a few more minutes, mainly about my four nieces and nephews. Although Danny and his wife Karen love being parents and are doing a brilliant job, I frequently feel a guilty gratitude that I have only Mouse to care for. At last, I check my watch.

'I'd better go,' I tell him. 'I'm due downstairs for the introductions.'

'Ooh, enjoy. Just one thing before you go . . .'

'Yeah?'

'Can you try to keep everyone alive this time?'

I roll my eyes and he starts laughing. 'Going now,' I tell him, and hang up.

Leaving Mouse to nap in his bed, I walk downstairs, taking in the view from each window along the way. These include the tulip tree and the sea, all framed by a blue sky without a cloud in sight.

Mike is waiting in the hall. I wonder if he's been there the whole time. He passes me a name badge with a crocodile clip, which I attach to the neck of my t-shirt. Gesturing towards the open door behind him, he says, 'Go on in and find the others.'

Stepping inside the Saloon, I discover it's far bigger than I'd thought from my earlier glimpse. Stretching away from me, it houses four sofas, several armchairs and even a piano, each in its own island of space. The room clearly projects out from the house like a promontory, because light floods in through the mullioned windows to the left and right as well as at the far end.

There are four people already present, standing in a group, holding drinks. A black woman of around forty breaks off as I enter, coming towards me with a warm smile. Of medium height, curvy, and in a houndstooth skirt suit teamed with an Ankara-print headscarf, she conveys chic individuality.

'Hello! Welcome,' she says, with an extended hand. 'I'm Addie Adebayo, the manager here at Coleton Fishacre.' Her voice is rich and deep, like the voice-over for a chocolate advert.

I tell her my name and she smiles and nods, turning to the other people present. 'Right, everyone, this is Steph Williams, queen of the garden restoration.' She turns back to me. 'We're excited to see what you come up with when you're creating a garden from scratch.' I don't point out that I had to submit my design plan when I entered the flower show. She gestures towards a tall, broad-shouldered white man wearing a Hawaiian shirt in a fuchsia pink that matches his flushed cheeks. I'd guess he's in his late thirties or early forties. From his slightly glazed expression, I also deduce that he's drunk.

'This is Toby Butcher. You'll recognise him from TV.' I don't, but I keep quiet on the matter, as I can google him later. Toby seems to have taken charge of drinks. He holds up a wine bottle in each hand, and I smile and point to the red, which he promptly pours into a glass and passes over to me.

I nod my thanks as Addie waves a hand towards a woman who looks vaguely familiar. Willowy, with a short, sharp bob that ends at pronounced cheekbones, she's very tall – at least two inches above my own five foot ten. Her long, lean frame in a cream linen shorts suit has the elegance of a catwalk model.

Addie says, 'This is Koko Yamada.'

'Oh!' I say with enthusiasm. 'I thought you looked familiar. I saw your photo at Fairview in Norfolk. Your wildflower meadows are amazing. They've taken so well.'

Koko smiles. At first glance, I had thought her close to my age, but now I recall an interview I read that stated she was in her fifties. This tallies with the air she has of self-assurance.

'Thank you so much!' she says. 'The first year was, in fact, something of a disappointment. None of the field poppies germinated. They can be such tricky customers.' Her English, though fluent, is quite formal. She beams. 'But yes, it all came together in the long run. We can have a proper talk later.'

'I'd love that.'

Addie smiles and says, 'It sounds like you're forming connections already.' She glances around again. 'Now, who's next?'

At that moment, another woman steps into the room. She's small, with pastel-pink hair as fluffy as dandelion seeds haloing her lined, tanned face. The knees of her bright pink dungarees are caked in soil. My heart does a little skip of joy. I never expected to get so close to Sonny Carden, celebrity gardener and garden designer. I used to watch her every week on *Gardeners' World*, and I have all of her books. Now in her late seventies, she puts her decades of experience into every garden she creates, making her a force to be reckoned with in the gardening world.

Sonny glances around at the assembled party. 'Well, don't stop talking on my account!' she says, in her strong, West Country accent, and there's a ripple of laughter. Then Koko and a man I've yet to meet both advance on her and start talking at the same time, eager to claim her attention. Although I'm dying to meet Sonny, I'm suddenly shy: I've never met one of my heroes before. I notice that Toby is also holding back. I wonder if he's starstruck, like me. Sonny holds up a hand, laughing.

'I'm going to be around quite a bit over the next few days, so we'll have plenty of time to get to know each other – starting tomorrow, when I'm looking forward to going over all of your designs.'

I exchange a look with Toby: this is news to us.

Sonny catches my eye and grins. 'Oh, you didn't know that? Well, I'll be checking in on your progress over the first three days of your build time.'

Addie chips in, 'That's right. You'll have the benefit of Sonny's guidance from tomorrow, Saturday, until close of play on Monday.'

I realise I'm grinning with excitement.

'So,' continues Sonny, 'we'll have a chance to look at how your gardens are starting to come together, and discuss any snags you might hit. The other judges will be doing a walk-through as well, to see *what you're up to.*' She wiggles her eyebrows suggestively and we laugh again, like daft schoolkids. Glancing around, though, I notice Toby Butcher has his arms folded and is standing po-faced as a judge at a bad comedy festival. I, in contrast, can't believe I'm going to spend time with Sonny Carden. This is the opportunity of a lifetime.

She walks to stand beside Addie, who addresses the gathering: 'I can see our celebrity judge needs no introduction. Though she might need a bit of protection from her fans!' We laugh again and Addie continues, 'We're obviously thrilled that Sonny has agreed to mentor you for this competition. I know you're all accomplished garden designers, but Sonny has won five golds at Chelsea, so advice from her is worth its weight in ... er ... gold.' We all groan at the pun.

There's a knock on the open door, and Mike steps inside.

'Sorry for interrupting.' He walks over to Addie and speaks to her in a low voice. She glances at the clock on the wall, then turns to us all.

'Right, everyone, apparently two of your fellow competitors have been delayed.' She nods to her colleague. 'Thanks, Mike.' He leaves with his clipboard, and Addie addresses us again: 'So, where were we with our introductions?' She looks at me. 'Steph, did I introduce you to Seb?' I shake my head. 'Aha. Well, this is Seb Burroughs. You may know him from his regular contributions to various newspapers.'

I nod. 'Hiya,' I say to him. 'Great to meet you.'

'You, too,' he says in a Birmingham accent. He's around six foot three, with blond hair and grey-blue eyes. I file him under 'thirties-ish white man' before remembering that my own categorisation may have changed from, 'early-thirties white woman' to ... what, 'mixed race'?

Bringing myself back to the moment, I take in Seb's lean frame, square shoulders and sinewy arms. Although we've never met, I know him by reputation. The journalism is just a side hustle: he writes about the garden design and build work he carries out for his clients, all of whom seem to possess enormous grounds. He must be raking it in. I wonder why he would need the win of a competition like this one.

I sip my wine and scan my companions. I hadn't realised I'd be in such illustrious company. Although my garden renovations blog has gained a fair amount of traction – and some media attention – over the past year or so, I am a long way from acquiring celebrity status in the gardening world.

'Right,' says Addie, 'everyone's got their drinks, so I think we'll go out to the Loggia and have our dinner.'

We follow her out of the Saloon, where she turns right and leads us through a dining room and on to a covered terrace, where a long table has been set for us. I stop for a moment, taking in the setting.

'Lovely, isn't it?' says Addie. 'The Loggia was where the D'Oyly Cartes had most of their meals.'

'It's breathtaking,' I say. 'In fact, this whole place is amazing. Do you think anyone would mind if I moved in?'

Mike laughs. 'The National Trust visitors might be a bit bemused to find you here when they look round,' he says, 'but I'm sure they'd get used to it. You and Mouse could be a live exhibit.'

With a grin, I pull out a chair between Toby Butcher and Seb Burroughs. The Brummie journalist is chatting to Koko on his other side, so I turn to TV presenter Toby, and see he is once again taking charge of the wine. We all pass our glasses to him, and he fills them with our choice of red or white. Koko turns down wine, instead pouring water for herself from a crystal carafe.

Mike takes a seat at the bottom of the table, leaving two seats free between him and Koko, presumably hoping the missing members will arrive in time to join us.

There's a starter at each place setting: melon, laid out in a fan on beautiful, gold-rimmed china.

Just as I'm taking my first mouthful, Toby leans close to me. 'Steph, was it?' His breath smells so strongly of alcohol, I have to force myself not to flinch. At least – despite his glazed eyes – his expression is friendly, rather than leering.

I smile, holding my breath against the fumes. 'That's right, Steph Williams. And you're Toby Butcher?'

He nods slowly and forks up some melon, allowing me to breathe again. 'Have you seen the show?' he asks. His voice is upper middle class, and I have to nudge away my ingrained inverted snobbery.

I remind myself that one of the things I love about gardening is that it's open to people from all walks of life.

I pull a face. 'I'm afraid I haven't seen it. I don't watch a lot of telly. What's it called?'

He looks surprised but not offended, and I like him for this, as it suggests a lack of ego.

'It's a Channel 5 show, *Butchering Your Garden*. It's a play on my surname.' Noting my shock, he bursts out laughing. 'Only kidding! It's called *Force of Nature*.'

I laugh, too. 'That's a relief! What do you do on it?'

He sips at his red wine before answering, 'The usual. I'm brought in to redesign a garden, according to the owner's needs and dreams. And there's a team to carry out the tasks.'

'Sounds like fun.'

'I do enjoy it – especially the part where the owners dance with joy upon seeing the finished product.' He swigs more wine then sets down his glass. 'But the formula's a bit tired. I mean, it's been done to death, hasn't it? The Alan Titchmarshes, Charlie Dimmocks and Diarmuid Gavins had all been there and got the garden makeover t-shirts, long before I arrived on the scene.' He glances around, but our companions are deep in conversation. Lowering his voice, he says, 'To be honest, I'm looking to move across to Channel 4. My wife Sarah and I could use the extra dosh.'

'Does Sarah work in TV as well?'

'Yes, she's a producer. It's how we met: I was a guest on a show she was producing. Nowadays she works on Sonny's show – you know, the one on the Beeb that's been going for years, *Sonny in the Garden*?' When I nod enthusiastically – this is the show that got me hooked on gardening – he lowers his voice still further and says, 'Well, I probably shouldn't say this, but Sonny's announced she wants to step down.'

'Really?' I exclaim. I can't imagine Saturday nights in summer without Sonny on my television.

He nods. 'Strictly hush-hush, of course.'

'Of course. I won't say anything.'

'Right, so the plan is to rebrand with a new presenter, and Sarah went for the job. Sonny knows Sarah's been desperate to get into presenting for years – not an easy transition, of course. But screen tests go well, the director's thrilled with Sarah's onscreen presence, etc., etc. You know the drill.' I don't, but I remain quiet. 'Anyway, we've just heard that madam over there is trying to veto her appointment. Of course, Sarah's devastated. It's a fine way for Sonny to repay Sarah's loyalty.'

He shoots an angry glance at Sonny, still in full flow with Addie.

I frown. 'Surely if Sonny's stepping down, she doesn't have the power to prevent them from hiring whoever they want?'

He lifts his eyebrows. 'Ah. But Sonny's an exec on the show.'

'OK . . . but why does she want to veto Sarah's hire?'

'The rumour is that Sonny feels Sarah doesn't have enough experience in front of the camera to be able to think on her feet for the live segments. But that's rot. She's a natural.'

'So, have they hired someone else?'

'It looks like it's going to be offered to some youngster no one's heard of.'

'You mean they've had no experience?'

'Oh, he's come from kids' TV,' he says, waving his fork dismissively. '*Blue Peter* or some such thing,' he says. I refrain from pointing out that even I know *Blue Peter* has been the launch pad for many a big name in the TV world. 'Anyway,' he says, 'it's pretty typical of her nibs over there. You see, Sonny's a total diva, has to have control over everything she touches. I think she feels threatened by Sarah, who might just do a better job than her.'

This doesn't make sense to me, especially when Sonny is TV gardening gold. 'If Sonny's retiring, why would she care?'

'Ah, she's only retiring from this show. She's still going to be doing segments for *Gardeners' World*, and plenty of other stuff.'

I try to process all of this. Sonny has always come across as warm and accessible, and happy to share the limelight. Back in the nineties, she even hosted a gardening show called *Down to Earth*, playing on her reputation as a woman of the people.

Sonny notices me watching her, and smiles. I smile back, wondering how much of Toby's dismissal of her as a diva might be down to disappointment on behalf of his wife. Perhaps the young man he mentioned was simply the better candidate for the role.

Our main course arrives, giving us a break in the conversation. The majority of us are served a delicious steak and mushroom pie, with mashed potato and green beans. Koko, who's a vegan, has a tempting-looking vegetable paella. Recently, I have been considering switching to a plant-based diet – or at least a less meaty one – and this particular fare looks especially good.

After a couple of minutes' silence, as we savour our food, I ask Toby, 'So, who else do you know here?'

He waves his fork in the air. 'Darling, I know *everyone*.' He continues, 'Seriously, though, I have met Koko before: she did a guest spot on *Force of Nature*, when we were creating a wildflower area in an urban garden. I wouldn't like to get on her wrong side, if you know what I mean?'

Meeting his gaze, I say, 'I'm not sure I do.'

'Oh . . . well, she's great at what she does and she's perfectly charming, but she's just very *certain*. There's no room for debate.'

I file this away for consideration. 'Who else do you know?' I ask again.

'Oh, Anil and I go way back.'

'Who's Anil?'

'Anil Ahmad, one of the two who've been held up. He and I did our horticulture degrees together at Writtle.'

'So, what's he like?' I ask.

'Oh, Anil's brilliant.' Again, he lowers his voice. 'I was actually pretty jealous of him in college. He always got top marks for everything, while the rest of us mere mortals could only look on in awe.'

I smile, finding his honesty disarming. 'What's he worked on?' I ask.

'He mainly takes on overseas commissions for corporations. That's where the big money is.'

'That explains why I haven't heard of him. Do you know who the final person is – the other one who's delayed, with Anil?'

He shakes his head and downs his wine, before refilling his glass. I put a hand over my own glass before he can top it up. I'm going to have to keep an eye on my alcohol intake around Toby.

I have a list of the competitors, which I pull from my back pocket.

Unfolding the A4 sheet, I scan the names. Koko, Toby, Seb, Anil, me and . . . 'Delilah Deville,' I say.

Toby, who has just taken another mouthful of wine, begins to cough. He puts his napkin in front of his mouth.

'Sorry, sorry! My wife's always telling me not to glug my drink.'

I smile. But I am sure his coughing has nothing to do with the wine. Keeping my tone casual, I ask, 'Do you know Delilah?'

'Sorry, what was the name again? Delilah Deville? No, never heard of her.'

Toby is a terrible liar, all fluster and averted gaze. Unable to resist a mystery, my interest has been piqued. I'm curious to meet Delilah Deville.

3

Anil and Delilah arrive while the rest of us are finishing dessert – a rich chocolate mousse that literally melts in the mouth. The pair of them appear, breathless and perspiring from their rush to make it in time for dinner.

Anil is of medium height and slender, with shoulder-length dark hair, prominent cheekbones and large brown eyes. He is handsome in an objective way, like a beautiful piece of art. I have always wondered if it's a gift or a curse, to go through life being admired without having done a thing to earn it. In Anil's case, if Toby's to be believed, it certainly doesn't seem to have held him back. I place him in his early thirties, like me, despite his having attended college with the older Toby.

Delilah, meanwhile, can't be in more than her mid-twenties, making it impressive that she's made the final cut for the competition. She's around five foot eight, with pale skin, jet-black hair and almond-shaped green eyes, like a cat. If the new arrivals were a couple, they'd make a striking pair.

But, from the moment they take their seats, side by side, in the two vacant chairs, it's clear they're in the middle of an argument.

'Sorry, everyone,' Delilah says, smiling sardonically around at the assembly, 'but *unfortunately* I spotted Anil on the Paddington Station concourse.' She regards him scornfully, adding, 'If I'd realised he thought he knew the timetable better than the station staff, I wouldn't have bothered going over. Thanks to him, we missed our train and had to change in the middle of nowhere.' She has a distinctly upper-class drawl. Anil sighs and closes his eyes briefly.

The smile on poor Addie's lips falters and she looks uncomfortable. 'Did you two know each other before today?' she asks.

Delilah tosses her dark hair over her shoulders. 'Oh, no. I'd read one of his books on . . .' she runs her fingers through her hair and screws up her eyes as she remembers, '. . . the intersection of garden design and architecture—'

'*Where Form meets Function*,' supplies Anil.

She shoots him an impatient glance. '*Anyway*, his photo was in the back. I recognised him from that.'

'Right,' says Addie, understandably keen to get past this hostility. 'Well, you must both be hungry.'

'Starving,' agrees Delilah. 'I'm hangry as all hell.'

Anil scowls. 'You mean it's just hunger? I was starting to think you were a harpy or something. I've been going over all my past mistakes, trying to work out which ones I'm meant to be atoning for.'

'Well, I'm sure you've got plenty of those,' she snaps.

Anil runs a hand through his glossy black hair and addresses the party with a sigh. 'Sorry, guys. I don't think you're seeing either of us at our best. It's been a long haul in this heat.' His accent is largely London, with a hint of other places, presumably from spending so much time working overseas.

Addie gets to her feet and says, 'Let me tell the kitchen you're here. They've kept food warm for you.'

'Thank heavens,' says Delilah, as Addie sweeps off. She passes her wine glass across the table to Toby without a word, and he fills it from a bottle of red and passes it back. If they don't know each other, how does he know her choice of wine? Or did he merely interpret her proffered glass as a cry for alcohol of any description? It still seems strange, for neither of them to have said a word to the other.

I have a growing sense that there is going to be plenty of entertainment here at Coleton Fishacre, even without the excitement of the competition.

Straight after dessert, Koko clears her throat and our eyes turn towards her. She folds her napkin before getting to her feet. 'I hope you will all excuse me,' she says, 'but I flew home to York on Wednesday after a job interview in the United States, and I am rather tired.'

She leaves the Loggia, waving over her shoulder in response to our chorus of, 'Sleep well!' and, 'See you tomorrow.'

The rest of us stay, to keep the newcomers company while they eat.

'What was the job interview?' Toby murmurs in my ear.

'No idea. We'll have to ask her. It sounds interesting.'

Thankfully, tensions diminish once Delilah and Anil have food inside them. Everyone has stories to tell of difficult clients, and soon we're all chatting and laughing together. It begins to get dark, and the setting sun paints the sky with stripes of apricot and deep pink. Mike turns on the outside light and I watch an elephant hawk-moth hover around the large bulb.

We finish the meal with coffee and liqueurs. Coleton Fishacre clearly likes to spoil its guests, and we're not complaining. At last, Addie bids us all goodnight, informing us that breakfast is at eight a.m. and that we need to be on the minibus to the show gardens by eight forty-five.

At that, the rest of us scrape back our chairs and head for our sleeping quarters. Back in the bedroom, I find Mouse still fast asleep, Mr Rabbit between his front paws. At least he hasn't been pining for that second walk. It's gone ten o'clock, and is fully dark now. We can return to our usual routine tomorrow, with a run before breakfast.

Despite the long drive, I find myself lying awake, sifting through the characters I've met this evening. I'm feeling pretty pleased with myself simply for remembering all their names. I'm looking forward to getting to know Koko better, especially as I love native flowers and am keen to learn more about their propagation and care, so that I can start incorporating more wildflowers into my own projects.

Toby had a lot of uncomplimentary things to say about Sonny, but he made me feel accepted and welcome. He evidently likes to drink, but, fumes aside, this didn't make him poor company. I do wonder, though, if the alcohol loosened his tongue. Would he have told me about his wife's issues with Sonny if he'd been sober? I make a mental note to be careful what I say around him. I'll be interested to see if he's in a bad state tomorrow – I reckon he downed a couple of bottles of wine single-handed. I remember his coughing fit at the mention of Delilah's name, and the casualness between them that suggested an acquaintance of some sort . . . Why play it down?

My mind flicks to the tension between Delilah and Anil when they arrived. I hope the truce they seemed to reach over dinner prevails. Anil and Toby clearly have history, too. I wonder if the rivalry is all on Toby's side.

My mind wanders, as it often does in the twilight hours, to my own intrigue: my missing ex-husband, Ben, whom no one, including his girlfriend Caroline, has seen for over a year. There have been alleged sightings over this period, but all of the images sent to the police have proved not to be him.

Thinking about photographs has me switching on the bedside light and reaching for the picture from Verity, which I placed on my bedside table earlier when I unpacked. Studying her smiling image, I am aware that my dark curls do not resemble her Afro. But, gazing into her large brown eyes, I see my own looking back. It's a curious sensation, both familiar and disconcerting. This is the first time in my thirty-two years that I've had someone with whom to compare family traits.

I need to talk to Mum, but it's too late to contact her tonight. Instead, I type her a message to let her know I've arrived safely. Checking the time on my phone, I see it's gone eleven. With a sigh, I remind myself that there's a minibus coming to pick us up at eight forty-five. Thankfully, I haven't needed to get a team together, as the National Trust has promised us volunteers to help build our show gardens. As I replace the photo on the little table, and turn off the bedside lamp, I feel a surge of excitement in anticipating the work to come. But, this time, exhaustion wins out over adrenaline, and I sink into sleep.

At one point, deep in the darkness of my dreams, Toby turns to me and says, 'Nobody can beat Anil in this competition. Should we just give up and go down the pub?' I'm about to object when I glance at the garden I've spent days creating and see it's made entirely out of toilet rolls.

When I wake at six to a robin's full-breasted song, it's with a great sense of relief that I have not made a toilet roll garden.

4

I almost leap out of bed to begin my stretches, fuelled by a determination to do my very best to win this competition. It could mark a turning point in my career, gaining me lots of free publicity, meaning I could hopefully have my pick of projects.

Mouse stirs at the sound of my movement, and I ask him, 'Shall we go for our run, boy?'

In a flash, he's out of bed and racing around the room, searching for his beloved lead. I gave him free rein (as it were) in a specialist canine accessories shop, after he took against the previous lead I'd bought. The new one, to my untrained eye, is identical to the old. Both are blue nylon, with reflective stripes woven through. However, according to Mouse, his selection is the finest lead around. When it's not clipped to his collar, he often carries it aloft, like a prize catch. He even takes it to bed sometimes, along with Mr Rabbit.

Now, he manages to unearth the lead from within a large tote bag of his accessories – causing a mini avalanche in the process – and I clip it to his matching blue collar.

We take the carpeted stairs down to the front door and let ourselves out, closing it quietly behind us. And then we're climbing the garden until we reach an upper path, where we begin to jog. The June air holds the haze that promises a fine, sunny day to come. After a minute or two, Mouse glances up at me and I interpret this as a request to switch up the pace. Soon, we're sprinting, our rhythm and strides perfectly matched, Mouse's tongue lolling in joy. I grow warm, and stop to tie my hooded sweatshirt around my waist, enjoying the early rays of sun breaking through.

I'd love to take Mouse off the lead, but this, understandably, is against Coleton Fishacre rules. I'll have to find a dog-friendly beach for tomorrow.

In the meantime, we climb a path through the lushly planted grounds until we arrive at a spot I've seen marked on the map as 'Tree Fern Glade'. Here, towering specimens of *Dicksonia antarctica* prove the mildness of the area's microclimate. Although generally sold as 'hardy', I've found tree ferns will rarely survive a long, hard frost.

Just past this glade, the land slopes downwards as we reach signs warning of an eroding cliff edge, where I slow for a moment, keeping away from the edge as I peer down into a valley filled with thorny gorse bushes. With a shudder, I respond to a bark from Mouse and move away, picking up my pace and joining him for a final sprint uphill to a view of the sea, where the heads of several seals form dark spots, bobbing amid the blue expanse. Mouse is once again entranced, and I feel a twinge of guilt as, upon checking my watch, I register that it's time to return to the house.

Back in the circular courtyard, I lead him through the front door of the stone house and up to our first-floor room, where I set out his food and water before having a wash at the sink and heading down to my own breakfast.

5

I'm the first to arrive out on the Loggia. The long table has been set with glass jugs of freshly squeezed orange juice, along with individual pots of fruit yogurt and a couple of large crystal bowls containing fresh fruit salad. There are also baskets of croissants and bread rolls, giving off the delicious smell of freshly baked goods.

However, none of this attracts me as much as the sophisticated-looking coffee maker, which I spy on a side table. As I approach the machine, the scent of the strong, rich brew assails me. Coffee is my drug, and I've never been tempted to cheat on it with cigarettes or actual narcotics. I've had the foresight to bring my thermos down with me, and I fill that for later, before placing a cup beneath the spout.

'Ooh, grab one for me while you're there.' I turn to see Toby arriving. He's dressed in another Hawaiian-print shirt, this time in shades of blue and green with splashes of fuchsia. From his fresh appearance, I infer that he's shrugged off last night's drinking like a cardigan.

'How do you take your coffee?' I ask.

'Any way it comes,' he says with a laugh. 'But I'll have milk and one sugar if they're going.'

I follow his directions, then carry both cups to the table, sipping from my own as I walk. The blend is delicious, layered with flavours, reminding me of walnuts and berries. Toby has taken a seat in the middle, facing the house. After handing him his cup, I pull out the chair opposite him and sit down, taking in the view before me of the semicircular pool and stunning flower borders.

'Do you not want to face the garden?' I ask.

'Oh, I thought I'd let other people enjoy it for now.' He passes me the bread basket and I take one of the warm rolls, sniffing it with pleasure. He laughs. 'You remind me of Chaplin, my Miniature Schnauzer. He has to sniff everything.'

'You have a dog? Is he with you?'

'He's up in my room but he'll be joining us on the minibus.'

'So will Mouse.'

'You have a . . . mouse?'

'No, he's a large, black, poodley dog.'

He laughs again. He has an easy chuckle. 'Poodley?'

'Hey, I'll have you know that's an official dog breed.'

'Ah, of course – I know it well. Chaplin is a pedigree. My wife Sarah's choice. I was all set to visit the shelter and pick out some ugly, neglected little chap, but she had her heart set on a Miniature Schnauzer. She'd had one as a girl. Sadly for Sarah, though, Chaplin is a daddy's boy through and through, and insists on going everywhere with me.'

'Poor Sarah,' I say.

'Poor Sarah,' he agrees.

'Why's he called "Chaplin"?' I ask.

'It's because of the facial hair,' he says, miming the bearded snout for which the breed is known.

'It's a great name,' I say, not pointing out that the drooping whiskers of a Schnauzer bear little resemblance to Charlie Chaplin's neat toothbrush moustache.

I butter my roll, spread some home-made raspberry jam on top and bite into the crispy bread just as Koko and Delilah walk out to join us. I wave my greetings with my mouth full. They nod and smile, and Koko helps herself to coffee before coming to sit beside me. Delilah sits next to Toby, whom she greets with a smile and a pat on the hand. Again, this seems pretty intimate, considering last night he claimed not to know her.

There's a momentary lull in the conversation. Toby is the first to speak again. He talks about the hot weather that looks like it's set in for at least the next week. 'I don't know about the rest of you, but I've brought a giant sun hat,' he says. 'I just hope I remember to take it off before Sarah films me – it's most definitely not a stylish item.'

We all laugh, then Koko says, 'Who is Sarah and why is she filming you?'

'Oh, Sarah's my wife.' He puffs out his chest like a proud cockerel. 'She works for Wild Path Productions, who, as you probably know, produce a lot of the gardening shows. They're loaning her a handheld so she can film our builds.' He looks around at us with a grin. 'So, it's not only me she'll be filming, folks.'

'Does that mean we're going to be on TV with our show gardens?' I ask, unable to suppress a grin myself, at the thought of how many potential clients this could reach.

'Provided the BBC give the go-ahead, but it's looking promising,' he says. 'Anyway, she'll be joining us for dinner later, and she's staying for the week, so you'll all get to meet her and she can answer any questions.'

Delilah spreads butter on a roll and asks, 'Sarah's coming here?'

'That's right,' says Toby.

'And she's staying all week?'

'That's the plan.'

After the revelation about the filming, most of us lapse into an easy silence. Toby, however, keeps up a stream of fairly inane chatter, without seeming to mind that none of us responds. After a second cup of coffee, I get to my feet. 'Right, I'm done.'

Addie checks her watch. 'We'll see you at the minibus out front in ten. You're bringing your dog?' I nod. 'Make sure it's on a lead while you're in the house and grounds.'

'Will do.'

I have to wake Mouse when I reach the room, but I don't want to leave him all day on his own. He takes the disruption well, even fetching his lead again.

'Good boy,' I say, stroking him. He wags his tail and looks up at me expectantly. I grab my green tool belt from the dressing table and fasten it around my hips. The belt was a Christmas gift from my brother and his family, chosen by my niece Alice. I don't know why I hadn't got one for myself before now – it makes it so much easier to locate individual tools than rummaging through my pockets.

Outside, a warm sea breeze is blowing little white clouds across a blue sky. I try to convince myself that the impending heat is still preferable to working in a downpour.

The minibus doesn't look much younger – or healthier – than my ancient Ford Transit, which is parked beside it. Painted the aggressive orange of a glass of Tango, the bus bears patches of brown rust like age spots.

Mouse tugs on the lead as we near the minibus door, and I see the reason why as soon as we've climbed on board: Toby's Miniature Schnauzer is already in place, sitting very upright on the seat behind Addie, who's at the wheel. Mouse stands in the aisle and pants an eager greeting at the smaller dog, adding a slight whine when the Schnauzer blanks him.

Toby, seated beside Chaplin, smiles an apology at Mouse and pats him on the head. 'Sorry, old chap, maybe later. Chaplin is working. He takes his transportation duties very seriously. He has to be ready to take over if the driver has a heart attack.'

I laugh and coax Mouse to the back of the bus, where there's room for his bulk.

Seb, the tall blond guy from Birmingham, gets on next. He walks through the little bus and takes a seat in the row in front of us. Mouse promptly abandons his disappointment with Chaplin and runs to put his paws on Seb's lap, who reels back, looking hunched and uncomfortable.

'Can you get it down?'

'I'm so sorry!' I get up and tug Mouse away from Seb by the collar. My friendly companion is bemused but obedient, returning to his seat with only a small whine.

Without turning to face me, Seb says, 'It's just . . . I had a bad experience with a dog in our street as a child.'

'I'm sorry to hear that. I shouldn't have let him put his paws on you like that. I forget some people are nervous.'

Thankfully, at that moment, Mike walks down to join us, taking the seat beside Seb and leaning over to stroke Mouse, who gives him a lick.

'You're a good boy, aren't you?' says Mike.

The bus starts to move and I strap Mouse in on the seat beside me.

Despite Mike's best efforts to include Seb in conversation, the latter is silent for the journey. I hope Mouse and I haven't damaged his mood for the day ahead.

Mouse, though, quickly forgets his rejection by Seb, distracted by the world going past in a blur. He sees a lot of trees, a great many exciting birds and cows, and the occasional, less interesting stone cottage.

Glancing around at the other passengers, I note that Delilah has seated herself beside Koko and is talking, but it looks like a pretty one-sided conversation: Koko doesn't even turn her head towards her companion. I wonder if they've got off on the wrong foot, or if Koko just isn't in a chatty mood. Anil is sitting on his own, making notes on a tablet. He's wearing large headphones, plainly signalling his lack of availability for a chat. I don't blame him. While Mike talks to me about Coleton Fishacre and future plans for the gardens and grounds, my mind is whirring in the background, processing the plethora of tasks that I need to get done over the next seven days.

The journey turns out to be a short one. After little more than ten minutes, Addie turns the minibus in at a sign for POPLARS FARM, where an A4 laminated sheet tied to the open gate announces 'Coleton Fishacre Flower Show'. She drives across a rutted car park and parks the van. We all pile out and stand together, surveying the site. We're at one end of a row of six identical plots, each surrounded on three sides by high wooden fences.

'Welcome to the inaugural Coleton Fishacre Flower Show show garden site,' says Addie. 'And don't try saying that in a hurry.' We all laugh. She gestures to knots of people of a variety of ages, standing at the edge of the car park. They're dressed in t-shirts bearing the words 'Coleton Fishacre Flower Show 2024', with the National Trust logo above. 'As you can see, we've had a lot of volunteers to clear the land and fence off the plot for the show gardens,' she continues. 'They've all worked tremendously hard.'

The volunteers smile as my fellow designers and I cheer and applaud them.

'Right,' she continues, 'this first field next to the car park is for the show gardens. The next field you can see behind it, and accessible via both the far end of the show garden area and this car park, is where you'll find the refreshments. Please help yourselves to water, tea, coffee, herbal teas and biscuits. There's milk and sandwiches – and ice creams – in the various cool boxes.' With a smile, she holds up her wrist, displaying her watch. 'And your time starts . . . now!' She makes a downward slicing action with her arm, and I feel a surge of excitement as the six of us head into the first field, to seek out our allotted areas.

There is a wide grassy verge to the right, and we walk along this, each looking for our name on the posts in front of the rectangular plots to our left. I stride with Mouse along the grass until I find my own plot, at the far end. Here, I stop and stand in contemplation of the blank slate before me – and find my brain immediately making small alterations to my plan. It's one thing to design a garden remotely; it's quite another to be inspired by the site itself.

Mouse looks up at me quizzically, wondering why we've come to a field but aren't going for a run. At that moment, Toby walks over with his Miniature Schnauzer, whose tail is now wagging. Mouse hesitates. He hasn't forgotten the recent rejection. But Chaplin is like a different dog, now that his duties as stand-in driver are over. Toby lets out the extendable lead, and Chaplin runs right up to the big dog and lifts his head to sniff his nose. Mouse's barriers crumble instantly; he gives Chaplin a lick on the nose.

'Do you think we could let them off the lead?' Toby asks me.

I nod. 'I emailed Addie before we came, and she said it should be fine with the farmer.'

'Perfect.' We smile at one another as we unclip the dogs' leads and watch the new friends run off to play. There's a beautiful oak just past my garden, casting glorious shade, and we set down the two dogs' water bowls beneath it and fill them, ready for when the dogs return.

Toby sighs and rubs his goatee. 'On with the show, I guess.'

'Are you not looking forward to it?'

He tilts his head to one side. 'I am . . . It's just, we're at the daunting stage, where it's all to do. And there's so much work.' He groans.

'You'll get there.'

It would be insensitive to tell him that I love this part: there's so much excitement in envisaging the creative process to come. He nods and wanders back to his plot, while I sit down cross-legged on the grass in front of my rectangle of bare earth, taking out my plan and starting to amend it. The plots are fifteen metres deep by ten wide. The most important part will be to disguise both the angularity of the plot and its small size. I'm aiming to use the standard trick of covering the fences in lush planting to hide the boundaries.

The main feature, though, will be that the entire garden is designed around a loose spiral. I plan to form the winding shape in a single path made from several tonnes of wood chippings that are being delivered in a couple of days. There will be a dew pond at the end of the spiral path, complete with benches on either side, to provide resting points and new angles from which to survey the garden. By strategic placement of specimen shrubs, I intend to create a peekaboo effect, by which specific features of the planting and furniture will be glimpsed from different viewpoints along the path. I'm calling my garden 'The Journey', and am hoping that visitors will feel like they've been on a journey of sorts by the time they reach the centre. It's a big demand on such a tiny plot, but I feel quietly confident that I can carry it off.

My phone rings while I'm pacing and measuring, deep in a world of spatial imaginings.

When I draw it from my pocket, I see it's Dad. 'Hiya,' I say.

'Hi, love. Is now a good time?'

'That depends how long you need.'

'I wanted to ask you about mealworms. I bought some for the hedgehogs but your mum says they're bad for them.'

Mum's voice sounds in the background, 'Because they are.'

'I'm sure we used to feed mealworms to the hedgehogs when I was a youngster,' Dad says.

I roll my eyes. 'Yeah, and I bet you also put out milk for them.'

'What? They can't have milk either?'

'They cannot.'

He calls to Mum, 'Did you put out that saucer of milk last night?'

She calls back, 'I did not. They aren't supposed to have milk.'

Suppressing a grin, I say, 'Dad, listen to Mum, would you?'

He sighs loudly, then says, 'How's it going anyway?'

'I have a large rectangle of bare earth at the moment.'

'Well, you'd better get on and fill it then, hadn't you?'

'Great plan. Thanks, Dad. Always good to have your input.'

He chuckles. 'Glad to be of help.'

There's a moment's pause before I say, 'Dad . . . I had a photo from my birth mother, Verity.'

'Ah. Let me fetch your mum.'

'No, I can talk to you.' But he's already gone.

I hear the murmur of voices before Mum comes to the phone. 'Hello, Louise,' she says, and I suppress a sigh. My family all still insist on calling me Louise, even though I changed my name to Steph several years ago, after my now ex-husband – the missing Ben Doughty – secretly gambled all our money on risky deals, and we lost everything, along with our house and marriage. I wanted to wipe out all of the bad associations from being married to him so, when changing my surname from Doughty back to my family name of Williams didn't seem quite enough, I switched Louise for Steph.

But the name battle is not my priority right now. I sit down on the ground and take a deep breath.

'Mum, did Dad tell you I got a photo from Verity?'

'He did, yes.'

'So, it turns out she's possibly mixed race?'

'Biracial,' she says at once. 'Verity's mother was white, her father was black.'

There's a familiar fist clenching in my belly. I focus on slowing my breathing and relaxing my muscles. 'So . . . you knew?'

'We saw a photograph of her with you, before we adopted you.'

'Why didn't you tell me?'

'You looked white,' she says. 'Wasn't it easier not to have to deal with all those questions of race?'

'Easier for who?' I ask her.

'Oh, Louise. Don't be like that. It's not like we didn't tell you anything about your family tree.'

'You told me I had a black great-grandparent on my father's side.'

'Did we? Well, we probably got a bit confused.'

I sigh heavily. 'I have to get on . . .' I hang up without saying goodbye, something I'd never normally do, and stuff my mobile back in my pocket.

Debates over my identity and my parents' failings will have to wait. I have a show garden to create.

6

I begin to measure out the spacing for the trellis panels, which are
due to be delivered on Monday to support the climbers for the fence.
This is a pleasantly mindless job, allowing me to drift off into images
of the spiral path and dew pond. A clear picture is emerging in my
head of how all of the planting, which is to be weird and wonderful,
will echo and reflect the spiral framework.

After a couple of hours, Mouse and Chaplin appear, while I'm
marking out the area designated for a mural on the back fence. I
stop for a moment to pour more water into their bowls, which they
lap up within seconds before settling down in the shade for a nap.

When Toby comes by a little while later, he stops on the grass beside
my plot, looking towards the oak, and says, 'Be still my beating heart.'

I turn from my measuring and walk to the edge of my plot to take
in the sight of our dogs, curled up together like an imbalanced Yin
and Yang. 'I know. They're adorable.'

He takes a metal flask from a back pocket. 'You fancy a swig of
the strong stuff?'

I shake my head. 'I've got a thermos of coffee, thanks.' I resist the
urge to check my watch, to see how early he's starting on the alcohol.
His hands shake as he puts the flask to his lips, and I look away. When
I turn back, he's screwing the lid back on the flask. He nods towards
my markings on the back fence. 'What's going on there, then?'

'That's the spot where there's going to be a trompe l'oeil frame
around a mirror.'

'I'm using mirrors, too.'

I shrug. 'It's Garden Design 101 really, isn't it, using mirrors to make a small space look bigger?'

He smiles. 'Yes. Except that my whole garden's going to be mirrored.'

I raise an eyebrow. 'Really?'

He nods with enthusiasm. 'All the fencing's going to be coated with adhesive-backed mirroring, and there will be reflective balls of different sizes placed throughout the flower beds. And that's just for starters.'

'In this heat, you'd better be careful not to start a fire,' I say, with a laugh. 'It sounds amazing, though.'

'What else are you planning?' he asks. 'Apart from the mirror and the painting?'

'The whole design's a spiral. And there'll be lots of climbers up the fence. Oh, and some big specimen shrubs. There are a few details I've yet to work out.'

He raises an eyebrow. 'You haven't got it all planned? You do realise we only have seven days?'

He's right, of course. Unlike Chelsea Flower Show, where the designers have two or even three weeks in which to construct their show gardens, we've been allocated a mere seven days for the much smaller flower show at Coleton Fishacre. Today, Saturday, is Day One. But I'm confident I can make the time work for me.

He squeezes my shoulder. 'Just stop planning and start work.'

'All right, Mr Patronising, I do have it all in hand, thank you.'

He laughs. 'You're not the first person to accuse me of that.'

At that moment, a pair of lorries pulls in beside the field gate.

'Plants!' I say at the same time as Toby says, 'Mirrors!'

'Maybe both,' I suggest. 'There are two lorries.'

'Maybe both,' he agrees.

We walk along the stretch of grass that runs in front of the six gardens, regarding each plot in turn. Koko's is next to mine. She is engrossed in dividing the area into perfect squares, using twine stretched between bamboo canes. It reminds me of botanical fieldwork, where an area is sectioned off into grids, in order to count the flowers in each section.

She is kneeling to tie a knot when Toby says, 'Ah, a giant cat's cradle.'

She shoots him a scathing look, so I ask quickly, 'Is the whole design going to be made up of these grids?'

She shakes her head. 'No, I just wanted to give myself equal-sized areas, for balance. I shall blend the edges once the plants have been put into their places.'

'Wildflowers?' I ask.

She shakes her head. 'Not this time.'

'What then?' asks Toby.

But Koko puts a slender finger to her lips and arches an eyebrow. 'You will just have to wait and see, Mr Toby.'

'Have you noticed the lorries?' I ask her.

'This delivery will not be for me. My plants are not coming so early. I want to get all of the structure into place first.'

We nod and move on. Next along is Seb's plot. There's no sign of him, but he's dug out large holes in various spots, which I suspect will be for small trees or shrubs. There's a carpenter's table set up near the back fence, and a pile of planks beside it.

'Do you think Seb's laying decking?' I ask Toby, pointing to the planks.

He peers at the planks. 'Rather him than me. Given the time frame, I'd have thought no one would put in too much in the way of hard landscaping. I'm installing a water feature, but it's nothing fancy.'

'Same here,' I say as we walk on. Then I remember his mirrors. 'Aren't all those reflective surfaces a form of hard landscaping?'

'Not the way I'm using them.'

'Fair enough.' With a sigh, I say, 'In another world, I'd have loved to make a herringbone path, using reclaimed bricks, but that's way too time-consuming.'

He does a double-take, one eyebrow raised. 'Really? You don't think herringbone's a little . . . old school?'

I grin. 'Don't knock old school. Aged bricks are pretty. And they make a great foil to foliage.' When he still looks unconvinced, I raise an eyebrow. 'You're a tough judge, aren't you?'

He laughs. 'Again, it has been said before.' We've reached the next plot, which belongs to him. He stops, and I see his face crease in a frown.

'What is it?' I ask.

'I left a couple of volunteers digging a trench for the water feature ...'

I have a flashback to my dream, in which Toby suggested we give up and go to the pub. In reality, he is a long way from that. 'Maybe they've gone to help unload the delivery,' I suggest.

'Maybe. Let's get a move on and see.'

But we only make it to the next plot, where I stop in shock. Anil's section is entirely masked by a giant portable screen.

'Is this standard practice in the competitions?' I ask Toby, who has also come to a halt.

'Er, no. I hadn't realised Anil had got so paranoid, to be honest.' He makes no attempt to lower his voice, so I'm not too surprised when Anil's voice comes from behind the screen,

'Hey, Toby mate, I can hear you!' I shoot a concerned look at my companion, who says quickly, 'I'm off to inspect the delivery,' and hastens towards the car park, leaving me to apologise to Anil, who emerges from his plot.

But he grins, dusting off soil-covered hands. 'I was only messing with you.'

'In that case, is there any chance of a sneak preview?'

He shakes his head. 'Nothing to see yet. And, when there is, I'll be keeping it under wraps till the judging.'

I raise an eyebrow. 'Why so secretive?'

He pulls a face. 'I didn't start out like it. But, early on in my career, I told ... this person ... too much about my ideas for a show garden I was going to be building for a competition. It was someone I trusted, a mate. When the gardens were all finished, theirs turned out to be almost identical to mine. There was no way it could be coincidence, you know? We're talking the same layout, the same specimen plants, the works. The judges couldn't decide who'd copied who, so we both ended up getting disqualified. It was only a small competition for new graduates, but it still stung.'

'Shit,' I say, and he nods. I can't help wondering who this person was. From the way Anil paused, it seemed as if he was about to name them but stopped himself. Is it someone well known? Or even someone who's here for the flower show?

I reflect on how Toby is openly awed by Anil's talent and success. And he was at college with Anil . . . But is it possible that Toby – the self-deprecating man who has made me feel so welcome within this group of strangers – could have resorted to foul play?

7

After leaving Anil, I head over to the lorries. Mike is standing between them, holding a clipboard. He greets me with a smile.

'I think your order's coming from Hope's Nursery?' When I nod, he says, 'That delivery's coming later today.' He consults his schedule and frowns. 'Or maybe tomorrow. What did they say to you?'

'They were quite vague, now you mention it. But, to be honest, I'm in no rush to get my hands on the plants – there's a lot to do on the structural side before I can think about starting on the planting.'

'Are you putting in any hard landscaping?'

'Not really. A bark pathway is my biggest project.'

He nods. 'Right. Well, I'm going to help Anil with some of his build, which sounds quite a big job from the hints he's dropped. And I've promised Toby I'll lend a hand digging trenches, if I have spare time after that. But I should be free either tomorrow or Monday, if you need some extra help.'

I feel a blush spreading across my cheeks as I catch myself gazing into his warm brown eyes. I'm not sure if he notices, as he simply asks, 'What volunteers have you got?'

'Oh! I haven't yet.' Pulling myself together, I glance around, catching the eye of a square-shouldered, middle-aged white woman with long grey plaits. She walks over wearing a big smile and one of the flower show t-shirts in an oversize fit, teamed with cycling shorts in a psychedelic print, lace-up, hand-painted ankle boots and bright pink socks gathered around her ankles. She is a walking piece of art, complete with tattoos of plants twining around both arms as well as up her sturdy calves, plus a piercing in one eyebrow. As she continues to smile at me, her big blue eyes are filled with warmth and good humour.

'You looking for a helper?' she asks, coming closer and flexing impressive arm muscles as she flashes me a cheeky grin. Her accent is Welsh and her voice soft and a little hoarse, reminiscent of a long-term smoker.

'Ooh, yes, please. I'm—'

'Steph Williams, I know. Your website's quite something. I've been holding out to work with you.'

'Really?' I can't help but feel flattered, that she would choose me out of the clutch of largely better-known designers competing.

'Absolutely. I'm Gertrude Jones, by the way.'

Looking back at Mike, I say, 'Thanks, but it looks like Gertrude here will be helping me.'

He smiles and nods. 'I'd say you're in safe hands there.'

'Too right,' says Gertrude.

She accompanies me back along the row of newly started gardens, until we reach my empty plot at the end.

'I just need to check on the dogs,' I say, continuing towards the oak tree.

'Oh, are they yours?' she asks, walking alongside me. 'I saw them playing earlier. They're such a pair of cuties.'

'Only the big, shaggy one's mine. He's Mouse. The little one is Chaplin. He belongs to Toby Butcher.'

As I say this, we reach the oak, where the dogs are now awake, chewing on either end of a long bone.

'Where did you get that?' I ask them.

'Oh,' says Gertrude, 'I saw Mike give it to them a few minutes ago. Don't worry, I checked – it's not been cooked, so there won't be splinters.'

'That's great. Right, in that case, fancy helping me with some measuring to start with?'

As I crouch to rummage in my backpack for my tape measures, I glance up at her and ask, 'How did you come to volunteer for this?'

Gertrude pushes a plait from her shoulder. 'Ah, you see, I'm going to start my training in September, to be a garden designer. The flower show couldn't be better timing.'

'Oh, fantastic! Ask any questions along the way – I'll be happy to answer.'

'Thank you. And by the way, I loved how you renovated those gardens – you know, first that one at . . . Beaulieu, was it?'

She pronounces it the French way, 'bow-lee-er', and I say, 'Believe it or not, it's "Bewley".'

Her eyes grow round. 'But the houses all looked so grand.'

I laugh. 'I was quite surprised when I first heard it. Anyway, I loved bringing that garden at The Chimneys back to life.'

'I couldn't believe how well the lawn grew, after you took out all those wild rhododendrons.'

'Yeah. *Rhododendron ponticum* is a beautiful plant, but it's a definite pest. It crowds out pretty much anything in its vicinity.' I locate two tape measures and hand one to her, with a pencil. 'We're marking up the fence, where the trellis will go. I've already started on the left-hand side, so could you start on the right? The panels need to be close together, as the aim is to cover the entire fence with climbers. They're one-point-eight metres wide and I'm only leaving five centimetres between them.'

'Is that to make the boundary blend in, so the space seems bigger?' She shoots me a grin. 'I've started the reading for my course.'

I smile back. 'It is, yes. And the orange-stained wood isn't exactly inspiring at the moment, is it? I'm hoping we can make it look as though the garden's quite mature, with green "walls" and large shrubs.'

'Ooh, exciting,' she says. 'I can't wait to see what shrubs you've gone for.'

'I'll show you the plan and the plant lists at lunchtime, before Sonny comes round.'

Her eyes grow wide again. 'Do you mean Sonny Carden, off the telly? I love her.'

'Me, too. She's going to pay mentoring visits to all of us for the first three days of the build.'

'Excellent.' She shoots me a beaming smile and I see she has an endearing gap between her front teeth.

'What did you do before?' I call across the plot, as we settle down to measure and mark.

'I was a teaching assistant in a primary school,' she calls back. 'But the little school I worked at got closed down, so I retired early. I'm only fifty-two. Then I thought to myself, hey, Gertrude, you like plants and gardens. Why don't you train to be a garden designer?'

'Great idea,' I say, sitting back on my heels and wiping the sweat from my forehead with the back of my arm.

'I can't wait,' she says. 'I reckon I'll be going from one brilliant job to another. I mean, teaching and gardening – they're both all about helping small things to grow bigger and better, aren't they?'

I laugh as I make my final mark on the left-hand fence where it meets the back. I stand up, stretching my legs. 'Fair point. I reckon you'll be great.'

I move over to the right-hand side, working outwards from the back corner, and we continue until we meet.

'Is it the back fence next?' she asks, as we both stand up, Gertrude with a loud groan as she stretches her back.

'I have other plans for that,' I say. 'We do need some climbers, but one large area will be left unplanted. It's going to be filled with a piece of art.' I check my watch. 'Hey, it's one thirty. We'd better have some lunch.'

Gertrude has brought a salad. I, meanwhile, head over to the refreshments table, where I look through a selection of tasty-looking sandwiches in one of the cool boxes. I've just chosen houmous and olives on tomato bread when Anil arrives.

'Anything good left in there?' he asks.

I go through the contents again. 'Yep, there's still a chicken salad baguette, a tuna wrap and another houmous with olives. Oh, and a Brie and redcurrant on sourdough.'

'Tuna sounds great.'

I pass the wrap to him and he nods in thanks.

'So, how's it going?' he asks.

'Slowly.'

'Yeah,' he says. 'This is the part that's all about the foundations, isn't it?'

'Yep.' A thought occurs to me. 'Unless you mean literal foundations, like a building?'

'Ah.' He winks. 'You'll just have to wait and see, won't you?'

'Really? You're not going to give me anything?'

'Nope.'

'OK, well, have you got anything to show Sonny?'

He nods confidently, then seems to falter. 'Well, not a lot, I guess. I mean, I've got all my plans. I've done them in 3-D modelling software, so she can see the end result. How about you?' He peels back the waxed paper on his wrap and takes a bite as I respond.

'I've only really got my plans. But she must be expecting that at this stage, don't you think?'

He meets my gaze and swallows his mouthful before saying, 'Just give her the spiel. She can be a bit of a tricky customer, you know? So, you might want to give her a bit of the old hard sell.'

'Oh, you know her? I didn't realise.'

'We first met on a gardening show that was filmed in Hong Kong. I was fresh out of college and a bit starstruck, to be honest. I was such a noob.'

I pull a face. 'I'm still there. I'm worried I'm either going to freeze in her presence or start gabbling.'

He grins. 'The celeb effect wears off. Anyway, I met her again at Chelsea, when I got silver to her gold a couple of years back, and we did press interviews together. Not being funny, but I reckon my design was better – more innovative, you know?'

I'm not sure how to respond, but he saves me the trouble by continuing, 'I wouldn't be that surprised if it turned out she'd blackmailed the judges. She's been around so long, I bet she's got dirt on everyone.' He laughs. 'Just kidding!' He pauses, then says with a frown, 'It's just, hers was this twee cottage garden – I mean, how does that deserve a gold medal?' He pauses for breath before palming his forehead. 'Oh, god! Please tell me you're not doing a cottage garden.'

I laugh. 'You're safe – no cottage garden will be appearing on my plot.'

'Thank fuck for that. Our firm couldn't handle another legal case right now, if you sued me for defamation.'

'Yeah . . . I'm pretty sure I can't sue you for insulting my show garden.' I hesitate before asking, 'What's the court case about?'

He pulls a face. 'Sorry, I shouldn't have mentioned it. I'm not allowed to talk about it while it's "ongoing".' He performs air quotes. 'My business partner would kill me. Suffice to say, I could do with a win right now – a bit of good press might help push the bad stuff out of people's minds, you know? And the ten k wouldn't go amiss either.'

'I second that part,' I say. 'Well, good luck with the competition.'

He raises his eyebrows. 'You don't mean that.'

'All right, I plan to win,' I admit with a laugh. 'But I wish you silver to my gold.' I'm still laughing as I wave goodbye and head over to the oak tree, to join Gertrude in the shade. The dogs have vanished, and I refill their water bowls before settling down with a sigh of pleasure to enjoy my lunch.

'Addie's just been round,' says Gertrude, as I pour us both coffee from my thermos. Gertrude has her own mug, with 'World's Best Granny' painted on it in red.

'You're a grandma?' I ask.

'I'm Granny,' she says firmly. 'The other one's Grandma. And you do not want to get me started on the grandkids . . . Unless it's your life's ambition to scroll through millions of pics of kids you're never going to meet?' She raises an eyebrow in invitation.

'Maybe another time,' I say quickly. 'What did Addie have to say?'

'Right, so, apparently, Sonny's on her way. She's coming from the BBC radio studios in Torbay, so Addie reckons she should be here in about an hour.'

'Great,' I say, taking a sip of the strong brew and swallowing. 'That gives us time to start marking out the pond.'

'What shape of pond are you putting in?'

'Oh, I said I'd show you the plans.' I'm about to stand up, but she waves for me to stay seated.

'No, I'll fetch them. Where are they?'

I point to my portfolio, a few metres away, and she walks over and extracts the papers.

While I savour my tasty sandwich and rich coffee, she sits poring over the designs. I watch as she traces the spiral path and circular pool with her index finger. At last, she sits back on her heels and says, 'It's bloody gorgeous.'

'Thank you.'

'It's so clever, how you've distracted the eye from the rectangular plot without resorting to the usual diagonals or separate rooms.'

'You know a lot for an alleged novice.'

'I've been reading gardening mags for decades, so I suppose I have absorbed a little along the way.'

I nod. 'Well, I decided there wasn't enough space to make rooms, if that makes sense?'

She nods. 'No room for rooms.' She collects up the pages and returns them to the portfolio case.

I drain the last of my coffee and stand up, clapping my hands. 'Right. Let's get on. Have you used spray chalk before?'

She shakes her head. 'I've seen it on the telly though, and it looked like fun.'

I smile. 'OK. I'll do the measuring and you can do the spraying. I've got a couple of masks in my backpack, so we don't inhale the chalk dust.'

Sonny arrives when we've just set up our makeshift compass, using a stick at the centre tied to a long piece of twine, which I've cut to the requisite radius.

'Cooeee!' she calls from the edge of the plot, waving madly, reminding me of a character from a camp eighties sitcom.

We abandon the compass and head over to meet her. The diminutive woman's pink dandelion-fluff hair has been left delightfully untamed, but she's wearing a fuchsia-pink t-shirt, with clean, pressed dungarees instead of her signature soil-covered ones.

'Sonny, this is Gertrude Jones, a volunteer who's about to start training as a garden designer.'

Sonny holds out her hand, but Gertrude says, 'Oh no! I'm filthy.'

The celebrity laughs and shakes Gertrude's hand anyway, saying in her broad West Country accent, 'I'd be concerned about what kind of help you were being to Steph here if you weren't getting filthy.'

She glances around the plot, then says, 'Shall we take a look at those plans, and you can talk me through your process?'

'Sure,' I say, hoping she can't tell that my legs are trembling. This fangirl thing is ridiculous. 'Let's go and sit under the oak, where it's shady.'

We lead Sonny over and find the dogs have returned and are once again fast asleep. 'Oh, this looks like my kind of spot,' says Sonny, sinking to the ground. 'Now,' she says, addressing me and rubbing her hands together, 'show me your plans!'

I open out my portfolio and sketchbooks, and pass them to her, explaining my thought processes and inspirations. I have mood boards, along with 3-D models that I've printed from the computer, plus sketches of planting schemes, and a drawing of the spiral, from above.

While I sit close by, Sonny invites Gertrude to sit beside her, and I hear her talking through parts of my plan with the volunteer.

At last, Sonny passes the materials back to me and says, 'This is wonderful.'

I can't help grinning. 'Really?'

She nods. 'Such a strong structure. My only concern would be the bark chippings: I'm thinking they might get kicked into the borders as each visitor walks along the path. You really need to dig out the path, so it's below the surrounding beds. I notice you didn't specify this on your plans.'

I push a loose curl back from my face. 'That is what I'd do on a permanent build. But, with only seven days to create this garden, I'm trying to cut my workload.'

'Well, I'm guessing you've built in what I like to call "hiccup time"?' At my bemused expression, she explains, 'Time to resolve any hiccups you might have along the way.'

I laugh. 'Oh! Yes, I've built in extra time. I normally call it "snagging time".'

'Potato, pot-ah-to,' she says. 'So, you might consider allocating some of it to digging out the path.'

Gertrude chips in, 'I can enlist some of the volunteers to help with that, if you like?'

I shoot her a grateful look. 'That would be great, yes please. We'll need more bark, in that case. I'll message the supplier later, to increase quantities.'

She nods.

'Well, thank you for sharing your vision with me,' Sonny says, as she levers herself to standing.

Getting to my own feet, I say, 'My pleasure. Thanks for the advice. I should probably admit that I'm a massive fan. I've been watching you all my life. You're such an inspiration.'

'Aww! Well, you're adorable, aren't you? You come to me any time you want advice, even after this competition, lovely. And I mean that.' She holds out her arms. 'Come on, let's hug it out.' She beckons to Gertrude to join us. Sonny's so much smaller than both of us, we all nearly lose our balance.

'Whoa there!' Sonny says with a laugh.

I ask her, 'Did Anil share his designs with you?'

'He did, yes. I was given access all areas, if you'll believe it! He wasn't in the best of moods, mind you.' She hesitates, then continues in a hushed tone, 'When I arrived, I found him all on his own, on the phone to someone. It sounded like they were arguing.'

Remembering what Anil told me about the lawsuit, I wonder if he was talking to his business partner, or perhaps their lawyer.

'Oh dear,' I say.

Sonny continues, 'Anyway, I should probably have told him I'd come back later. I don't think he was in the right frame of mind for my critique.'

'Did he not take it well?' I ask.

She sighs and runs a hand through her pink hair. 'Don't get me wrong, he's a very talented designer, but he overcomplicates things.' She tilts her head thoughtfully. 'His design is amazing. It's just that it's very . . .' she pauses, clearly searching for the right word, 'flashy.'

I raise an eyebrow and she shrugs. 'It's not very organic. It feels more *architect*ural than *horticult*ural, if you catch my drift? It's probably his background, with the commercial contracts.' She sighs again. 'I'm afraid he really didn't like my suggestion that he tone it down – he got quite cross.' She pats my arm. 'Anyway, that's quite enough about our wunderkind over there. You need to stop standing around talking to me and get on with building your fabulous garden, or you won't have anything to show my fellow judges when they pop by on Monday.'

'Who are the other judges?' I ask. 'We haven't been told yet.'

'Frank O'Connor and Gillie Goudge.'

My mouth drops open at the mention of these tours de force of the gardening world. 'Those are big names.'

Sonny smiles at my awe. 'Yes, so you need to make a good impression. They'll be coming round after our final mentoring session, to get a feel for your builds.'

As soon as Sonny has left, I exchange an excited grin with Gertrude before texting my brother, Danny:

I just showed my designs to Sonny Carden and she loved them!

Danny, who knows how I feel about Sonny, messages back within seconds:

You go, sis!

He follows this with a GIF of a cheering SpongeBob SquarePants. I respond:

You need to spend more time with grown-ups. Your references are all kids' TV.

I add a laughing emoji, to show I'm just teasing. He responds so quickly, I can sense his eagerness from here:

You offering to babysit?

With a smile, I type:

Let me get this flower show and my meeting with Verity

47

> out of the way and then we'll talk about me giving you and
> Karen a couple of nights off.

Danny and I are siblings by law, not blood. Not that the lack of a genetic connection has affected our bond: he is my most loyal friend and supporter. If anything, I wonder if we get on better for not being blood relatives. Most of the other siblings I know can't spend time in the same room as one another.

He sends another GIF – this time of a blue cartoon dog jumping up and down and cheering in excitement.

> Remind me who that is?

> That would be Bluey. 150 episodes. And I know every single one inside out, upside down and back to front. I am losing my mind.

I smile and shake my head as I put away my phone and join Gertrude back at our compass, where I tie a second stick to the loose end of the string. Then, with the first stick marking the centre, I move the second stick in a circle, as Gertrude sprays chalk from the can to mark the periphery.

'Good job,' I say, as we finish the circle and step back.

'I like the spray chalk,' she tells me.

I smile at her. 'You can use it again when we mark out the spiral path, if you like.'

She nods enthusiastically, then says, 'How are we going to dig out the pond? Do you want me to line up some other volunteers for that as well?'

I shake my head. 'Tomorrow, we have a digger arriving.' Her eyes grow wide. 'And yes, it's only a miniature model, so you can have a go at driving it,' I tell her, laughing. 'If it was a full-sized machine you'd be needing a licence, which I have.'

Checking my watch, I see it's nearly five. 'We'll be heading back to the house in a few minutes,' I tell Gertrude. 'Thanks so much for your help.'

'I've never created a garden from scratch before,' she tells me as she fetches her bag from the corner. 'Well, except my own, but I've taken years to create that. It's not the same as having all the ingredients right from the start.'

'This is my first show garden,' I admit. 'It's a different challenge from anything I've worked on before.'

'We'd better make sure you win in that case,' she says with her cheeky grin.

'Sounds good to me!' I smile back. 'Thanks again for all your help today.'

She gives me a wave before leaving. Then, after stowing away my measuring and marking tools, I call Mouse and put him on the lead. Chaplin appears behind him, and I lead the two dogs slowly back to the minibus, taking in the other designers' progress as we walk.

At the moment, like mine, the other plots mainly resemble rectangles of bare soil, although Seb's wooden deck is already taking shape at the back and there are large holes and trenches dug out in several of the plots. Toby obviously managed to round up his missing volunteers, as his planned water feature now has a very neat rectangular channel excavated.

We assemble at the minibus hot, grubby and tired. While we're waiting to mount, I notice Delilah is holding a transparent drinks bottle which bears her name in large cursive letters, surrounded by painted flowers. The bottle is full of leaves.

'What are you drinking?' I ask.

She holds it up. 'It's an infusion of borage and nettles, so it's packed with vitamins and minerals.'

'You need to be careful,' says Koko, standing behind us.

'Excuse me?' says Delilah, turning towards her.

Koko shrugs. 'Borage contains specific alkaloids which, over the long term or in large quantities, can damage the liver. But I am sure that you are aware of this fact.'

I watch as Delilah's smile wavers. 'I only added a few borage leaves,' she says uncertainly.

'In that case, I daresay you will be fine,' says Koko, nodding for us to climb on board. Delilah goes first, then I follow with Mouse and we walk to the back, passing her en route. She's sitting by a window, holding up her bottle and inspecting its contents. I wonder if she is feeling less confident in their nutritional properties.

On the short journey to Coleton Fishacre, Toby insists we all sing 'One Man went to Mow'. Despite our initial reluctance, he somehow cajoles us all to join in. Seb turns out to have a beautiful voice, which soars above the rest of us. I wonder if he used to be a choirboy. To everybody's great amusement, Mouse gets into the spirit and sings along. As I watch him, head back, howling along with enthusiasm, I mull on the fact that all dogs originally descended from wolves. There are some occasions when this is more apparent than others.

Chaplin refuses to be drawn into song, instead determinedly keeping an eye on Addie the driver.

Belying the brevity of the trip, twenty-eight men have already been to mow when we pull up alongside my van in the small parking area. We all file out, with Mouse and me at the rear.

I think we're all desperate to wash off the earth, sweat and sunblock and have a rest, so we agree to separate until dinner time, which will again take place outside on the Loggia. Up in our room, I set out food for Mouse. Then I cross the corridor to the glamorous bathroom which I've been allocated for my personal use. This bathroom, like everything at Coleton Fishacre, is finished to a luxurious standard. The cream wall tiles are interspersed with pictorial tiles by the artist Edward Bawden, depicting D'Oyly Carte-appropriate activities, such as hunting and riding. The original bath, sunk into the floor, is deep. I run cool water and climb into it.

As my body soaks, my mind flicks to Anil, and his explanation for keeping his build a secret. I wonder again if the person who plagiarised his garden design all those years ago might be one of the contestants in the Coleton Fishacre competition. It would explain his concern.

Rubbing myself dry after my wash, I pull on a pair of clean khaki shorts and a white vest top. Standing in front of the mirror, I draw my thick hair back into a ponytail on top of my head. Now that I've cooled down, I'm determined to stay that way.

8

When I walk into the dining room, I immediately feel underdressed. Everyone else is in their finery tonight, milling about, drinks in hand. There's the scent of mingled perfumes and aftershaves, and the women have applied fresh makeup.

Koko is in a gold-patterned trouser suit, teamed with long gold earrings; Seb is wearing a white shirt with smart grey trousers; Addie has donned a beautiful off-the-shoulder sundress in a blue and red Ankara print with matching headscarf; and Delilah is wearing a knee-length red slip dress with matching lipstick. Although Anil is in shorts, like me, his are smart, belted chinos, which he's teamed with a rose-pink shirt. Even Toby – who has donned another of his Hawaiian-print shirts, this time in orange and yellow – has paired it with cream linen trousers. He hands me a glass of red wine, which I accept with thanks. Standing beside him is a woman of no more than five foot, with an abundance of red curls rarely seen outside of Pre-Raphaelite paintings. Toby has his arm around her shoulders.

With a proud smile, he says, 'Steph, I'd like you to meet Sarah, my lovely wife.'

I hold out one of my large hands, engulfing her tiny one as we greet one another. She's wearing a calf-length wrap dress in an emerald green that complements her hazel eyes and red hair, and hugs her curves.

'Good to meet you,' I say. 'Toby has told me a lot about you.'

She smiles. 'It's good to meet you, too.' Her voice is deep and husky.

She raises an eyebrow. 'Although what exactly has my husband been saying about me?'

Glancing at Toby, I see he's gazing at her in besotted fashion.

'Oh,' I say, caught on the hop, 'only that you're a TV producer on gardening shows, and that the pair of you . . .' I tail off. 'Well, that's about it, really,' I say with a laugh. 'Oh! And that Chaplin was your choice, as you wanted a Miniature Schnauzer.'

'Daddy's little boy,' she says of the dog.

'He told me that, too,' I admit.

'Do I have any secrets left?' she asks, looking up at her husband.

Toby smiles indulgently. 'Darling, I speak nothing but the truth about you, and it's all good. And I will tell it to anyone who'll listen. Honestly, I'm quite the bore – I'm surprised the others are still speaking to me.'

'It's early days,' says Anil, lifting his glass as if in toast, and we all laugh.

'Shall we head outside?' says Addie. She leads the way out to the Loggia, which feels deliciously cool after the heat of the day. As per the previous night, our entrées are already set out. Most of us are having a mozzarella, avocado and tomato salad. Koko's plate bears a salad featuring green lentils.

Taking a seat on the far side, facing the house, I gesture to my vest and shorts and say, 'Sorry, everyone, I feel like I'm letting the side down. I'll make more effort tomorrow, I promise.'

'Oh, you look fine,' says Sarah, pulling out the chair to my right. She sits down and leans in closer to whisper, 'At least you're not wearing your nightdress.'

I glance around the table until I see that Sarah's gaze is directed at Delilah, in her red slip dress. Torn between defending Delilah – along with any woman's right to wear what she chooses – and shutting down the conversation, I settle for, 'Oh, I think she looks lovely. When do you start filming?'

'Tomorrow.' She clears her throat to get everyone's attention. 'I was just telling Steph that I'm going to start filming tomorrow. So, I hope you've all got some interesting jobs planned.'

'I've got a tree coming,' says Delilah. 'I've had to hire a crane to lift it into place.'

'I was asking about jobs you're doing yourselves,' says Sarah. 'Are you driving the crane?'

Delilah's face falls. 'No, but—'

'Anyone else?' asks Sarah, reminding me of a strict head teacher.

Toby, seated on the far side of Sarah, reaches across the table to pat Delilah's hand. 'A tree sounds marvellous,' he tells her, and she shoots him a grateful smile.

A second later, several people leap up from the table as Sarah's glass of red wine topples over. 'Oh god, I'm such a klutz!' she says, reaching to right the now-empty glass. 'Did it get anyone?'

They shake their heads and take their seats again as the wine trickles harmlessly away between the central slats of the table. Toby refills her glass and the conversation moves on.

But I'm left watching my neighbour closely. It seemed to me that, as soon as her husband showed attention to a pretty young woman, she made sure to bring it back to herself. I'll be interested to see if there's a repeat performance during our stay.

There's a momentary awkward lull, during which all that can be heard is the scraping of forks against china.

At last, Anil says loudly, 'Toby, mate, *please* tell me the mirrors I saw being unloaded earlier weren't for you.'

'Why shouldn't they be?' asks Sarah.

'Oh, come on, Sarah,' says Anil jovially. 'You know he *always* uses mirrors.'

With a chuckle, Toby says, 'I'll tell you I'm not using mirrors if you tell me *you're* not making another bloody urban garden.'

Anil laughs and pats his chest. 'Ow! Touché,' he says, and the two men lean across the table to chink glasses, both shaking their heads and laughing.

'I am going to win, though,' says Toby.

'Not if I win first,' says Anil.

Just when I'm thinking you could cut the testosterone at the table with a knife, Koko clears her throat. 'Actually, I believe you will find that *I* may be the winner on this occasion.'

Addie breaks in. 'I'm quite sure the most deserving designer will win the competition. Now, who would like a top-up? Toby, will you do the honours?' As Toby makes a tour of the table with the wine bottles, she says, 'I'd love to hear what you all made of Sonny's feedback. We're thrilled that we were able to procure her for this project.'

Seb speaks first, in the lugubrious tone that I am already beginning to associate with him. 'She didn't much like one part of my design.'

'What was it?' asks Toby.

'This deck I'm making – did any of you see?' When we all nod, he continues, 'It's nearly done, and it took the best part of the day.'

'What didn't she like about it?' asks Delilah.

'Oh, she said it "jarred with the rural intent and prevented the design from being cohesive",' he says, adding air quotes. His Birmingham accent seems, if possible, to grow stronger with his indignation.

'Ouch,' says Anil.

'Are you going to change it?' I ask.

He shrugs. 'It's pretty integral, actually. I think I'm just going to go ahead.'

'Is that a good idea, though?' asks Delilah. 'If one of the judges isn't keen on an aspect of your design, wouldn't it be better to alter it now, to improve your chances? I mean, that's why Sonny's coming round to see us.'

Seb rubs his hair. He looks exhausted. 'It'd be so much work, and it's not like we've got any spare time on these builds. And don't forget, she is only one of three judges. The other two might love it.'

Koko nods. 'I understand. I think I might do the same, if I was in your position.' Seb shoots her a grateful smile.

'I take it she liked yours?' Anil asks Koko.

She tilts her head. 'In fact, she was not completely happy.'

'Oh?' says Addie, sounding surprised.

'Yes, she said my design was beautiful, but that there was no focal point.'

Anil leans forward. 'So, will you be changing it?'

Koko sips some water before answering. 'I am not sure. Like Seb says, it is hard to make a change at this stage, when everything has been planned to fit the schedule.'

Anil says, 'You two aren't the only ones she said negative stuff to. She reckons I'm being too ambitious. But, as far as I'm concerned, with any competition it's go big or go home. I don't enter to play it safe.' He looks around for approval, and receives one or two nods.

But Toby says, 'I think there's a balance to be struck between creating something novel and striking, and being deliberately controversial.'

Anil smiles. 'Damien Hirst wouldn't agree with you there, mate.'

Toby reaches again for the wine bottle. 'Oh, well, if Damien Hirst's your role model . . .'

We all laugh.

But, after a brief pause, Sarah says, 'Anil, I don't understand why you've entered this competition. Isn't it a bit . . . *small fry* for you?'

There's a moment's silence. Then, clearing his throat, Anil says, 'I'm not sure what you're getting at.'

She leans forward, and I see Toby shoot her an anxious look. 'Couldn't you just let Toby have a win, for once?'

'Sarah,' says Toby quietly.

She turns to her husband. 'What? I mean, he's been busy, out in Dubai, winning all sorts of awards as usual for his grand designs. Why on earth did he need to come back and enter a teeny National Trust contest – one which could be a great bit of publicity for you, but which he, frankly, can't possibly need?'

I glance at Addie, to see how she's taking this belittling of her competition. She's wearing a fixed, tight smile.

Keen to defuse the situation, I say, 'If you ask me, it's pretty prestigious – especially if you manage to get it on the telly, Sarah.'

Sarah smiles at me. 'Well, yes, televising it would obviously be a giant plus.' Turning back to Anil, she says, 'You can't let Toby have anything, can you? You never could.'

'What? I . . .' Anil looks thoroughly bemused as Sarah downs her remaining wine and reaches past Toby for the bottle to refill her glass.

Beside me, Anil says under his breath, 'I *might* need the win,' but I'm not sure anyone else hears. I hadn't envisaged Anil's lawsuit to be too serious for his company when he mentioned it earlier. Now, I wonder . . . He certainly seems to be invested in winning this competition.

The remainder of the meal passes without incident. Sarah drinks a lot of wine rather quickly and falls quiet, which is a definite plus. The rest of us chat about the challenges of working in the heat, the enthusiasm of our respective volunteers, the beauty of both Coleton Fishacre's grounds and those of nearby Greenway – Agatha Christie's holiday home – as well as what, if any, adaptations we're having to make due to the site's aspect, the heat or the time frame.

Koko says, 'Everything from that point of view has been planned for. I do not envisage that I will have to make any accommodations.' She tops up her water from the crystal jug and takes another sip.

Delilah says, 'I know I'm changing the subject, but I'm excited about my tree!' She pushes her long dark hair back from her shoulders and leans forward eagerly.

'I think we've booked the same company for the crane,' says Anil.

'You're using one, too?' she asks, in evident surprise.

'I pretty much always use one,' he says. 'You're lucky you've got the first plot, next to the car park. I reckon they're going to have to come at mine from the refreshments field. We're going to have to take the back fence down.'

'I'll almost certainly have to remove the side fence for access,' she says. 'But I'm sure between me and the volunteers, we'll manage.'

'A tree's quite a statement,' says Seb to Delilah. 'What are you planning?'

Delilah smiles. 'A woodland garden.'

'Oh, that sounds lovely,' I say, amid a general murmur of approval. As I look around the table at my fellow competitors, I feel warmed by more than just my second glass of red wine. There's such a sense of camaraderie and good will that it seems to be having a positive effect on even the more competitive members of our party.

'Has anyone been to Sonny's nursery in Torquay?' I ask.

'I'm hoping to make it before I go back to Brum,' says Seb. 'She really does know her plants, doesn't she?' I suppress a smile at the grudging note in his voice. He continues, 'I was showing her some photos from other builds I've done, and she spotted this rare plant I'd had to get imported. She knew what it was and everything.'

'She's amazing,' I say. Something in my tone must give away how much I idolise her, because everyone laughs.

The group conversation breaks into smaller chats, and Delilah turns to me with a smile.

'Do you have any plants in yet? With my plot being the first one, I can't see much of what everyone else is doing.'

I shake my head. 'No. I want to get the structure built first. What's going in yours, apart from the tree?'

She smiles. 'I'm recreating my grandparents' back garden, from when I was little. It's where I fell in love with gardening. They lived in a little cottage, where the main garden was underneath deciduous trees. There was a riot of foxgloves in the spring.'

'That sounds gorgeous.'

'I spent so much of my summer holidays climbing those trees . . . and being told off for scraping my knees and tearing my clothes!' She laughs.

'It sounds idyllic.'

'It really was.' Her expression turns solemn. 'And those were the only times I got away from my father. He was such a bully. He threw a long shadow over our family.'

'I'm sorry.'

She nods. 'Thanks. It's been quite liberating, admitting his lasting influence on me and my brother.' There's a moment's pause, when she looks in danger of falling back into bad memories, so I say, 'Tell me more about your garden.'

She pushes her hair off her shoulders and sits forward. 'This is the first time I've done anything really ambitious for a show garden. I decided to push the boat out. I really need this win.'

'How come?'

She blushes. 'I'm getting married next year, and we want to get a place together.' She sighs. 'Everything's so expensive.'

I nod. 'That's true. I'm also saving for a place of my own. I really hope Sarah does manage to get the show on the BBC. That would be amazing publicity.'

Her smile fades for a moment, but then it's back. 'I know! So exciting!' Her manner is lacking some of her former conviction.

'Congratulations on the nuptials.'

'Thank you.'

Her face falls, and she whispers, 'I agree with Sarah about Anil not needing the win, though. I mean, I've read his book. He creates these really high-end gardens.'

'That doesn't mean he's going to win,' I tell her quietly, remembering Sonny's description of Anil's design as 'flashy'. 'You never know, a woodland garden might be exactly what they're looking for.' She brightens instantly, and I give her shoulder a squeeze before tucking into my main course, which has just been brought through by Addie. We meat eaters have smoked salmon with salad, which is delicious. This doesn't stop me from shooting an envious glance at Koko's plate, where a mix of multicoloured salad leaves forms the base for a selection of dips, with pitta bread and olives on the side. She catches me looking and places her hands over her plate as if to fend me off. We both laugh.

As soon as we've finished our main course, Anil pushes back his chair and stands up.

'Sorry, everyone, but my partner wants me to look over some paperwork tonight. I need to get on.'

'No rest for the wicked,' says Toby, earning a playful shove on the shoulder from Anil. The rest of us stack our dinner plates and tuck into a tasty dessert of orange sorbet with fresh mint. Afterwards, I go up to my room feeling pleasantly full and with a sense of excitement at the work to be done tomorrow. Mouse is snoring quietly in his bed, his lead and Mr Rabbit both tucked lovingly beneath his chin. It's quarter to ten, and the sky, as I draw the curtains, is suffused with a delicate pink from the last rays of the sun.

After cleaning my teeth and climbing into bed, I pick up the photo from Verity and study it again. My mind flicks to Mum, and I feel a pang of guilt for how I left things. It's too late now to call her, so I record a quick voice message instead:

'Hiya. Sorry about earlier. I'm just having trouble processing everything. But I keep remembering what a happy childhood Danny and I had. You and Dad did a great job.'

Mum is not the best with emotional stuff, and I nearly delete the message before she has time to play it. But Mum needs to know that my desire to meet Verity is no reflection on her. She will always be my mum.

9

I wake full of energy and ready to return to work. There's already a typed response from Mum, which reads:

> Thank you for your message. I am missing you. Good luck with your competition.

I can't help but smile at Mum's predictably formal phrasing. Putting away my phone, I pull on shorts and a vest, plus socks and trainers, before waking Mouse for our run. I've looked up the nearest dog-friendly beaches online, and have settled on Scabbacombe Sands. We access it by jogging across fields, arriving happy and relaxed by the time I let Mouse off the lead at the beach.

I had been planning a run along the sand, among the scattered pebbles, but Mouse races straight into the sea. With his love of water – dislike of rain notwithstanding – I'm ever more convinced he's got some retriever in his mix.

I've read that the secluded nature of Scabbacombe Sands means it attracts some nude sunbathing. But we're the only ones on this wide expanse so early in the day. A delicate mist hangs over the sea and the salt-scented air has yet to heat up. Removing my trainers and socks, I paddle, laughing whenever Mouse comes back to me and shakes water off his curly coat on to my bare legs. He is so happy, tongue lolling, I make the decision to bring him here daily for the rest of our stay.

A little while later, after returning to our room at Coleton Fishacre, I put out Mouse's food before enjoying a shallow wash in my sunken bath. Then, freshly dressed, I walk out to the Loggia for my breakfast and find Koko and Delilah sitting side by side at the table, chatting.

'Morning,' I say, and they both nod, but continue their earnest discussion while I stand at the coffee machine, filling first a cup and then my thermos. Crossing to the table, I pull out a chair opposite the pair of them, so that I'm facing the view. They're still deep in conversation, so I help myself to a croissant and a bowl of fruit salad and soak in my glorious surroundings as I eat.

It's when I sip my coffee that I hear Koko say, 'There's no excuse for ignorance.'

I close my eyes wearily against the conflict. I'd been so looking forward to spending time with like-minded people, who wanted to talk about plants all day long.

But Delilah responds calmly, 'I completely agree. Peat farming is out of control at present. The current measures just aren't stringent enough.'

Opening my eyes, I see Koko observing me. 'What is the matter?' she asks.

I hesitate, but then admit, 'I was worried you two were arguing.'

Delilah laughs. 'Arguing? No, we're discussing the impact of the peat trade on the environment.'

'Oh,' I say. 'Well, that's all right then.' I laugh, too, and agree with them about the need for greater controls to ensure the conservation of this precious resource.

We're soon joined by the rest of the party, and there's the pleasant atmosphere I'd been anticipating, with people sharing their experiences of difficult clients and awkward landscapers. I sit back, savouring both my coffee and the experience of being among my peers. While I love spending time alone with plants, it's a rare treat to be surrounded by others who understand both the joys and the tribulations of gardening as a profession. Only Anil seems distracted. His phone keeps pinging and, each time, he frowns at the screen before typing a response.

Toby, meanwhile, begins to hold forth on the merits of reflective surfaces, and it occurs to me, looking round, that there's no sign of his wife. Addressing him, I ask, 'Did Sarah not want breakfast?'

'Oh, she had it early, so she could get over to the site and get in a bit of filming before we and the rest of the crowd descend. She thought it would make a good contrast: the early-morning deserted spaces, and then the hum as we all get to work.'

'Very atmospheric,' says Anil, looking up briefly from his phone.

As the others make noises of agreement, my gaze lands on Delilah. She's fallen quiet, and I see she hasn't eaten any of her breakfast.

'Delilah, are you all right?' I ask.

She sets down the spoon she's been using to push the fruit around her bowl. 'Yes. I'm just not very hungry.'

'You need to eat something,' says Toby. 'We've a long day ahead and you need fuel.'

When she shrugs, Seb asks, 'Nerves? I know I'm feeling stressed. So much hangs on this build.'

Delilah is rubbing her stomach, but I don't want to put her on the spot, so I keep quiet.

Having finished my own breakfast, I get to my feet and say, 'I'm off. See you all on the bus.'

Inside the bedroom, I grab my backpack and put Mouse on the lead. As we leave the room, Sarah comes out from the next door along.

'Oh!' she says, upon seeing me. Then, laughing, she adds, 'Sorry! You just gave me a shock.'

'I thought you were at the site. Toby said you wanted to get some filming done before we all showed up.'

'Yes, that was the plan. But I was halfway there when I realised I'd forgotten the spare battery packs.' She holds up a small black kitbag. 'What a pain.'

We exchange a smile and then head downstairs and out to the car park, where she gets into her smart white Volvo XC60 and drives off, while I climb on to the rusty orange bus with Mouse.

He and I walk through the vehicle, stopping briefly en route so he can have a cuddle with Mike. The under-gardener meets my eye. 'Morning,' he says, in his rich Devon accent. He gives me one of his warm, eye-wrinkling smiles, and I smile back, slightly entranced when I notice he has a dimple in his right cheek. It's only Mouse pulling on the lead that reminds me we need to get to our own seats. I feel a flush heating my cheeks as I nod to Mike and walk quickly to the back.

Delilah is the last to appear. She sits near the front, behind Toby and Chaplin. I hope she has the energy to supervise her tree installation today, after her lack of appetite at breakfast.

I notice Toby turn around to look at her at one point during the journey, but I can't tell if any words are exchanged.

My phone rings when we're five minutes out, and I see Dad's name flash up. I hit the red button to block the call and type him a quick message:

> Sorry, can't talk right now. On minibus to build site. Can you text me?

A moment later, my phone pings with a response:

> URGENT! SOS! ALLOTMENT TOO SMALL! NEED HELP CONVINCING UR MUM TO LET ME DIG UP FLOWER BEDS TO GROW MORE VEG!

With a laugh, I type back: Never going to happen.

We're just pulling in at the car park at Poplars Farm when there's another ping. I check my phone and read: FEEDING THE MASSES SHOULD TAKE PRIORITY

I respond: What masses are you feeding, Dad?

Hopefully, that will keep him quiet for a while.

After we've climbed down from the minibus, I walk with Mouse to the show gardens, where Toby is waiting by the gate with Chaplin. We let the dogs off the lead to play, and they run off together.

'Phew!' says Toby, wiping his forehead with a large handkerchief. He's already red in the face. 'It's going to be another scorcher,' he says, with a sigh. 'How do you manage to look so fresh?'

'Check on me around midday. I'll be decidedly cooked by then.'

'I'd better let you get on while you're still raw, then,' he says, with a smile. He raises a hand in farewell as he heads to his plot.

I walk over to Delilah, at the first plot. She is sitting on the ground, going over her plans.

'Are you OK?' I ask quietly.

She pulls a face. 'I'm feeling a bit sick and I have to keep running to the loo.'

'Have you taken anything for it?'

She holds up her transparent water bottle. 'No, but I've switched my leaves to peppermint. I'm hoping that will help settle it.'

'I hope so. Let me know if you need anything.'

She manages a smile. 'Thanks, Steph.'

Back at my plot, I fish my sun hat and water bottle out of my bag and place my backpack out of the way, beneath the oak tree. This tree is so beautiful, I'd love to incorporate it into my design. Walking back inside my rectangle, I check, but there's no way of creating a sightline that would include the tree.

Gertrude arrives a few minutes later, bright-eyed and excited. Clearly, we're both looking forward to the job we've lined up for today: digging out the dew pond. The digger is due to be delivered mid-morning, so we busy ourselves with preparation, putting down planks to avoid crushing the earth beneath the digger's treads.

Sonny appears at ten. Gertrude and I are both covered in soil, and we attempt to brush ourselves off as we get to our feet to greet our mentor.

'Hello, girls,' she says, walking towards us with a smile and giving us each a squeeze of the hand. 'Don't clean yourselves up on my account. You know me: the dirtier, the better.'

'I wasn't expecting you till later,' I say. 'There's nothing new to see!'

'Yes, timing has gone awry today,' she says. 'I've been booked in to do a local radio interview this afternoon, so I'm afraid there was nothing to do but rejig the timetable. How's it going? You're looking busy.'

'Not bad, thanks,' I say. 'We're nearly prepped for the little digger, which should be here soon for digging out the pond.'

'Could you use it for the path as well?' she suggests.

I pull a face. 'With the path being a spiral, I think we need to do it manually.'

She nods. 'Makes sense. And you're putting in a bog garden, I believe. Remind me what's going in there?'

'I've planned a mass planting of the corkscrew rush, *Juncus* "Spiralis".'

'Excellent choice,' she says with a smile. 'Spiral plants for a spiral garden.' Glancing around, she says, 'Do you think you'll get your path marked out today?'

'Probably not,' I say. 'But we should be able to do that tomorrow, and get it dug out, like you suggested.' I catch Gertrude's eye. She's bright red and perspiring. 'Though, in this heat, that won't be a fun job.'

'We'll get it done,' says Gertrude, flexing her impressive arm muscles and causing the morning glory tattoos to bulge at the same time.

'I'm very lucky with my co-worker,' I tell Sonny. 'She's hard-working and undauntable.'

'So far,' says Gertrude, pulling a face.

Sonny places her hands on Gertrude's shoulders. 'Listen, girlie, take the compliment. You'll find they're few and far between over the years, so you need to learn to enjoy them when they happen your way.' Her tone is firm but kind. 'OK?' she says.

'OK,' says Gertrude quietly.

'OK?' says Sonny again.

'OK,' says the volunteer, laughing.

'Good. Now, make sure you pay attention to this one,' she says, gesturing to me. 'This may be her first time creating a show garden, but she knows her stuff.'

I'm too busy blushing at this praise to answer, so I'm relieved when a loud engine noise starts up, causing a distraction.

Gertrude frowns. 'What on earth's that?'

'That will be the crane, for Delilah's tree,' says Sonny.

'She's putting in a *tree*?' Her tone and expression are filled with awe.

Laughing, I tell Sonny, 'I think she's having trouble getting past that.'

Sonny nods. 'It's a bold move for a show garden. And Anil's booked the crane for tomorrow, I believe. He's got some large structures going in. I don't think I'm allowed to say more than that.' She mimes zipping her mouth shut. 'Though it is going to be quite dramatic,' she whispers.

'Not to mention "flashy"', I deadpan.

She grimaces. 'I forgot I'd said that. Oops!'

'Oops indeed.'

We all laugh.

'Did you have anything you wanted to run by me?' she asks. 'I can't believe it's Day Two already. Time is just whizzing by. Of course, it goes faster where the company is pleasant and receptive.'

The way she says this has me asking, 'Was Anil in a bad mood again?'

With an arched eyebrow, she says, 'Oh, it's not just him. Another is building a deck that clashes with his bucolic dream, and yet another has designed a gorgeous mass of planting with nowhere for the eye to settle. But do they want to hear about it from me? You can bet they don't.'

'It sounds difficult,' I say, remembering the conversation over last night's dinner.

'Hmm,' she says. 'Anyway, never mind. Are you happy you've got everything under control here?'

'Yes – if anything, we're a little ahead of schedule,' I say, 'though I feel like I'm tempting fate by saying that out loud! Thanks for all your encouragement.'

'You are most welcome, my love. Right: until tomorrow, then. We'll be back to the afternoon then.' She squeezes my shoulder, then we walk with her to the grass verge.

'Adieu,' she says, giving us a wave.

Gertrude sings, 'So long, farewell, *auf Wiedersehen*, goodbye,' and I laugh before calling, 'See you tomorrow!' to Sonny's retreating back. She lifts a hand and continues on her way.

We return to laying the remaining few planks. 'What are your plans for all the excavated soil?' Gertrude asks, as we finish laying the last one.

'I'd originally thought about using it to create a sculptural landscape. I had this vision of mounds, like giant anthills or the surface of a strange planet.'

'That's interesting,' she says. 'Why did you decide not to do it?'

'The main design is the spiral, which is almost 2-D. I didn't want to draw attention away from that.'

'Ah, I see.' She nods and shoots me a grin and I can't help grinning back. I had a trainee for a while, at Beaulieu Heights, and I'd forgotten how much I enjoy passing on my knowledge and experience.

'Anyway,' I continue, 'Addie's checked with the farmer, and he's given us permission to dump the excavated soil in the next field along from the refreshments. He seems really kind – he's even volunteered to use his own machinery to empty the pond after the show and refill the hole.'

'Well, that makes our lives easier!'

We take a quick coffee break beneath the oak, and we're just walking back to the plot when I receive a text to say the digger's been delivered to the car park. I drive it to the plot while Gertrude walks alongside. We then spend a thoroughly enjoyable few hours, taking turns to steer and operate the neat machine, scooping out earth from our chalk circle, then driving past the oak tree and the refreshments field to deposit it in the allocated spot.

By half twelve, we have a large, circular hole. I park the digger in the car park for collection, then Gertrude and I set to work, first neatening the hole with spades and then positioning the pond liner centrally before burying all of the excess liner in the surrounding soil. It's a fiddly job but, once completed, we're rewarded with a neat cavity that needs only filling with water to become the perfect dew pond.

We finish by puncturing the buried edges of the pond liner to create a boggy environment for the corkscrew rush. It will thrive here, forming a knee-high forest of fabulously twisted stems.

We break for lunch beneath the oak just after one. I'm just finishing today's tasty choice – a roasted vegetable and houmous wrap – when, glancing towards the car park, I spot a large blue van.

'I wonder if that's my plant delivery,' I say to Gertrude. 'I'm going to check.'

'I'll come with.'

On our way, we glance at the other plots. I'm keen to see how my fellow competitors are progressing with their creations.

Koko is doing something complicated with pacing and measuring sticks. There's still no sign of any structure or plants. Seb is looking very focused, crouching at the far end of an undulating trench that several volunteers are busy digging out. He is placing pebbles along its base, to replicate a natural mountain stream. Sarah is crouched opposite him with her handheld camera, filming his process. I wonder how he can focus with her so close. I see that his deck is already finished.

'What do you think?' asks Gertrude, nodding towards his plot. 'I love the stream bed.'

'Yeah, me, too. But as you heard, Sonny told him the deck jarred with the natural surroundings and I have to say, I agree.'

Gertrude puts her head on one side. 'I'm biased because I do like a nice deck,' she says as we walk on.

Toby and his volunteers are busy at the next plot, employing a pair of giant spirit levels, presumably to ensure the trench is completely horizontal before they insert the stainless-steel water run. Anil's garden still has the screen, of course. But Delilah's tree, when we reach it, is a thing of beauty.

'Wow,' says Gertrude.

'Wow indeed,' I say. There's no sign of Delilah, so I'll have to wait till later to compliment her. I hope her stomach's improved since this morning.

Finally, we reach the car park where I experience a thrill of excitement upon seeing the words 'Hope's Nursery' painted on the van's blue sides. Gertude and I collect a barrow each from a rank at the edge of the car park, then we walk over to the van.

A man and woman climb down. 'Steph Williams?' asks the woman.

'That's me. And this is my helper, Gertrude.'

She smiles and holds out a hand. 'I'm Hope and this is my husband, Graham.'

We shake hands.

'We've got your plants,' says Graham. 'Some beauties in there.'

'Great, thanks! As we discussed, you can have them back when I'm done. And I've made sure you're credited in the programme for the show.'

Hope and her husband climb into the back of the van and pass out the plants to Gertrude and me. Part way through filling our first barrow loads, Gertrude holds up one of the plants. It's a toad lily, which boasts several small flowers with deep-violet speckles. The five separate petals, to my mind, resemble the spokes of a wheel, thus continuing my circular and spiral theme. It's a plant I love, so I've ordered a lot of them. En masse, they will provide the perfect underplanting to my larger specimens.

'Whoa, this is weird!' Gertrude says, turning the pot as she examines the curious flowers.

'Weird good or weird bad?' I ask.

'Definitely good,' she says. 'I've just not seen any like it.'

I smile. 'It's a toad lily, *Tricyrtis* "Blue Wonder". Isn't it an eye-catcher? It likes damp shade, so it's a bit of a rare beast.' The plants from Hope's Nursery are just as I'd imagined – all slightly eerie and otherworldly. I can't wait to see them in situ.

We wheel the first load around to the oak tree and deposit them in the shade before going back for the rest. When we reach the car park, Hope and Graham have finished unloading and are turning the van, on their way out. They wave farewell and we wave back.

It's only after they leave that I notice a plant I didn't order at the back of the collection. It's a multi-stem silver birch, whose white bark gleams in the sun.

'What is it?' asks Gertrude, seeing my uncertainty.

'I didn't order this.'

'Really?' She strokes the bark. 'It's gorgeous.'

'I know. And I can immediately see where it would go. I wonder if it's an extra. I'd better check with Hope.'

I stop to send a quick text to the nursery owner:

Is this *Betula utilis* for me?

While waiting for Hope's response, Gertrude and I transport the remaining plants over to my plant store beneath the oak. I wonder how the other designers are managing without the overflow area, which I'm finding so useful. Mouse and Chaplin are curled up together in the shade, asleep but panting from the heat. I refill their water bowls ready for when they wake.

Then Gertrude and I examine the plants. I've selected a number of shrubs and small trees, all of which have globe-shaped or otherwise unusual flowers. The cream, delicately scented spherical blooms of the button bush, *Cephalanthus occidentalis*, will provide a perfect foil for the vibrant yellowy-orange of a large *Buddleja* x *weyeriana* 'Golden Glow', which bears its flowers in spherical clusters. I also have a number of specimens of corkscrew hazel, the twisted branches of which fit my theme perfectly. A few *Hydrangea paniculata* and three bottlebrush trees, *Callistemon Laevis*, provide excellent complements.

'Why have you gone for such weird plants?' asks Gertrude, watching a bee on one of the buddleia's orange globes. 'I mean, they're fantastic, but your garden's called "The Journey", isn't it?'

I nod. 'It's about the plants reinforcing the circular walk, so that as you walk in the spiral, they give the impression of rotating as well. I want the journey to be a slightly disorientating experience.'

'What about soil type?' Gertrude asks me. 'Isn't it ericaceous in this area? I've noticed everyone around here grows rhododendrons and azaleas.'

I smile. 'At one point, I did consider creating a rhododendron garden. I love Sonny's book from her TV series *What's Your Type?* back in the nineties. Do you know it?' She shakes her head. 'It's all about being led by soil type and location. But, for the show garden, I'll just be burying the plants in their pots, so I don't need to worry about the site's low pH.'

The nursery has done me proud, supplying beautifully balanced plants in glossy good health. With the help of Gertrude and a couple of other volunteers, we test some of the larger shrubs in their intended positions. I can feel excitement mount as I stand back and take in the overall effect. It's amazing what a difference it makes, placing these plants. Hope has supplied some large pittosporum balls as well as some box plants trained in a spiral, and they immediately give a framework to the spiral pathway to come. I have an image of each of these shrubs as a wheel in a pinball game, with the visitor as the ball, moving between them.

I pour coffee for us both and sit down in the shade to go through my list of tasks. The priority will now be the creation of the garden's framework, before the rest of the planting goes in. I've arranged for a local artist to paint the trompe l'oeil frame I've sketched out for the large mirror, which won't be delivered until Thursday, along with two small wooden benches. The mirror and benches have been carved by a talented local craftswoman. She's sent me photos and they look phenomenal, all fabulous carvings in uncanny shapes, and I can't wait to see and touch them.

I show Gertrude, who's sitting close by, stroking a dozy Mouse, and she says, 'Oooh, they're like thrones in some fairy tale of wicked queens.'

I laugh. 'I love that! I'm hoping the whole garden will have that kind of weird and wonderful vibe.'

I check my phone throughout the afternoon, but no response comes from Hope about the unexpected plant. Eventually, I mark the spot where I'd like to site it, before measuring the pot. Then Gertrude and I dig a hole to the right dimensions. It's hot work, and we have to stop regularly for water until it's finally big enough. Then we round up another volunteer, and the three of us stagger down to my garden with the birch tree. It may not be a full-size tree but, like all pot-grown specimens, it's a weighty object.

Once we've lowered it into the hole, I stand on the grass at the front, calling out directions for the other two to turn it, until it has its best face forward. Plants, like humans, definitely have a front and back. The three of us backfill the hole, then we thank our extra volunteer and she heads off, leaving Gertrude and me to stand back to admire the effect.

'What do you think?' I ask her.

'It's fantastic,' she says.

I nod. 'It's going to be a great focal point when the garden's finished. Right: coffee break?'

'Yes, please! I'm parched.'

We take the thermos and mugs and walk over to join the sleeping dogs in the shade beneath the oak. While we sit and sip our drinks, I answer her questions about the craft of designing a garden from scratch, and we discuss the work ahead. I'm grateful for her easy company.

We're still in this spot a few minutes later, when we hear something close to a roar.

'What on earth is going on?' says Gertrude.

We both stand up and walk warily towards the sound. As we approach my plot, Seb comes storming out of it, wheeling around until he spots me, his face purple with fury.

As I begin mentally sifting through my possible crimes and coming up empty, Seb advances upon me like a man possessed.

10

During Seb's charge, I try to push Gertrude behind me for safety, but she resists, and I feel a surge of gratitude.

'You fucking thief!' he roars, bearing down on me.

At that moment, a large, snarling black dog inserts himself between the angry man and us. With relief, I see uncertainty flicker across Seb's face. He slows, taking in Mouse's bared teeth and hunched shoulders.

Chaplin comes to join Mouse. Together, they present a ferocious front. 'What is it?' I ask Seb. I have to shout over the growls. 'Why are you so angry?'

'You've stolen my fucking tree!'

'Ohhh.' I share a look of understanding with Gertrude. 'The silver birch is yours?'

'Of course it's fucking mine! I've been looking all over for it. Then one of the volunteers said you'd taken a tree like that from the car park.'

'It was in my delivery, and Hope just left it standing there. All the other plants were for me, so I thought it must be an extra. I did ask, but she hasn't been answering my texts.'

'Her phone's off. I had to call Graham. He said they left it in the car park for me.'

'I didn't know.' A thought occurs to me. 'Anyway, why do you need a silver birch? I thought your garden was set on the Yorkshire Moors?'

I regret this question as soon as it's spoken. He rolls his eyes. 'Oh, don't you start. I'm not creating the literal Yorkshire Moors, am I?

73

I mean, we're in bloody Devon.' He gestures around us, as if I need help locating myself.

'Right . . . Anyway, I'm sorry.'

Seb's face is hard and mean. He's almost unrecognisable as the quietly spoken man with the lovely singing voice.

At that moment, Mike, Toby and Koko appear.

'What's happening? Are you all right, Steph?' Mike asks, coming to my side. I nod weakly and he turns to Seb. 'Why are you yelling at her?'

Seb's eyes flick to Mike but quickly return to me. 'She's stolen my tree,' he says.

'I'm sure it was an innocent mistake,' says Mike. 'There's no call for raising your voice like that.'

Seb spits out, 'I've been round the block too many bloody times to believe in innocent mistakes when there's a prize up for grabs.' His tone is so harsh that Mouse starts to bark loudly.

I pull him back, murmuring reassuring words but not taking my eyes off Seb. I have to raise my voice to be heard over Mouse. 'Grab some volunteers and you can take the tree.'

'I'm going to take it back right now,' he says, in a combative tone that implies I haven't already suggested he do that.

After he's stridden off to find help, Toby and I lead the dogs back over to the oak tree where we stroke them and talk to them in soothing tones. Chaplin had really just been providing moral support to Mouse, so Toby calms him easily. Mouse, though, who was thoroughly invested in my protection, takes a while to stop growling. While I murmur to him, Gertrude sits on his other side, pale and shaken. Koko and Mike stand watching us, looking concerned.

With her hands on her hips, Koko pronounces, 'He should be disqualified for that behaviour.'

Toby says, 'She has a point. That was distinctly threatening. I was worried he was going to hit you, Steph.'

'Me, too,' says Gertrude quietly. I reach around Mouse to squeeze her hand.

We all watch warily as Seb returns with two volunteers, to dig up the tree. Mouse starts grumbling at once, and I keep stroking him while still holding on to his collar. Mike, Toby and Koko line up protectively in front of me. There's no way I would let them get hurt on my behalf, but I'm touched. At last, Seb's back recedes, along with those of his helpers, all working hard to carry the heavy tree in its pot, and Mouse finally relaxes his vigil and allows me to give him a big cuddle.

'You're a brave dog,' I murmur into his fur.

'He's amazing,' says Gertrude, earning herself a lick from Mouse.

Mike says, 'If you're OK, Steph, I'll go and discuss the situation with Addie.'

'Thanks,' I say. 'But I had taken his plant, even if he did overreact. I don't want to make it into a big deal.'

Mike raises an eyebrow. 'I think Seb's done that for himself.'

As Mike strides away, Toby sits back down beside me. 'Seb really Hulked out, didn't he?'

Gertrude laughs wanly. 'That's a good way of putting it.'

'He was terrifying,' says Koko. 'Addie will have to do something.'

Toby says, 'You never really know someone till you've seen them angry.' I wonder if he's right. Studying him, I try to picture what he'd be like enraged, but my mind balks at the concept. He seems so affable. Mind you, until Seb's outburst, I would have said the same of him. Or, if not affable, then gentle, at least.

'We should get on,' says Koko.

I give Mouse a final pat and get up. 'Yep. I need to work off some adrenaline.'

'Me, too,' says Gertrude.

Toby says goodbye to Chaplin then turns to me. 'Well, you know where we are if you need us.'

'Thank you both so much for coming over,' I say. 'I really appreciate it.'

'Hey, we have your back, girl,' says Koko, swinging her bob. I smile and she smiles back before stalking over to her plot.

My hands are still shaking as Gertrude and I set to work, filling in the hole left by the removal of the silver birch.

'Are you OK?' Gertrude asks me, after we've finished and tamped down the soil.

I nod. 'Yeah, I'm OK, thanks. I was just missing the birch. Did you see how it was casting some lovely, frothy shadows?'

She smiles, dusting soil off her gardening gloves. 'Don't forget you've got a load of gorgeous plants lined up.'

Thinking of the ranks of striking shrubs and perennials awaiting us in the shade of the oak tree, I say, 'You're right.' Checking my watch, I say, 'Oh, it's nearly time to go home.'

'That went fast.' She meets my gaze and asks, 'Will you be all right on the minibus, with Seb and everything?'

I hadn't even thought about that. Reflecting on his flare-up, I say, 'I can't help feeling there's something more going on. It can't just have been about the tree.'

She nods. 'You're probably right. He's maybe under some other stress.'

I slip my tools back into my belt and remove my gloves. Then I make up my mind. 'If he's calmed down, I'll see if he wants to talk about anything on the way home.'

'You're a brave woman!'

'More like, I don't want to spend the next week being on my guard.'

'That's fair,' she says. 'Hey, did you see the woman filming earlier?'

'That's Toby's wife, Sarah. I saw her on Seb's plot, while he was laying pebbles.'

She raises an eyebrow. 'She had her camera out when Seb was throwing his tantrum as well.'

I stare at her. 'I didn't notice her. Does Seb know?'

She shrugs. 'No idea.'

Remembering the scene, I feel a stab of concern for my own reputation. If shown out of context, far from gaining me clients, it could make me look like some kind of plant thief. I'm going to have to talk to Sarah, to persuade her against using the footage.

But that will have to wait. My first priority is speaking to Seb. Determined to get a chance to do this, I make sure Mouse and I are the first on to the minibus. We pass the digger in the car park, still awaiting collection by the hire company. I guess they must be planning on picking it up tomorrow. I can't do much about it tonight, so I climb aboard the bus with Mouse and we take our seats at the back.

When Seb gets on, I beckon to him to join us.

Mouse grumbles as the man approaches, but I stroke him while addressing Seb brightly, 'Can we have a quick chat?'

'If you keep your dog in check.'

'I promise.'

He nods and takes a seat in the row in front of us, but he keeps an eye on Mouse.

'Seb,' I say, waiting until he meets my eye. 'I'm sorry for what happened earlier.'

He nods. There's a moment's pause during which he pushes his blond hair back from his face. Clearing his throat, he says, 'I'm sorry, too.' There's another pause, which I don't attempt to fill. His gaze wanders away but returns to mine. 'I always promised myself I wouldn't turn out like my dad, who was a total a-hole, always going off at the slightest thing.' He sighs, rubbing his face, then says, 'It's just, this competition's so bloody important.'

'Why's that?'

He pulls a face. 'My girlfriend wants me to move out. I'd hardly get to see our daughter, Millie.'

I frown. 'How does the competition fit in?'

'If I win it, I should be able to land more work locally, so I won't have to travel so much. At the moment, I'm all over the country from one week to the next. That's what Kerry's so fed up about, me never being there. She says it's like being a single mum, having to do everything herself.'

I'm not sure his reasoning around the competition makes sense, but my heart goes out to him.

'I'm sorry for losing it with you,' he says. At my side, Mouse has stopped grumbling, though he's still watching Seb closely. I continue to stroke the dog's head to reassure him.

Without my noticing, Mike has come to sit nearby, also keeping a close eye on Seb. Accustomed though I am to being self-reliant, it's still good to see others watching out for me. I shoot Mike a grateful smile before turning back to Seb.

'Did Addie speak to you?' I ask, and he nods.

'She said I'll be disqualified if it happens again.' He sighs. 'Seems fair enough. To be honest, I'd have disqualified me already, if I was her.'

'She seems pretty fair-minded.'

He nods again. 'Yeah. She really listens . . . like you.'

'We're all here together for the next five days, plus the show itself,' I say, as Addie starts the engine. 'Just seek one of us out, if you need to talk. It's much better than storing it up until you go off like a pressure cooker.'

He laughs in embarrassment, running a hand through his hair again. 'You're right, you're right.'

Glancing at Mouse, I say, 'Shall we forgive him, boy?'

Mouse barks once, and I have to restrain him from poking his head between the seats. With a small whine, he settles back beside me, placing his head in my lap.

'Good boy,' I murmur. He rumbles an agreement in his throat.

For the short remainder of the journey, Mike moves nearer and makes a fuss of Mouse, while chatting to Seb and me about our careers so far.

'What about you?' I ask Mike.

'Oh, I've been with the National Trust practically since I was born.'

'That long?' I ask with a raised eyebrow.

'I was at Greenway before this, Agatha Christie's old holiday home, not far from here. Have you been?' I shake my head. 'It's another beauty. I can't see why I'd ever want to move from this area, and I love working at Coleton Fishacre. Every part of the garden is spectacular. Have you seen the area known as Kent's Border?'

'I don't think so.' I draw the map of the gardens from my pocket as he continues, 'I think it was named after the original foreman who constructed the house. It's one of my favourite parts of the garden.' The bus has just arrived back at Coleton Fishacre and we all start getting to our feet. 'Have you got time to see it now?' he asks.

'Absolutely. That sounds great.'

Seb says, 'I'm going up to my room for a bit of quiet before dinner.'

We descend from the bus and Mike escorts Mouse and me the short distance to an area of the garden so beautiful that I stop short, drawing in a breath. Mouse at my side looks up and makes a questioning sound in his throat. I pat his head as I take in the scene.

A cardoon provides a spiky backdrop to what is otherwise a soft watercolour planting of white *Rosa* 'Desdemona', clipped domes of *Ilex crenata* and mounds of silver-leaved and pink-flowered *Lychnis coronaria*, all interspersed with splashes of dark Sweet William 'Sooty'.

I catch Mike's eye and he smiles. 'Told you it was good.'

'It's beautiful.' I draw out my phone, so I can take photos for my inspiration gallery. 'I'm already working out how to create a similar effect in the future, when I have my own garden.'

He looks appalled. 'You don't have a garden?'

I shake my head. 'I'm an itinerant gardener at present. But one day I will have my own place again. How about you?'

'I have the ground-floor flat in a Victorian terrace, so the plot is narrow but it's long. I've had a lot of fun, playing with diagonals to create a sense of width, and making separate rooms and hidden surprises.'

'It sounds lovely.'

'You'll have to come and see it.'

I meet his eye and can't help but smile at his warmth and enthusiasm.

We walk on in silence, enjoying the birdsong and the continuously changing vistas. It's a while since I've felt this relaxed in a man's company. My mind flashes to Ben, my ex-husband, and I find myself telling this kind new acquaintance about his disappearance.

Mike stops walking and turns to stare at me. 'He's gone missing?'

I nod. 'He came to ask me for a loan in April last year. I should say at this point that this is the man who gambled all my money as well as his own on risky deals, so we lost the house and I had to fold my business. I turned him down for the loan.'

'I should bloody well hope so.'

I nod. 'Anyway, no one has seen him since I ran him off.'

His eyes grow wide. 'So, that was it? He just . . . vanished?'

'Yup. His girlfriend Caroline keeps me informed whenever there's a "sighting" but they always prove to be false. I guess one tall, red-haired white man looks pretty much like another to the uninformed public.'

Mike lets out a whistle as we walk on, climbing a path to a crumbling wooden structure which gives a different view out to the ocean from the one at Scout Point.

'Oh my god,' I murmur, staring out to the rippling expanse punctuated by two rocky outcrops, resembling the head and spine of a sea monster. Mouse is excited by the sight, ears twitching as he tries to take it all in.

'It's something else, isn't it?' says Mike. 'You can see why I don't want to leave this place, can't you?'

'I really can.'

'This is the old gazebo. Though I'm not sure why all the seats have their backs to the view.' We both laugh.

'Maybe no one used them,' I suggest. 'I mean, you wouldn't want to turn your back on this view, would you?'

He checks his watch and sighs. 'I'm afraid we're going to have to. It's half five and I'm out tonight, so I need to scrub up. I guess you could stay longer, if you want?'

Holding up my filthy hands, I say, 'I really must remember to wear my gloves the whole time I'm gardening. Anyway, in this heat, I definitely need a wash before dinner.' Reluctantly, I bid farewell to the view, and we turn back, walking in silence to the house.

'Thanks for the tour,' I say as we reach the front door.

'You're very welcome.' I watch as he heads to his car, the vintage Mini in racing green which I've admired in the car park.

This evening, after my soak in the bath, I don the one dress that I've brought with me: a white jersey halterneck, which I like to think shows off my toned arms from all the gardening. If nothing else, it makes me feel like I'm on holiday. The gathered skirt swirls around my legs and I feel a little like a D'Oyly Carte lady as I descend the main staircase and cross the hall.

Addie is already there, and she hands me a glass of red wine.

'Cheers,' she says, holding up her own glass. As we chink glasses, she murmurs, 'How are you doing?'

I pull a face. 'I'm so sorry about that plant mix-up with Seb. I had no idea it was his tree or I'd never have touched it.'

'It's not your fault. And he really shouldn't have spoken to you like that.' I don't point out that he didn't speak so much as shout.

Instead, I say, 'We talked it through on the bus back, and he's apologised.'

'That's good. I came pretty close to sending him home, but he was so remorseful...'

I nod. 'Yeah. I think he's feeling up against it with the competition.'

'I got that impression.' Frowning, she says in a low tone, 'There's a lot more tension here than I'd expected, given that the prize pot is fairly modest compared to what I've heard top landscape gardeners can earn.'

Remembering Sarah's rather scathing comments at dinner the previous night, I say, 'Don't underestimate the kudos and publicity. A win like this – especially now it might be televised – can go a long way towards boosting reputation and expanding a client base. I know it would be a real boon for me. And ten grand isn't just a drop in the ocean for a small business like mine.'

She sips her wine thoughtfully before saying, 'I can't think what's in it for Anil, though. He's obviously big news in the gardening world, especially overseas. And those commercial commissions are major money. Of course, the judges jumped at the chance to include him.'

'I can imagine,' I say cautiously, not wanting to mention Anil's lawsuit in case Addie doesn't know about it.

Most of the others trickle in, including Delilah, who immediately finds a chair and sits, while the rest of us stand with our drinks, chatting and asking Sarah about her plans for filming. I make a mental note to ask her to delete the footage from the Seb incident.

Suddenly, the buzz of conversation stops and there's a tautness in the air. Searching for the cause, I see that Seb has stepped into the room.

He's looking nervous, so I walk over and engage him in conversation about his progress, until the tension slackens. Anil joins us and slaps him on the back. 'Got that out of your system, mate?'

Seb flushes. 'Yeah. All done.' He scans the faces before him and says with an embarrassed frown, 'I'm sorry, everyone. Won't happen again.'

The party nods and, on a signal from Addie, we file outside to take our seats at the table. Delilah is slow to rise, and I see Toby check on her, offering her an arm which she refuses.

When I step outside, the late-evening sun is illuminating sections of the hillside like spotlights. I stand in awe for a moment, admiring the view, before taking my seat. Delilah sits beside me, on the end.

'Are you OK?' I whisper. When she answers with a grimace, I ask, 'Is your stomach still bothering you?'

She nods.

'I think you should see a doctor.'

'Maybe, but I need to get on with the build.'

'Well, see how you're doing tomorrow.'

She nods again, and I don't press my point.

Part way through our entrée – some kind of whipped delicacy for Koko and a delicious Stilton brûlée for the rest of us – Koko, sitting opposite, addresses me:

'How are you getting on with your garden?'

'Oh! There's loads still to do, of course, but I'm on track.'

She nods. 'It is the same for me. I have completed all of my measuring and placed my markers for the features. I am hoping I can commandeer some volunteers to help with carrying the heavier items.'

'You want to watch out that Seb doesn't accuse you of stealing his volunteers,' quips Toby, and everyone laughs, including a sheepish-looking Seb.

'I'm pretty sure the wheelbarrows all belong to you, don't they, Seb?' chips in Sarah, glancing his way.

Seb is starting to blush again, looking down at his plate. Addie holds up her hands, palms out. 'Enough,' she says, though she's smiling. 'Seb has apologised. Let's move on, shall we?'

Anil tactfully changes the subject. 'Is anyone starting their planting tomorrow?' To Seb's evident relief, the conversation turns to everybody's progress on their gardens.

'Koko, your plants were arriving today, weren't they?' I ask her.

'That is correct. I am keeping them under wraps for now.' She meets my eye as if challenging me to ask further questions.

'I'll wait to see,' I say, even though I'm itching to discover what types of plants she's chosen. I wonder if she's aiming to specialise in a whole new area. This thought reminds me of her wildflower expertise and I add, 'I'd like to pick your brains at some point, about incorporating wildflowers into my planting schemes, if that's OK?'

'Of course. I am exhausted right now, but perhaps we can have a coffee break together tomorrow. Around eleven?'

'That sounds perfect. Thank you.'

When I reach our room after dinner, Mouse is already curled up, fast asleep in his bed.

It feels a bit late to call my brother Danny, so I type him a quick message:

How's it going with baby Stevie and the little monsters? Hope you and Karen are getting more sleep. All good here, although there are some 'interesting' characters.

He messages straight back:

Stevie slept through the night last night! Really, really, really hoping it's the start of a new habit. Luke's latest hobby is climbing up the tallest bookcase, so we're making sure everything is fixed to the wall. Not sure how we got away with it for the other two. Alice wrote a brilliant story, which she got to read out to the whole school. #ProudDad. Will send you a copy. And Frankie is being Frankie, getting on with life in his own individual and frenetic way.

Love you, sis.

I still find it amazing that my own little brother has four children. Alice, the precocious eldest, is eight. Cheeky Frankie is next, with less than two years between them. Then there's Luke, a boisterous tot. And of course there's Stevie, the baby. I send love back and change into my night things.

My phone rings as I'm climbing into bed.

Checking the caller ID, I answer, 'Hi, Dad.'

My mum's voice corrects me: 'Actually, it's your mum.'

'Oh! Hi!'

'Can you please tell your dad he does not need more space for his vegetables? We get far too many as it is. He ends up having to put them on a table out the front, with a note for the neighbours to take what they want.'

I sigh in sympathy. 'OK. Put him on.'

Dad doesn't bother with a greeting. 'Exactly,' are his first words.

'Exactly what?'

'I'm feeding the masses!' he says, with pride. 'I'm not just growing enough for your mum and me – I'm feeding the neighbours.'

Picturing the neat environment of suburban semis that is my parents' road, I doubt very much that any of the neighbours need feeding by my father. I say, 'Right . . . Well, I think you'll find there's more than enough to do with the allotment, Dad, without introducing more veg beds to maintain. See how this year goes before you start expanding your empire.'

He makes a noise that's somewhere between a grunt and a sigh, then Mum comes back on.

'Thank you, love. He wasn't going to listen to me. How's it going where you are?'

I fill her in briefly, leaving out Seb's tantrum, and she gives me her own news about various day trips she has planned with the local U3A educational organisation, to public and private gardens. It's a shame Dad's more recent obsession with growing veg has taken over from Mum's love of flowers. A natural showman, Dad has a large presence, which often crowds out Mum's less showy nature.

There's a pause before we finish the call, and I can sense she's working up the courage to ask me something. I can guess what and I feel tension prickle the back of my neck. At last, she asks quietly, 'How are you feeling about meeting Verity?'

'Nervous, if I'm honest.'

'Oh, Louise. She's going to love you.' As ever, I let slide her use of my former name, especially as, coming from my mum, this statement is the equivalent of an emotional outpouring.

'Thanks, Mum. And you know you'll always be my mum, right?'

'I should hope so.'

With a smile, I say, 'Night, Mum.'

'Goodnight, love.'

Once we've hung up, I pick up my book from the bedside table.

It's called *Chelsea Gold*, and features award-winning gardens from Chelsea Flower Show over the years. Although I've already planned my current show garden, I've been enjoying learning about the inspiration behind the various show winners, alongside the glorious photography. But I can't focus on the book.

The fact that my parents knew about my racial heritage and chose not to tell me still feels like a betrayal. I lie awake, wondering what else they might have kept from me. If I thought Mum would give me straight answers, I'd confront her.

When I eventually get to sleep, my dreams are stressful and I wake at six, drenched in sweat and feeling like I've been chasing shadows all night.

One dream comes back to me. I was busy planting up my show garden, but Seb was dogging my steps, digging up and removing each plant the moment I moved on to the next, saying, 'That's mine. And that's mine, and that's mine . . .' in the voice of Cat from the comedy series *Red Dwarf*.

With a sigh, I roll out of bed, keen to run off the unpleasant sensation left by my nightmares.

11

My phone rings just as I'm closing the front door softly behind us. Fishing in my pocket, I see Caroline's name flash up. The girlfriend of my ex-husband Ben, who went missing in (probable) inaction, she and I have nothing in common. But a phone call might mean news of Ben, so I answer promptly.

'They found a body,' she says matter-of-factly, in her nasal whine.

I feel a knot in my belly at the news I've been expecting but am still somehow unprepared for.

My heart starts thumping and I sink on to the ground at the edge of the courtyard. The earth is damp with dew, which seeps through my shorts. Mouse pushes his head into my lap, looking up at me with concerned eyes.

'It wasn't him,' Caroline says after a moment.

I take a deep breath, trying to calm my racing heartbeat. 'You didn't think to lead with that?'

'Look, I didn't have to ring you, did I? I could've just not bothered.'

I shake my head at Mouse in disbelief. I'm sure he understands. 'So, what happened?' I ask.

'Police found a body. Got me all worked up. Then rang me back to say it wasn't him, 'cos they'd got some DNA or dental records or something.'

I am glad we are on opposite sides of the country. I am not too sure I could have held my temper if she were standing in front of me. And I really don't fancy my chances in a shouting match with 'the whiner' as my brother Danny has generously named her.

'So, it's not him?' I say, pushing down my anger. 'Are there any new leads?'

I hear her turning pages in a notebook. 'Only that some old biddy saw him in a cabaret show on a cruise ship.'

'Now, that does sound like Ben,' I say.

She actually laughs. 'Yeah, I thought that! I thought, *Trust him to be having fun on a cruise ship while I'm pining away and imagining the worst.*' She continues, 'D'you know, I wouldn't put it past him to be doing a bit of gigolo stuff on the side?'

'I know what you mean.' For a moment, I wonder why I was so upset at the idea of his being dead. 'I take it that wasn't him either?'

'No. Turned out to be a good tip for the police, though. Apparently, this other guy was wanted for some breaking and entering jobs. Oh – and the red hair was a wig. Awful quality, too – I dunno why anyone thought it was real.'

'Anything else?' I ask.

More page turning. At last, she says, 'A nun with red hair, a boy of eighteen, a sixty-year-old man with hair dyed ginger . . . I think that's the lot.'

'How does a person just vanish?' I say, not really wanting a response.

'They pay the right people to make it happen,' she says.

I do not want to know how Caroline possesses this information. I thank her politely for the update and end the call.

It's only now that I realise my spare hand has been digging in the earth of the flower bed beside me. I sit and stare at the dirt under my nails and wonder if Ben himself has turned to earth by now.

12

It's amazing, the power of a run to shake off negative feelings. As Mouse and I take the paths across the fields to the beach, we're surrounded by wildflowers: early purple orchids, delicate ox-eye daisies and the tall spikes of teasel. When we reach Scabbacombe Sands, the sea is the hazy blue of a perfect morning. While Mouse plays chicken with the waves, I jog along the beach and back, stopping when a large bird glides over my head from the cliffs behind. I've read about these birds in the local literature. Related to the albatross, the fulmar is quite a sight with its huge wings spread. By the time we return to the house, I feel revitalised, and ready to take on the day.

Most of the party is already at the table chatting happily, when I reach the Loggia. I fill a coffee cup and my thermos, then take the seat next to Koko, facing out to the lush gardens and the hills beyond.

'Morning,' I say, and they all respond in kind. I notice that Addie and Delilah have yet to appear. I hope Delilah is feeling better this morning.

Anil fills me in. 'We were just discussing Koko's plan to branch out from her wildflower focus.'

Toby adds, 'I'm not sure I'd say we were "discussing" anything. You and I were speculating, and Koko was refusing to tell us. This, despite my offering an extremely tempting bribe.'

Beside him, Sarah bursts out laughing. It occurs to me that this might be the first time I've seen her laugh. I've been thinking of her as a stunning yet sulky creature, like a temperamental pedigree cat.

'What?' asks Toby, all mock innocence.

Koko raises a sardonic eyebrow. 'I am not so certain that anybody would consider your offer to be tempting, Toby.'

'What are you talking about, woman?' he says. 'These are fabulous socks. It's not my fault you have no taste.' He sticks one leg in the air to display a bright pink sock covered in large yellow spots.

'I'm sorry about my husband, Koko,' says Sarah, shaking her head. 'I've tried convincing him to apply subtlety to his wardrobe.'

'Yeah. I can't see Koko wearing those socks,' I say to Toby, reaching for a bread roll. 'Now, if you had a beautifully tailored jacket . . .'

Koko, outfitted today in cream linen shorts with a matching V-neck vest, is looking both cool and chic. She shoots me an appreciative smile. 'Thank you, Steph. I am pleased there is at least one person who recognises style.'

I gesture to my own denim shorts, lace-up gardening boots and white t-shirt. 'I recognise it. I just don't apply it to myself. My main concerns are practicality and comfort, especially for gardening.'

Toby says, 'Well, it's not my fault if none of you appreciate a snazzy dresser.'

'I love you in spite of your clothing, not because of it,' Sarah tells him, patting his hand.

'A backhanded compliment if ever I heard one,' he says, kissing the top of her head.

'What have I missed?' asks Delilah, wafting on to the Loggia like a forlorn ghost. With dark shadows beneath her eyes and a slight yellowy tinge to her skin, she looks unwell.

She pulls out a chair beside Koko, who promptly stands up, saying, 'I must leave now,' before stalking back indoors.

'Did I say something wrong?' asks Delilah, looking around at us. We all shrug to signal our ignorance. I notice that she has a hand on her stomach again, but I don't get a chance to ask about it before she says, 'Actually, Koko did go a bit . . . weird over something I said yesterday.'

Anil puts a hand to his forehead. 'What did you do?'

'What?' She looks offended. 'I didn't do anything. It was her. She got all *off* with me. I only said that she ought to do a Japanese garden.'

There's a moment's silence while we look at one another, then Anil says, 'Why should she?'

Delilah flushes. 'Oh, now you're all at it. I can't see what's wrong with suggesting someone use their heritage in their designs.'

'That doesn't mean they *have* to though, does it?' says Anil.

Delilah sighs loudly, her eyes round with indignation. 'I didn't say she *had* to, did I? Only that she . . .'

'Should,' I say quietly.

'Oh, for god's sake!' Delilah shoves her chair back from the table and slinks back into the house, just as Addie comes out. I refrain from pointing out that, with all the people leaving and arriving, it's beginning to feel like a farce.

Addie stops short, watching Delilah's retreating figure, then turns to us.

'What was that about?'

'Unconscious racial bias,' says Anil flatly, scraping his spoon around the bottom of his yoghurt pot.

'Oh dear,' say Addie. 'Where's Koko?'

'She left the minute Delilah got here,' he says.

Addie sighs. 'I'd better go and check on them.'

'First, come and have your breakfast,' says Toby, patting the seat on the other side of him from Sarah. 'You can't solve all the world's problems on an empty stomach.'

'Good point.' With a smile, she joins us at the table. Anil fetches her a cup of coffee from the machine while Addie helps herself to a roll. Today, she's left off the headscarf and her hair is coiled like a crown on her head. She's wearing a sleeveless summer dress in an African wax print in shades of orange and yellow, with matching beaded earrings.

'What a beautiful dress,' I say, taking in the neatly fitting bodice and full, pleated skirt.

'Thank you. My granny makes them for me.'

I reflect on my own grandmothers. The one on my mother's side lives in Portsmouth, so we rarely saw her growing up – although I suspect that our absence had less to do with the distance from Peterborough and more to do with her belief that physical affection, such as hugs, makes children weak. Even now, Mum is awkward and stiff when I hug her. My dad's mother died of cancer when I was five, and all I remember of her is those iced rings on a floral plate, set atop an embroidered tablecloth.

I haven't realised Addie is watching me until she says, 'Why the long face?'

'Oh, nothing.' I shake my head to dismiss the sad thoughts, like Mouse shaking off the sea water. 'I was just thinking how nice it must be to have a grandmother like that.' The image of Verity pops into my head and I find myself thinking, *Perhaps I will soon have a whole new set of grandparents.* Downing my coffee, I stand up and say, 'Right, I'll meet you all at the bus.'

I've just climbed the stairs and reached our door when there's a distinct sob from one of the bedrooms.

Turning around, I stand on the landing, listening for more sounds. When there's another sob, and it's clearly from the room next to mine, I knock on the door.

'Are you all right in there?' I call.

'C-come in,' the voice stutters between sobs.

Pushing the door open, I step inside with Mouse. Delilah is lying on the bed, face down.

'Oh, Delilah! I'm sure whatever you said to Koko, she'll forgive you if you apologise.'

She pushes herself up and turns to face me. Her eyes are red, her face bloated from tears.

'Oh, it's not just that,' she says. 'My stomach's really bad still.'

I frown. 'Do you think it's something you've eaten?'

She shakes her head. 'I only had a cheese sandwich on the way here on Friday. And we've all been eating the same food.'

'And you're not prone to stomach upsets?' When she shakes her head, I say, 'That's really strange.'

She nods. 'But I've picked a load more peppermint leaves this morning and used them to make a fresh infusion.'

'It looks like the peppermint isn't helping. I really think you should see a doctor, Delilah, or at least a pharmacist.'

She nods meekly. 'I'll ask Addie or Mike to drive me into Kingswear later, if the peppermint still hasn't helped.'

I'm about to leave when a memory comes back to me: Sarah, leaving this room yesterday morning.

'This is your room?' I check.

She stares at me. 'Of course.'

'It's just, I thought I saw Sarah coming out of here yesterday.'

'Sarah? What would she be doing in my room?'

'I don't know. She said she was fetching a battery pack.'

Delilah wrinkles her nose as if a battery pack is something undesirable. 'Why would she come in my room for that?' She pauses before saying, 'Sarah was probably just passing my door and you made a mistake.'

Glancing around, I spot Delilah's drinks bottle on the table by the window. 'Do you take that to meals?' I ask, walking over to it and holding it up.

She looks baffled. 'No. Why?'

'OK if I examine it?'

Clutching her stomach, she says through gritted teeth, 'Do what you like. I have to go again.'

While she runs out of the room, I move to sit on the chair by the window, where I tilt the bottle so that the leaves separate. I try to examine each one, but they keep settling at the bottom before I have a chance.

By the time Delilah returns a few minutes later, groaning and still clutching her stomach, I'm at her basin, sifting through the leaves, having emptied the bottle.

'Steph, I really don't feel well,' she says in a weak voice.

I turn and, seeing she's wobbling, begin to run towards her. But her legs buckle before I can reach her, and she falls, striking her head on the footboard of the wooden bedframe.

I reach her side. She's unconscious but breathing. It's a harsh sound, as if she's inhaling through sandpaper. Her skin has a bluish tinge around her lips and there are dark shadows beneath her eyes.

I check her pulse, and it's erratic, first too quick, then barely detectable. I place her on her side in the recovery position before sitting beside her and calling for an ambulance. As soon as I'm assured the paramedics are on their way, I call Addie, who answers on the first ring.

'Steph, are you with Delilah? We're all on the minibus, waiting.'

'Delilah's not well.'

'Oh no! Is it her stomach? She said it was troubling her.'

'I think so. She's unconscious. I've rung for an ambulance, so I'll wait here for them, and I'll catch up with you later at Poplars.'

'Unconscious? Oh my goodness. I'd better come up. Mike can drive the others.'

'Can you make sure the front door's propped open for the paramedics?' I say.

'Of course. I'll be right there.'

In fact, it's Mike who enters the bedroom a few minutes later and comes to crouch beside me.

'Hey. How is she?' he asks quietly.

I tell him about Delilah's fall. 'I'm not sure if she's knocked herself out, or if she was unconscious before she hit her head.'

'Poor thing,' he says, looking down at her. 'She's so pale.'

'I know. And her pulse is irregular.'

'I wonder what it is. Do you think it could be a bad case of Covid?'

'I don't think she's got a disease,' I tell him. 'Have a look in the sink and tell me what leaves you can see among the mint.'

With a bemused frown, he gets to his feet and walks over to the basin. He comes back a moment later, saying, 'I don't understand. What have the leaves in the sink got to do with anything?'

'They were in her drinks bottle.'

His expression turns to horror. 'What? Are you sure?'

I nod. 'I emptied out the bottle, and all of them were inside.'

There's the sound of the front doorbell, and Mike runs from the room to meet the paramedics.

When he returns, he holds the door for two people in uniform, a male and a female, bearing a stretcher.

As they busy themselves around Delilah, the woman asks questions, which I do my best to answer. I state that her symptoms have been going on since at least the day before, and that I'm pretty sure she's been suffering from diarrhoea as well as vomiting. I finish by repeating what I told Mike:

'I'm not sure whether she was unconscious before she fell, or whether she knocked herself out. Her legs gave way and she hit her head on the wooden bedframe.'

The woman says Delilah's name repeatedly and bends over her, but Delilah remains as pale and unresponsive as Snow White after biting the apple.

'Looks like heatstroke,' says her colleague. 'We'd better get her into the ambulance and straight on some fluids.' He looks from me to Mike. 'Don't worry – your friend will soon be right as rain. We've had several cases recently, in this heat.'

The female paramedic lifts each of Delilah's eyelids in turn and shines a torch on to her pupils. She doesn't tell us what she finds but says, 'We'll ask the hospital to monitor her for concussion.'

I haven't wanted to interrupt their examination. As a result, they're already lowering her unresponsive form on to the stretcher when I finally say, 'It's not heatstroke.'

'Hold on,' says the man, 'let's get her strapped in.' As soon as they've fastened the straps to hold her in place, they both stand and face me. 'What makes you believe it's not heatstroke?' he asks. 'Do you know what's wrong with her?'

'Yes,' I say with conviction, meeting Mike's worried eye. 'Someone's been putting foxglove leaves in her water bottle. She's been poisoned with digitalis.'

13

There's a moment's pause after my revelation. Then the female paramedic says, 'You need to be very sure. We don't want to omit treating her for something else, if you're wrong.'

I grab a tissue then run over to the sink and pick up the foxglove leaves that are lying among the peppermint. Wrapping them quickly in the tissue, I hold it out to the female paramedic.

'Here. You can get this tested if you have a toxicology lab. If not, you can take our word for it, as trained horticulturists who know our plants, that this is definitely digitalis and the leaves came out of the patient's water bottle. And, as I said, I'm pretty sure this has been going on since yesterday.'

The paramedic takes the wet parcel of leaves from me and places it in a small plastic bag which she slips into the breast pocket of her jacket, zipping it closed. I also hand her the drinks bottle, which she puts in her bag.

'I'll ring the police to report the poisoning, so they might want the bottle,' I say. 'Though it will be covered in my fingerprints.'

'We'd better get her on oxygen and a saline drip,' she says to her colleague.

When she nods to him and they lift the stretcher, I say, 'I don't know what your protocol is about dealing with the police.'

'Our first priority is the patient,' she says, watching the space behind her colleague as he reverses towards the door which Mike has run ahead to open. 'The police will have to liaise with the hospital if they want to pursue a case.'

Mike goes to see them out. Just before the door closes behind them, I hear her say, 'If it's digitalis poisoning, we need to take her to Torbay for activated charcoal treatment.'

By the time he reappears, having seen them off in the ambulance, I'm downstairs with Mouse, who is watching me anxiously as I pace the hall, reporting the case on my mobile via the non-urgent police phone line.

The woman on the other end takes down my statement and both my details and Delilah's. I tell her about seeing Sarah coming out of her room, and she notes that down, too.

'Will you take Sarah in for questioning?' I ask.

'Someone will be in touch from a local station, probably Brixham,' she tells me.

After I've ended the call, I look at Mike. His hair is on end from running his hands through it, and he looks haunted.

Mouse greets him and he crouches to pet him while looking up at me. 'Who put those leaves in her bottle?' he asks. 'Do you know?'

I pull a face. 'I think it was Sarah. I saw her coming out of Delilah's room. And Delilah's drinks bottle was in there at the time.'

'Are you serious?'

When I nod, he says, 'I don't understand. What could make Sarah want to harm Delilah?'

'You've not been at meals here since the first night, so I'm guessing you haven't noticed how Sarah treats Delilah. She really doesn't like her. I think she feels threatened by how attentive Toby is to her.'

'But . . . isn't Delilah about twenty?'

'Mid-twenties, I think.'

He grimaces. 'Toby's in his forties.' He hesitates before saying, 'He's not been inappropriate with her, has he?'

'Not that I've seen. He adores Sarah. I reckon it's all in his wife's head.' I think back to the times I've seen Toby with Delilah and add, 'I'm sure it's more fatherly than anything. And Delilah responds in kind.'

'Well, that's something, at least. Where are we up to? Have you reported the poisoning?'

I nod and he stands up. 'Come on, I'd better take you and Mouse to Poplars Farm. And I need to get on if I'm going to tackle Delilah's build in her absence. We'll take Minerva.'

'Minerva?' I ask as we approach the Mini.

'What? She was a goddess. It seems quite fitting.'

Mouse jumps happily on to the back seat of the little car with Mr Rabbit and I strap him in before returning my seat to its upright position and getting in.

Thankfully, Minerva hasn't yet reached full heat. We crank down the windows and enjoy the breeze as Mike drives. The engine is nearly as noisy as my old Ford Transit. We don't speak at first, and I'm sure his mind is as busy as mine, remembering Delilah's pale form and trying to process the implications of Sarah poisoning her.

Sure enough, after about five minutes, he says loudly, above the engine noise, 'I'm still reeling from the idea that Sarah could have poisoned Delilah.'

'I know. It's possible I'm wrong, but *someone* put foxglove leaves in that drinks bottle.'

'Maybe she did it herself, by mistake.'

'Does the mint even grow near foxgloves in the gardens here?'

I glance at him and he shakes his head.

'I'm sorry, Mike – I wish I could tell you Delilah's poisoning was accidental, but it just doesn't seem possible.'

'I know. You're right. I just don't want to accept it.'

'I get that.'

We travel the remaining short distance in silence, until he turns in at Poplars Farm and parks alongside the minibus. As I let Mouse out from the back seat, I glance to the corner of the car park where I left the digger the day before. For a moment, I think the machine has been collected, but then I see that it is in a different spot, several metres from where I parked it. I'm about to mention it to Mike, until it occurs to me that someone may have needed to move it, to make way for the crane, which is back, this time in the refreshments field.

'That'll be Anil's scaffolding going in,' says Mike as I release Mouse from the back.

'What's he doing with scaffolding?' I ask.

'I am sworn to secrecy.'

'Of course you are.'

Addie comes over as Mike's locking the Mini. The jauntiness of her bright clothing belies the anxiety in her expression.

'How is she?' she asks.

'She was still unconscious when the paramedics took her,' I say.

Mike adds, 'They said she might be all right, depending on how fit and healthy she was to start with, and how much of the poison she imbibed.'

Addie looks horrified. 'Wait, what? You're suggesting she's been poisoned?'

I start to fill her in on my discovery of the foxglove leaves and my belief that Sarah is responsible, but she puts up a hand to stop me.

'I refuse to believe that anyone here could have harmed her deliberately,' she says firmly. 'I'll hear no more about it. And please don't share this . . . malicious gossip with anyone else.'

Mike and I exchange a look of uncertainty. He says slowly, 'Addie, how do you think those leaves got into Delilah's bottle?'

She lifts her chin. 'As I say, it must have been accidental.'

'I've already told the police otherwise,' I say, and take a step back from the anger that flares in her eyes like a struck match. 'The hospital would have reported it anyway,' I say, with more confidence than I feel.

'Let's keep a lid on this,' she says, more to Mike than me.

'Talk later,' he says to me, before turning his attention to Addie. 'Can I grab some of the volunteers? And do you have Delilah's plans? I want to make sure she doesn't fall behind.'

As the two of them walk away, I'm left wondering what I should say if I encounter Sarah.

Variations on, *Oh, hi! Do you realise you may have killed Delilah?* or, *Hey, Sarah, I've just reported you to the police!* don't seem like the wisest approach with a potential murderer. After all, who knows how she might react?

14

Toby brings Chaplin over when Mouse and I have just reached the grass verge beside Delilah's deserted plot. We let them off the leads and they slope off. I would not be surprised to see them dozing beneath the oak tree when I reach my plot.

Not wanting to spend time with the husband of a poisoner, I make a move to walk on.

But Toby puts a hand on my arm. 'How's Delilah?' he asks in a low, urgent tone, looking around as if we're conducting a drug deal.

'Not good. She was unconscious when they took her in.' I watch his face, checking for signs he had any idea of his wife's actions. But his eyes fill with tears.

'Oh my god! Is she OK? I mean, will she be?'

I shrug. 'I honestly don't know.'

'What do you think is wrong with her?'

There is still no indication that he knows the truth, so I start with the basics. 'She's consumed foxglove leaves, so she has digitalis poisoning.'

'Good god!'

I give him a moment before asking, 'Why is Sarah so jealous of you and Delilah?'

'What? Why?' He rubs his face. 'What?' he says again. Then he takes a deep breath. 'Why are you asking?'

I decide to place the bombshell to one side for now, and say, 'No reason. I just noticed she was really short with Delilah at dinner on Saturday night.'

He sighs, then leads me into his plot, which is currently empty of people.

'Steph. You have to understand, Sarah is my second wife, and we've only been together for six years.'

I'm surprised at this but I simply say, 'Go on.'

'Sarah is quite jealous of anyone I knew before her. I've tried to reassure her, but . . .'

'Wait – so you knew Delilah before you met Sarah?'

He nods. 'She used to present a segment on my previous show. The camera loved her.'

'And Sarah thought there was something going on between you?'

He scratches his bearded chin. 'By the time I started seeing Sarah, Delilah and I were firm friends. But Sarah was always convinced we were more than that. It's ridiculous – I mean, look at the age gap, for one thing. I'm old enough to be her father.'

'Why did Delilah stop presenting?'

'The official story was that she wanted more time for her burgeoning design business.'

'And the unofficial story?'

His face fills with sadness as he says, 'I believe she couldn't cope with Sarah. My wife is lovely but rather possessive, and she used to find excuses to visit the set when we were filming. Although Delilah didn't tell me everything, I got the impression Sarah made her life quite . . . difficult. You've seen how she can be.'

I don't ask why he would stay with someone who could behave that way. After all, I stayed with Ben for a long time, even once I knew he was a gambler and a schemer.

Love can be a bittersweet companion.

15

'Toby? What's happening?' Sarah's voice comes from behind Toby. I am on his far side, so that he is thankfully blocking my expression.

He smiles and says, 'Nothing, darling. I was just telling Steph about Seb.'

When I look confused, Toby adds with a meaningful look, 'Awful about his garden being vandalised. Such a nasty business.'

'Yes, terrible,' I say, wondering what I've missed.

She puts her hands on her hips. 'That's what you were talking about?'

He nods.

'Well, in that case, you can let poor Steph go, so she can get back to her own plot. I've told you before, Tobes, you make a far better wall than a door.'

'Sorry, sorry.' He laughs, putting his palms up and stepping to one side.

'Oh Steph, before you go, how's Delilah?' she asks. 'I heard it was you who looked after her.'

'I really don't know. She was unconscious when the paramedics took her.'

'My god. Koko told me she suspected it was borage leaves. Something about alkaloids? Over my head, I'm afraid.'

'No,' I say, watching her closely for any signs of guilt. 'It was foxgloves.'

She doesn't miss a beat. 'Are they bad, too, then?' Her expression is all wide-eyed innocence.

101

'Yes,' I say slowly, 'they are bad, too.'

'So . . . what? Delilah just didn't know? Picked them by mistake?'

'No. There's no way she'd have made a mistake like that. Someone must have put them in her drinks bottle deliberately. She was poisoned.'

Sarah does a convincing show of being shocked.

Feeling a sudden urge to remove myself from her vicinity, I say, 'I need to get back.'

'She'll definitely be all right though, won't she?' This is the first time I've seen her express genuine concern.

'I don't know,' I say, walking away and leaving her to speak to my retreating back.

'I'll be around later to film you!' she calls. I nod and continue on my way.

I don't make it far, though, as the next plot along belongs to Seb. I come to an abrupt stop as I survey the damage. Toby wasn't exaggerating.

Seb's garden – with its carefully made decking and intricately placed pebbles – has been torn apart. There are big holes and mounds of earth, as if a giant, angry mole has spent the night grubbing ineffectually for worms. Only the silver birch remains standing, no doubt because it would have been inordinately difficult to dig up, even with a digger.

Thinking of diggers has me remembering the digger that is still in the car park. I try not to feel guilty for having supplied the tool of destruction.

There's no sign of Seb himself as I stand there, wondering who could have done this.

Koko appears from the next plot along and comes to join me, surveying the wasteland. 'It appears that Sebastian is not the only person among us to have tantrums,' she says.

'You think this was an attack of rage?' I ask her.

She shrugs. 'It seems quite likely.' She turns her gaze from the debris to me. 'Are you OK? I heard that it was you who had to call for the ambulance for Delilah.'

'I'm all right. She's not so good.'

'Is her sickness because of the borage which she was putting inside her drink? I did warn her that these leaves contain alkaloids.'

'You did. But no, it wasn't borage. It was foxgloves.' I'm starting to wish we had an online chat group in which I could have typed all this information, to save repeating it.

Her eyebrows shoot up. 'Really? I know she is young, but does she not know that these are dangerous plants?'

'She thought she was drinking peppermint.'

'Ah.'

We look at one another for a moment in silence. Then she says, in a thoughtful tone, 'It is not easy to mix up these leaves – peppermint and foxglove are different sizes, different shapes, different—'

'Yes,' I interrupt, not wanting to hear all the ways in which the leaves differ.

'You believe that Delilah has been poisoned,' she says, matter-of-factly.

'I do.'

'Are we all in danger?'

'I don't think so. But, to be on the safe side, don't leave any drinks unattended.'

She seems satisfied with this response and simply nods before saying, 'I need to get on with my work.'

'Me, too.'

As we walk together towards our plots, I say, 'Where is Seb now?'

'I believe he has gone to sit inside the refreshments field to try to calm himself down.'

She steps inside her rectangle, where she appears still to be deep in complex calculations involving string, measuring tapes and pea sticks. I notice she has yet to employ a single volunteer.

Approaching my own plot, I wonder about the vandalism. Was it an attack of rage, as Koko suggested, or a premeditated act of sabotage? After all, Seb's garden was an ambitious design, which was already looking impressive after two days' work. Was one of the designers feeling threatened, and keen to axe the competition? My mind flicks through the suspects. I recall Delilah's desire to acquire funds for her wedding; Seb's desperation to hold on to his partner and daughter; and Anil's resolve to attract positive press to drown out his firm's lawsuit. I wonder what, if anything, Koko might have riding on a win. There is certainly more than one contestant with a serious investment in winning this event.

'Morning!' Gertrude greets me with a cheery smile, drawing me out of my reverie.

'Oh, hi! I didn't see you in that corner.'

'Wonderful: I am officially dressed in camouflage.'

I laugh but don't respond, as her romper-style suit is, indeed, in a rather earthy shade of brown. She has a long measuring tape stretched out between the edge of the pond and the garden entrance, and has managed to acquire a can of spray chalk, which she has yet to use.

'I was extra early today,' she says, 'so, I hope you don't mind, but I thought I'd get cracking on the measuring for the pathway.' Walking towards me, she stops upon seeing my expression.

'Is everything all right?'

I fill her in on Delilah's poisoning, and she whistles before saying, 'Is there an antidote for that?'

'Not as such, but the paramedics talked about using a form of charcoal which I think prevents the body from absorbing the poison if administered in time.'

'God, I hope it works. Do you know who might have poisoned her?'

I hesitate. Until the police have investigated – and I'm starting to wonder if I might need to chase them – I don't want to say too much.

Sensing my inner conflict, she holds up a hand. 'Don't say another word.'

'Thank you. I just want to be sure before I name anyone.'

'Of course. I understand.'

'Have you seen Seb's plot?' I ask her.

'It's a bit of a mess,' she says.

'Well, that's an understatement.' I stand for a moment, thinking about the destroyed garden, until I reach a decision. 'Listen, I'm going to go over there and offer to help him put his garden back together.'

She links her arm through mine. 'In that case, I'm coming with you.' I offer her a smile of gratitude as we walk towards Seb's plot.

There's still no sign of him. Gertrude stands for a moment, gazing in evident horror at the decimated ground, which yesterday was already starting to resemble a slice of rural Yorkshire – albeit with a decidedly non-bucolic deck.

'Can I be honest with you?' she says.

'Of course.'

'I didn't take in earlier quite how bad it was. I thought he'd just thrown a few things around, you know?'

I see she's turned red. 'How could you not have noticed the garden had been trashed?' I shoot her a sideways glance. 'What were you up to?'

'I was dancing!' she admits, flushing an even brighter shade of red. 'I like to get here early and use this whole grassy area to dance to the *Footloose* theme.'

'That is brilliant,' I say. 'Tomorrow, I'm going to see if I can get Sarah to film it.' I don't mention that by tomorrow Sarah might be in police custody.

'Don't you bloody dare!' she says. 'Anyway, not to change the subject or anything, but . . .' She gestures to the abandoned plot.

'He must still be in the refreshments field,' I say, leading the way along the grass verge.

We find him, slumped at the refreshments table, head bowed.

'We've come to help you fix your garden,' I tell him.

He lifts his head briefly, gives me a doleful look, then lowers it again. 'What's the point?' he says. 'Whoever did it will just do it again.'

Addie appears at that moment, her phone clutched in both hands. 'Actually, no they won't. I've just hired some security cameras, which will be installed after we finish today. I'm only sorry I didn't think of it sooner. Although, to be honest, it never occurred to me that anyone would be so vicious.'

Seb lifts his face to meet my eye. 'It wasn't you, was it?' he asks in his lugubrious voice, reminding me of Eeyore from *Winnie the Pooh*.

I feel Gertrude bristle at my side and I say quickly, 'No, of course not.' I decide now is not the best time to mention the digger, which I'd left parked, with its key beneath a front tyre.

Seb says, 'It's just . . . I'd understand if you had done it, after how I treated you yesterday, you know?'

'I'd never do anything like that,' I say softly. 'And you apologised. Come on, let's get your garden back to its former glory.'

'You'd really do that?'

'Of course.'

Shaking his head, he mutters something to himself, of which I catch only the phrase 'too good'.

Addie says, 'That's very kind, Steph, but you have your own garden to build.' Addressing Seb, she says, 'I've rounded up four volunteers, two of whom are coming in by car and should be here any minute, so you need to get cracking.'

Amazingly, her schoolmarm approach does the job, and he gets to his feet. 'Thanks for your kindness,' he says. 'I really appreciate it.'

I wish him luck. Then, as Gertrude and I start to leave, he says quickly, 'Delilah! Is she OK?'

I turn back. 'I'm not sure.'

Addie says, 'I'll be calling the hospital later, and I'll update you all at dinner, if there's news.'

Seb nods and strides away.

'Thank goodness for that,' says Addie. She claps her hands. 'Well, I think I'm due a cup of tea.'

'You've definitely earned it,' I say. 'Meanwhile, Gertrude and I are going to cut loose.' I give Gertrude a sly glance to check she's caught the *Footloose* reference.

'Only after I put on my Sunday shoes,' she replies, deadpan.

We link arms and skip off to work, with the occasional sideways 'grapevine' dance move thrown in. When I glance back, I see Addie watching us with a bemused expression.

16

As soon as Gertrude and I arrive back at our plot, she says, 'Oh! I forgot to say, your trellis has been delivered.' She points to the back left corner, where there are two tall piles of wooden trellis stained a brash orange.

'Are they meant to be that colour?' she asks me, as I walk over to examine the panels.

'Awful, isn't it?' When she looks confused, I say, 'It really doesn't matter. Remember, we're going to cover it with the climbers. Anyway, thanks so much for lugging it over. That must have been quite a job.'

She wiggles her eyebrows somewhat suggestively and lowers her voice, despite the fact that there are only the two of us present. 'I had help from a rather fetching young man called Ryan.'

'How young are we talking?' I ask her.

She laughs. 'Oh, don't worry: "young" to me is anything between thirty-five and fifty-five. I'm no cradle snatcher.'

'Good to know.'

She nods. 'Right, well, I've been going by what I saw on your plans. I remember you had the path starting in the front corner there.' She points to what will be the front right corner of the garden, from the point of view of people arriving.

'Actually,' I say, 'I'm sorry but I've decided to move it. It's now going to start front left. That will give us a longer path, spiralling round to the back right, where the finish line is.'

'By "finish line", you mean the pond?'

'Sorry, yes! There's obviously no actual finish line.'

'Or,' she muses, 'we could make it into a race to the finish, by timing people's trip around the spiral.'

'With "trip" being the operative word,' I say, and we both laugh. 'Right – to work!' I say. At that moment, my phone rings with an unknown number. With an apology to Gertrude, I answer it:

'Steph Williams.'

'Ms Williams, hello,' comes an older male voice, with a strong Devon accent. 'I'm ringing from Brixham Police Station. You placed a call earlier, reporting your concerns about a friend who's been taken ill?'

I stride to the edge of the plot to check that Sarah is not close by. In fact, she is only two plots along, filming Seb on the grass verge, presumably getting his reaction to the destruction of his garden. A little too close for comfort in more than one sense. I walk towards the oak to extend the distance.

Taking my silence as a signal to continue, he says, 'We've spoken to the hospital, and I have permission to tell you that Ms Deville is responding well to treatment.'

'Oh! That's such a relief.'

I sit down on the ground, close to the two sleeping dogs.

He clears his throat. 'So, if there's nothing more . . .'

'Wait! I'm pretty sure she was poisoned.'

There's a pause, then he says, 'Do you have actual proof of this accusation?'

'The poisoner's fingerprints will be on Delilah's drinks bottle, which I gave to the paramedics.'

'We have a note about that. I'm sorry, but it doesn't sound like enough to go on.'

There's yet another long pause, while I try, and fail, to come up with something substantial. At last, close to tears, I say, 'You can't just let her poisoner off the hook . . .'

'Let me stop you there. I can assure you we have reason to believe the poisoning was entirely accidental. Apparently, a Ms . . .' there's a pause while he checks his notes, '. . . Adebayo has told the hospital that Ms Deville is using foxgloves in a garden that she's creating.'

'Yes, but she wouldn't have picked them and put them in her drink!'

'I'm sorry. As I say, with nothing tangible to go on . . .'

After the call has ended, I sit for a moment, in a disbelieving stupor. It's only when Gertrude comes to find me that I pull myself together.

'What happened?' she asks as I get to my feet.

'That was the police. They didn't want to hear about Delilah being poisoned. Apparently, the whole thing was accidental, because she's been handling the plants for her woodland garden.' My tone is bitter. 'Maybe I should ring back and see if I can talk to someone else.'

But Gertrude shakes her head. 'I'd leave it for now, if you don't have anything new to tell them.'

I consider her words, then sigh. 'You're right. I'm sure the police have enough to do, without fielding repeat phone calls from an amateur detective with no concrete proof. Let me just tell Addie and Mike that Delilah's on the mend, and then we'll get on with our measuring.'

I find Addie helping Mike in Delilah's garden, so I'm able to give them both the good news at the same time.

'So, you see, it was all perfectly innocent,' says Addie with a big smile. Resisting the urge to contradict her, I just give them a wave and head back to my plot.

At least there's plenty of work to take my mind off the poisoning.

We take a lot less time than I've allowed, to mark out the dual outlines of the winding path, which is to be two feet wide. I like to use imperial measurements for walkways, as I figure I need to fit actual feet on them. As with the pond, I measure while Gertrude sprays the chalk lines. We make an efficient team.

Once the marking is done, I check my watch and see it's nearly eleven. 'I'm about to meet Koko for a chat about wildflowers,' I tell Gertrude. 'Do you want to come?'

Her eyes grow wide as she pushes a grey plait back from her shoulder. 'Oh my god, is she *that* Koko? I read about her in *Gardeners' World*. I'd love to, if that's all right?'

'Of course.'

I grab my thermos and we meet Koko beside her plot before walking to the refreshments field together. As we pass Anil's plot, we hear him on the phone, behind his screen, saying, 'No, that's not what I said. Look, I haven't got time for this.'

I exchange a look with Koko, and she whispers, 'I think he is dealing with a lot of stress from his business partner.'

I whisper back, 'It sounds tough,' and she nods gravely before brightening and saying, 'Addie came to tell me that Delilah is doing well, which is good news.'

'That's right. She's responding to treatment, thank goodness.'

'Has she fingered her poisoner?' asks Koko as we enter the next field.

When I look surprised at her use of the vernacular, she says, 'I have watched a lot of the old detective films.'

'Ah. No, they seem to think it was her own mistake.'

'This does seem like a strong possibility.'

I say nothing, and we take our seats opposite one another on the benches on either side of the long refreshments table, Gertrude next to me.

'So, what do you want to know about growing wildflowers?' Koko asks me, as I pour us all coffee from my thermos.

'I'm keen to incorporate more native varieties into my designs. But I'm a novice in this department and I'm not sure which ones would work well,' I say. I sip from my mug while Koko considers.

'Are you looking to create entire wildflower borders or meadows, or simply to interplant your borders with them?'

'All of those, if possible.'

She nods and runs a long, slim finger around the rim of her enamel coffee cup while she considers. 'This last thing is, of course, a lot more complicated.'

'It's kind of a given that, within a perennial border, I'd have to use wildflowers that don't need disturbed ground to germinate,' I say.

'That's right. But there are definitely some species you could introduce, provided you do not mind that you would have no control over where they would reappear, from one year to the next. Borage, for example, or viper's bugloss, are both very pretty inside perennial borders, but you cannot dictate where they might seed down the line.'

I nod. 'And all the annual poppies, which I love, would be no good, of course, if I'm not digging the ground over between seasons.'

'Actually,' says Koko, 'I have had a surprising amount of success with the opium poppies, in places where I have carried out very little digging.'

'Oh, that's good to know. And what about cow parsley?' I ask, thinking of the way these white flowers turn the hedgerows to a glorious froth of lace in spring.

Koko pulls a face as she sips her drink. 'This plant is short-lived, and will self-seed almost too prolifically.' She sits back. 'If I am being honest with you, it would be better for you to allocate an area for these wildflowers, rather than to try and introduce them into a perennial border. You might decide to sow a few annuals among your perennials each year. But, as a long-term design plan, there is very little to be gained by setting yourself such a difficult task.'

'Ah, OK. Thanks so much. That's really helpful.'

She raises an eyebrow. 'Dashing your dreams is helpful?'

Gertrude laughs and I smile and explain, 'You've saved me from a lot of potentially disheartening work.'

Addie appears. She makes herself a cup of tea, before sitting down beside Koko, on the bench opposite Gertrude and me. 'How are you all getting on?'

'Good, thanks,' I say. 'Gertrude's a wonder.'

Addie nods, smiling at the volunteer. 'Yes, we're lucky. We've been very impressed with the standard of our volunteers.' I turn and see Gertrude blush beside me.

After a moment's silence, Koko leans towards Addie. 'Did you speak to her?'

'Not yet, no.'

'This woman needs to be curbed.'

I don't like the sound of 'curbed'.

Addie says, 'I'm sure you're getting this out of proportion, but I will speak to her.'

Curiosity overcomes me, and I say, 'Can I ask who you're talking about?'

Addie shakes her head, but Koko says, 'Sonny Carden. I am fairly sure that she has been having conversations already with the two other judges, influencing them against my garden.'

'Oh, really?'

She nods. 'In fact, she has told me this, that she is giving information to them about our progress. I do not like this idea. They should be free to judge our designs from the finished products. I am being considered for a lectureship at a university in America, and the board has informed me that I do not have enough prestige.' She sighs. 'I hate this word, "prestige". The board members have said that they would be willing to overlook my limited number of publications, if I win this competition. They are very impressed with the National Trust.'

'So, you're worried Sonny's biasing the judges against you?' I check.

She nods. 'She is like this: she says everything without thinking.'

'I suppose she can be a bit impulsive,' I say, 'but I'm sure Frank and Gillie will make up their own minds.'

Koko huffs and I give up.

Thankfully, Toby chooses that moment to come strolling towards the table and Addie says, 'Let's leave it for now.'

'Thanks again for the advice,' I say to Koko, getting to my feet. Gertrude stands up, too.

'Something I said?' Toby asks, as he comes to sit beside Koko.

'No. You just smell really bad,' Gertrude tells him, holding her nose, and he roars with laughter.

As we pass the car park, I spot a flatbed truck leaving with the digger on board. At least that should put paid to any repeat performance by the vandal.

As promised, Gertrude has enlisted two additional volunteers to help with digging out the path, and they are waiting beneath the oak tree when I get back. Jay and Alex are young and somewhat androgynous in appearance, both with oversized black clothing and long hair that obscures their pale faces. Alex does the introductions and tells me that they both prefer 'they/them' pronouns. After this, they speak little – to me, at any rate – but set to work with their spades as soon as I've issued my instructions. While Gertrude and I start digging the path at the pond end, Alex and Jay begin at the front left corner.

At one point, I look up to see Sarah filming us. At least this time

I'm engrossed in my work, and not in a stand-up row with a fellow competitor.

At one o'clock, Alex comes to find me, their long, straight brown hair concealing their expression. 'Is it OK if we take a break?' they ask, so quietly I have to lean closer to hear them.

'Of course,' I say with a smile. 'You're a volunteer – you don't have to ask.'

After they've left, I walk over to inspect the area the pair have dug so far. It's a neat, shallow trench. I check it with a tape measure and see it's exactly the depth I specified.

'They're past halfway already,' I say, as Gertrude comes to look. 'This is going to make our lives a lot easier. We can leave them to finish the path while we get on with installing the trellis. Let's have some lunch first.'

I fetch an avocado and tomato sandwich from the cool box in the refreshments field and meet Gertrude beneath the oak, where I'm surprised to see there's no sign of the dogs.

'There's some woodland two fields over,' says Gertrude. 'I reckon they probably go in there every day, to play in the shade.'

'I wondered how they were coping in this heat,' I say. 'It's a shame we can't build our garden in the woods.'

'Oh, it's *our* garden, is it?' asks Gertrude, looking delighted.

'Of course it's *our* garden,' I say. 'You're doing half the work.'

She beams with pleasure for a moment, but then shakes her head. 'Nope. This is your design. You're the brains behind it. I am just the hired muscle.' She flexes one of her impressive biceps and we both laugh.

After our sandwiches and coffee, we step out from the shade of the oak tree and I'm struck, once again, by the intensity of the heat. It's like standing beneath a heat lamp. I envy cold-blooded creatures, such as snakes and lizards, which rely on warmth to move; it seems to have the opposite effect on me.

Glancing at Gertrude as we walk the short distance to the plot, I can tell she's struggling, too.

As we have already marked the trellis positions, we each now take a small pile of the panels and retreat, she to the right-hand fence, and I to the left. Then we set to work with electric screwdrivers, fixing the trellis in place. My phone pings just as I'm tightening the last screw in the top of my final panel. I draw my mobile from my pocket and glance at the screen, and see it's a message from Dad:

Your mum's having a meltdown.

A fist of anxiety tightens momentarily in my stomach, until I remember that this can't be a reaction to anything I've done. I sent her that voice message after I hung up on her, and she responded and seemed fine. The fist relaxes as I type a response:

What did you do?

He responds immediately:

I only dug up one of the hydrangeas. She's still got two others.

With a sigh, I step away from the trellis and call him. He answers on the second ring.

'Your mum won't speak to me.'

'Put her on.'

I hear Mum in the background, saying, 'Leave me alone, Nigel.'

Then he says something I can't catch, and she comes to the phone.

'Hello, Louise. I didn't realise he'd involved you in this mess he's made.'

'Yep. I hear he's dug up a hydrangea.'

'Not just a single hydrangea,' she says, sounding angrier than I've heard her in a long time. 'He's laid waste to a whole section of my garden.'

'Seriously?'

I hear Dad in the background, joking as he tries to win her round.

I sigh again. 'Do you want to put him back on?'

She doesn't say goodbye but I hear her tell Dad, 'She wants to talk to you.'

'Hello again,' he says, in the too-cheerful tone he uses when pretending he hasn't done anything wrong.

'Put it all back,' I say.

'But I need the extra space for the salad garden.'

Gertrude turns from fixing a trellis panel and catches my eye with a querying look. I mouth, 'Tell you later.'

To Dad, I say, 'You have an allotment.'

'Yes, but won't it be nice for your mum when we can just pick salad leaves outside the kitchen door?'

'No, it won't,' comes Mum's voice in the background. 'I liked my flowers.'

'Put it all back,' I say again.

'I can't. I might have . . . er . . . taken it all to the garden waste section at the tip.' This last comes out in a rush.

'Oh, Dad! You'll never make it up to Mum, you do know that?'

He whispers, 'You don't think she'll forgive me, when she sees the lovely salad leaves? Some of them are rainbow colours!'

'No, I don't.'

There's a long pause, then he says, 'I'd better go shopping for another hydrangea, hadn't I?'

17

It's only after Dad's hung up that I realise Alex and Jay are waiting to talk to me.

'Sorry!'

'No worries,' says Alex. 'Only, we've finished the digging. Do you want to check it's all right before we head off? We've promised this guy we'll help him with something to do with stones?' They say this like a question.

'Maybe Seb needs help laying more pebbles for his stream?' I suggest.

Alex turns a questioning face to Jay, who nods. 'That's it,' they say.

'I can't believe you've finished already,' I say. 'That's brilliant. I'm sure it's great.'

I follow them to the spiral pathway and we meander along its edge, which is as neatly and evenly dug as if it had been done by machine.

'You two are stars,' I say. 'Honestly, I'm in awe. Thank you so much.'

Jay smiles shyly but Alex says, 'We enjoyed it. We could come back tomorrow?'

'Yes, please! I could definitely use the help.'

The two young people look pleased. They each raise a hand in farewell as they lope away. They remind me of foals, all long, skinny legs. It makes me feel protective and also somehow bereft, though I can't say why.

'It's nearly two thirty,' I say to Gertrude. 'Fancy a final coffee?' She and I drain the last of the coffee from the thermos and drink it while taking stock of the jobs on our list.

'Did you say there's a painting going on that back fence?' asks Gertrude.

'Yeah, it's my pièce de résistance,' I say with a grin. 'An artist called Mattie Le Roy is coming to paint a mural for me.'

Her eyes grow wide. 'You mean the artist who was on Grayson Perry's show?'

'That's the one. I saw she was from round here, so I got in touch.'

'Did you see the giant painting she did, with the woman gazing out of the window?'

'I did. It was phenomenal. That's why I commissioned her for this.' I check my watch. 'She's due at three and it's five to now. Let's go and meet her.'

As we walk along the grass verge beside the plots, I take in the other competitors' progress, while Gertrude chatters amiably.

'I was quite excited when I heard I'd been picked for this event, but to be honest I had no idea it would be such a big opportunity. I mean, aside from meeting all the famous gardeners, I'm loving helping you with the show garden build. It's such a different process from making a long-term garden.'

'True,' I say. 'Though there are a lot of overlaps. It should still be good practice for when you design gardens for clients. OK, so you won't be mixing plants that can't grow in the same soil, you won't be forcing them to flower out of season, and you won't be sticking them in the soil in their pots, but the overall idea – of shape and process – are pretty much the same.'

We've reached the car park while talking, and I spot the artist immediately, at the wheel of an ancient, metallic-blue Citroën Berlingo, which seems like the perfect artist's car. Climbing out, Mattie runs a hand through her short hair, which is bright blue and spiky, creating a striking contrast with her dark skin (while going rather well with her car). With her cropped vest beneath orange and pink dungarees – a tattoo of a humpback whale visible above the bib – any observer would know without asking that she was creative.

She gets out as we approach. 'Hi, are you Steph?' she asks.

I nod. 'That's me. Hi, Mattie. And this is Gertrude, my colleague. Thanks so much for agreeing to this.'

She shakes my hand. 'Oh, this is exactly my kind of project,' she says, with a grin. Her voice is deep, and her accent pure Yorkshire. 'Let me grab my stuff, and you can show me where you want the piece.'

She takes a large canvas holdall from the back of the vehicle and slings it over one shoulder before accompanying Gertrude and me through the gate to the show gardens. Delilah's garden is filled with activity, as Mike directs his small team of volunteers. There is, of course, nothing to see of Anil's plot, still hidden behind the screen. Toby, meanwhile, is preoccupied with laying out long, stainless-steel sheets, with the help of two volunteers.

At Seb's garden, we see Sonny standing among the remains of the broken deck. He's close by and they're talking in urgent tones, but I can't hear what they're saying. He's red in the face, and I wonder if they're disagreeing about whether he should rebuild the deck.

Finally, we pass Koko's plot, where she's deep in concentration, making notes on a clipboard as she regards her grid of string. She reminds me of a spider at the edge of its web. I can't imagine what she's planning for her design.

When we reach my plot, where the trellises are, to my eye, grating in their nudity, I show Mattie to the back fence.

'Here's your spot,' I tell her. 'I've marked it out. I'm putting in a lot of large shrubs, with gaps between some of them, through which your mural will be visible, and then again at the end of the spiral path, of course.'

She studies the fence for a moment before checking: 'So, I can do what I like, so long as it works as a mirror frame?'

'Absolutely,' I assure her. 'I've seen enough of your work to know I'll love anything you paint, and it'll be a great match for the mix of formal and informal we're going for. Do bear in mind that it will be directly above the pond, so you can create some fabulous reflections.'

Mattie stands still for a moment, gazing at the fence beside the large, lined hole, a smile slowly suffusing her face. 'I like that idea.'

'Don't forget spirals,' Gertrude blurts out.

Mattie turns to look at her, raising an eyebrow. 'What about spirals?'

Gertrude blushes charmingly. 'It's just . . . the whole garden . . . I mean . . .'

I decide to rescue her. 'Well, as you know from our chats and the designs I sent over, I've created the whole garden around a spiral shape and theme. Even the plants have something heltery-skeltery about them.'

The artist grins. 'I love "heltery-skeltery". I might be borrowing that one.'

'Trademark Steph Williams,' I say.

'Obviously.'

She sets the holdall down at her feet. 'OK, got it. Spirals, circles and reflections.'

'But don't feel you have to be too literal,' I say.

'Can I get you a drink?' asks Gertrude.

Mattie smiles at her. 'I'm OK, thanks.' She draws out a drinks bottle, displaying an orangey-yellow liquid within. 'Peach and mango smoothie, made fresh earlier.'

'Cool. Let me know if you need anything,' says Gertrude eagerly. I love how she's as excited around Mattie as I am around Sonny. Thinking about the grande dame reminds me that she should be joining us soon, for her third and final mentoring visit.

I feel suddenly nervous.

'Let's start planting the climbers,' I say to Gertrude, hoping to work off some of the excess adrenaline that's just kicked in, as well as to leave the artist in peace to work.

Although clearly reluctant to leave Mattie, Gertrude accompanies me to the car park, where we grab a wheelbarrow each, to fill at our plant storage area beneath the oak tree.

Then, while Mattie works, we start to position the climbers along the fence. It's nearly three, and we probably won't have long before Sonny reaches us, but I'm keen to have some of these boundary plants in place.

About an hour later, I'm kneeling on the ground, so engrossed in uncoiling a passionflower from its canes that I jump when I feel a warm hand on my shoulder.

Sonny laughs loudly.

'Sorry,' she says, sounding anything but, 'I didn't mean to give you a scare.'

It's my turn to laugh, despite the onset of nerves at finding myself once again in close proximity to my horticultural heroine. 'I was away with the plants,' I tell Sonny, standing and turning to face her.

'Best place to be. They're far nicer than a lot of humans. Ooh, look – you've already got a fruit on that one,' she says, pointing to the passionflower in my hands, which bears an orange fruit, presenting a contrast to the white and purple flowers.

'Yeah, there's a few with fruit already. I'm not sure how I feel about the way nurseries cheat the seasons.'

'Hey, that's my livelihood you're questioning!' Her smile fades as she takes my gloved hands. 'I hear you had to call an ambulance for Delilah earlier?'

I nod. 'It was pretty scary, but the police have rung to say she's doing OK.'

She pats her chest. 'Yes, Addie told me. What a relief! She's such a sweet little thing, and a real up-and-comer . . .' She frowns. 'Hold on – police, not the hospital?'

I nod. 'I reported it as poisoning and they were getting back to me.'

'And?'

'Not enough to go on.'

'But you really think it wasn't an accident? I assumed it had something to do with her handling the plants for her woodland garden.'

'That's what Addie thought, too. But someone had put foxglove leaves in her drinks bottle. She had an infusion in there, so she didn't notice.'

'And you think it was someone here?' She looks horrified.

I nod. 'But let's not talk about it now. According to the police, I don't have any proof.'

At that moment, Sonny notices Mattie, who has donned large headphones and is sketching intently on the back fence. I can't make out a lot from here, but I feel a thrill of excitement at the prospect of an original piece of art, visible first from a distance, and then in detailed close-up as a reward to those who take the time to follow the spiral path to its end.

'Is that our local celebrity, Mattie Le Roy, over there?' asks Sonny.

'In the flesh. She's painting a trompe l'oeil mirror frame for me.'

Sonny looks surprised. 'How did I miss that in your plans?'

'It wasn't in the plans.' I become flustered and feel a blush creep up my neck as I correct myself. 'I mean, the mural was in the plans, but not who was painting it.'

Sonny either doesn't notice or kindly overlooks my repeat performance of Steph the Fangirl, who seems to have stolen back into my body without warning. 'How did you manage that?' she asks.

Shrugging, I say, 'I just emailed her and she agreed.'

'Charm *and* modesty,' she says, patting my shoulder.

'Or brazen cheek,' I suggest, as the blush intensifies.

Gertrude breaks in, providing a welcome distraction. 'Do you want to meet her?'

Sonny shakes her head. 'She's in the zone. You should never interrupt an artist when they're in full flow – it's like waking a sleepwalker.'

She talks with confidence. Sonny's relationship with her artist husband Paul has been well documented in the press. If their shared public persona is anything to go by, they fit together like a pair of jigsaw pieces. Their own garden near Torquay in Devon is filled with Paul's expressionist sculptures, which lend a multicolour background to Sonny's lush plantings.

'So,' says Sonny, clapping her hands. 'Final visit from me. How do you feel it's going?'

'OK, I think. As you can see, we're busy with the climbers at the moment. By the time we've disentangled them all from the canes, there should easily be enough greenery to create the green "wall".'

She nods. 'It's looking good. And I see you've taken my advice and dug out the path. Well done. How did that happen so quickly?'

Gertrude tells her about Alex and Jay.

'The exuberance of youth,' says Sonny, sounding slightly sad.

I squeeze her shoulder and she gives me a smile. Checking her watch, she says, 'It's nearly four already. Time is just whizzing by. And don't forget you have the other two judges coming along shortly. Last time I checked, they were with Seb.'

Gertrude and I share a nervous look.

'Is that today?' I ask. 'I forgot all about it!'

'Ah. I think Addie reminded everyone on the bus this morning, so you missed it.'

'Oh, right.' I pull a face.

'You'll be fine,' she says.

'I can't believe this is the last visit we get from you,' I say.

'Better make the most of me then,' she replies, smiling. 'Any questions we haven't covered?'

While I'm reflecting, Gertrude says, 'Actually, there was something I was hoping to ask you, if that's OK with Steph?'

'Of course it is,' I say.

She nods and continues, 'It's just, I saw on your website that you run a summer school at your garden every August. I was wondering how I might apply for it and if I'm too late for this year?'

'Email Katie, my assistant,' says Sonny. 'Her email address is on the website. Tell her you're preapproved by me.'

I feel quite emotional when I see the look of joy that lights up my colleague's face.

'Really? You mean it?' she says.

'Of course I mean it!' Sonny looks at me. 'What about you?'

'I won't be here in August.'

She laughs. 'No, I mean did you want to ask me anything?'

'Only . . .' I take a deep breath. 'Do you think I stand a chance in the competition? Of winning, I mean.'

'Everybody here has been chosen because they stand a chance,' she says. She must note my disappointment because, lowering her voice, she adds, 'But yours is one of the best designs here, in my opinion.'

Gertrude and I share a grin. 'We'd better get on with it then,' says my co-worker.

'And I should leave you to it,' says Sonny.

'Oh! Before you go . . .' I run to my backpack beneath the oak and bring back a Chelsea Flower Show brochure from 1996, when Sonny won her first gold medal. Feeling a new blush begin to suffuse my cheeks, I hold it out to her with a pen. 'Please would you sign this?'

She laughs. 'I'd be delighted. I can't believe you still have this. In fact, were you even born then?'

'I was a tot,' I admit. 'My mum attended, though, and she held on to the catalogue. She has a whole shelf of them.'

'How wonderful,' says Sonny. 'I'm pretty sure my own mum stuck hers straight in the bin.'

'It's weird. Mum never talked to me about gardening, and it's only recently, since I've had a few commissions, that she's opened up about her own love of plants. I mean, I knew she had a nice garden . . .' I tail off, aware I'm babbling.

Sonny pats my hand and comes to my rescue. 'Your mum must be really proud of you, my love.' As she signs her name on the cover with a flourish, I feel unexpected tears prick my eyes. I'm relieved when Mattie chooses that moment to call over to us:

'I'm going to have to finish tomorrow, if that's all right?'

'Of course,' I call back.

'Do you want to see the work in progress?'

Sonny, Gertrude and I walk over. The fence is already transformed. She's used coloured chalks to mark out her design, and it makes my heart speed up with excitement to see it. An intricate illusion of an old scrollwork gate with honeysuckle and ivy growing around it, the mural already looks 3-D.

Sonny whistles. 'Well, will you look at that,' she says. Catching Mattie's eye, she holds out a hand. 'Hiya. Sonny Carden.'

But the artist's eyes have grown wide. 'I know who you are,' she says, in an awed tone. 'You're like my most favourite out of all the people they've had presenting *Gardeners' World*.'

Sonny grins. 'And you're like my most favourite out of all the artists I've come across. Apart from my husband, obviously.'

Mattie wipes her chalky hands on her dungarees. I note that it's not the first time she's done this today: the orange and pink print of the fabric is daubed with the greens and blues of the chalks, turning her clothing into abstract art. She shakes Sonny's hand vigorously.

I nearly laugh at the volume of mutual admiration and respect filling the small space between us. If only the world was always like this. If it was, I might not have had to deal with the brutal manifestations of greed and jealousy in my previous placements.

Pulling my thoughts back to the current challenge, I tell Mattie, 'That mural is incredible. It makes me want to put a door there instead of the mirror, suggesting an entrance to another world.'

Her face lights up. 'If you want, I could paint a door, and you could leave off the mirror?'

I stare at the drawing, narrowing my eyes as I visualise the effect. 'Yes, please!' I say at last, with a grin.

She grins back, then nods decisively.

'Well,' says Sonny, 'it's been a pleasure, girls, but it's time for me to take my leave until the judging.' She takes one of my hands and one of Gertrude's, giving them a squeeze. 'You're going to blow them out of the water.' She pauses, looking thoughtful. 'Or some appropriate gardening metaphor.'

'Compost them out of the bin?' Gertrude suggests.

'Turnip them out of the veg patch?' I say.

Shaking her head, Sonny says, 'I'm glad you're gardeners and not novelists or poets, or I'd be worried about your futures. Now, is there anything you need from me, before I go?'

I shake my head. 'You've been brilliant. Thanks so much.'

'Well, you and Gertrude here have been pretty brilliant yourselves. It's been a total pleasure.'

We have a group hug, Sonny beckoning to Mattie, who drops her bag and gets in on the action. Just as we're breaking up, Mouse appears with a bark, closely followed by Chaplin, and everyone makes a fuss of them.

Once the dogs have been suitably stroked and patted, Mattie and Sonny walk back to the car park.

The other two judges arrive a few minutes later, when Gertrude and I are on the last few climbers. The pair approach slowly, making notes on their clipboards as they glance around at the plot.

'Hi,' I say. 'I'm Steph and this is Gertrude.'

Gillie and Frank introduce themselves, an act which is somewhat redundant, given their celebrity status.

'How's it going?' asks Gillie in her soft voice that still bears traces of her Glaswegian childhood. With her slight build, pale skin and blonde hair, she reminds me of a china doll. Frank, by contrast, is broad and rugged, with messy hair and a rumpled appearance. He's one of those white men who always look like they need a shave and a good scrub. I don't know how he gets past the wardrobe departments.

As they walk around the plot, I resist the urge to run ahead, pointing out where different landmarks and sightlines will be placed. Frank stops abruptly, pointing to a copy of my design on his clipboard. 'I see you've dug out this spiral path. How will you stop the path from seeming disjointed, disparate from the rest of the design?' His clipped speech doesn't fit with his scruffiness. It seems to me that he might need some work to avoid his own elements seeming disjointed and disparate. But I explain to him and Gillie about my spiral leitmotif, and how the plants and furniture will all reflect that in some way, bringing the whole design together as a unified whole.

He stares at his clipboard as I speak, making the odd note and giving nothing away.

'And don't forget the mural,' says Gertrude.

'Ah, yes,' says Frank, finally looking up from his clipboard and stepping closer to the chalk drawing. 'And how does this tie in?'

Gillie is right behind him. With a raised eyebrow to Gertrude and me, she says, 'Well, as you can see, with the curls of ivy around the scrollwork gate, it's full of Steph's spiral theme.'

He says nothing, but makes another note.

'Thank you,' I mouth to Gillie.

She nods, and says, 'How are you getting on with the mentoring process? Are you finding Sonny's feedback useful?'

'Very,' I say. 'She's so generous and helpful.'

She and Frank exchange a smile and Gillie says, 'Sonny's always been that way, wanting to share her experience with younger or less experienced gardeners.'

The pair depart soon after this exchange, leaving me uncertain as to their opinion on my build.

'He's a gloomy old so-and-so, isn't he?' says Gertrude brightly. 'I mean, not a word about how much we've got done already.'

Glancing around, I'm reminded that most of the climbers are in their spots, tied in to the trellis, with only three panels remaining uncovered.

Reading my mind, Gertrude says, 'Shall we get those last ones in? We've got twenty-five minutes before your minibus leaves.'

We complete the green wall, made up of passionflowers, *Clematis tangutica* – the nursery has cleverly managed to get these to the fluffy seedpod stage – and the truly weird *Clematis florida* 'Taiga', the flowers of which mimic the passionflower in purple and white, but have a dense white centre surrounded by myriad pointed petals.

Gertrude and I walk out to the grass verge, to get an overview.

'Apart from at the back, you can't see the fence at all,' she says, sounding a little surprised, as if we hadn't spent hours working to create precisely this effect.

'We've done a great job,' I say. We each remove a glove so we can share a high five.

Checking my watch, I say, 'Ooh, it's five. We'd better pack up.'

'You go,' says Gertrude. 'You'll be late if you hang around here – and you don't want to miss out on that posh wine I've heard they serve.'

'You make a good point,' I say, with a smile. 'If you're sure?'

She nods and I thank her before calling to Mouse and Chaplin, who come at once. I clip on Mouse's lead and, with a last wave to Gertrude, take the dogs to the minibus, meeting Toby en route. From his red, perspiring face and sweat-drenched shirt, he looks even more wrung out than I feel. As we climb on to the minibus, reeling at the heat, Mouse whimpers.

'I know, boy. I feel the same.'

'We all do,' says Koko, patting Mouse on the head. Although she's holding a little battery fan to her face, she shows no visible sign of overheating. Her short bob is shiny and her face is not.

'How do you look so cool?' I ask her.

She gives a Mona Lisa smile. 'My mother is the same. She used to be a model, you know? For the catwalks and for magazines and billboards. She is quite famous in Japan.'

'Ah, so that's where you get it from,' I say. Addie starts the engine, so Mouse and I make our way to the back of the vehicle. Koko's mention of her mum has me remembering my own mum's initial resistance to my wanting to make contact with my biological mother. Although she's come round to the idea in theory, I don't know how or if Mum will adapt, should Verity become a fixture in my life.

I wonder again why Mum kept Verity's biracial heritage from me. Was it, as she claimed, because she believed it would be easier for me to grow up as a white girl in a predominantly white society?

Or was it from something more deeply rooted in herself – the desire to raise a child whose identity was unquestioningly white?

18

There's an atmosphere of relief at the start of dinner. Addie has spoken to the hospital again and announced that Delilah is conscious and will make a full recovery.

Addie says, 'Let this be a lesson to you all, to be aware of what you're handling. Such an awful accident. Thank goodness she'll be all right,' and the others murmur their agreement, before we toast Delilah.

I watch the activity during the meal, keeping an especially close eye on Sarah, who seems louder and brighter than anyone else present. I wonder if she is feeling extreme relief at Delilah's recovery.

After the initial euphoria at the good news, it doesn't take long for fatigue to set in among the majority. We're shattered from working for hours in the heat, and most of us run out of words. Only Toby maintains his usual chatter. Seb peels off first, straight after dessert, then Koko. I follow soon after, my legs like heavy weights as I mount the stairs.

Mouse is out for the count when I reach our room. Checking my watch, I see it's only nine fifteen, but bed beckons. I pull on a long t-shirt, clean my teeth and climb in, relishing the smooth, cool sheets against my arms and legs.

It's as I'm lying back that I hear a scream. It's distant and faint, but Mouse wakes up instantly and starts to bark, so I know it wasn't some trick of my exhausted mind.

With a groan, I scramble out of bed and run to the window,

parting the curtains to peer out, but I can't see anyone in this section of the grounds.

Grabbing a pair of denim shorts from a drawer, I pull them on, slip on my trainers, slide my phone into my back pocket and look down at Mouse.

'Shall we go and investigate?' I ask him.

He's making a strange, low rumbling sound that I've rarely heard before. Whatever has happened out there, it's bad. I feel my heart begin to speed up in anticipation of what we might find.

As he and I race down the main staircase, I spot Addie leaving the dining room and switching off the light. She turns in surprise as first Mouse and then I land at the foot of the stairs. I make rather more of a thud than my dog.

Taking in the fact that she has her jacket draped over one arm and is carrying her handbag as if ready to head home, I ask, 'Did you not hear the scream? We're going outside to see what's happened.'

A concerned frown creases her brow. 'I didn't hear anything. Hold on, let me leave my things.'

She hangs her jacket on a coat stand in the hall and stashes her bag beneath it before opening the front door and saying, 'Oh!'

Koko is standing on the doorstep, one hand outstretched towards the door handle. She looks momentarily wrong-footed but recovers her poise almost instantly. She must have been listening to music on her phone; she presses the button to stop it before asking, 'Where are you going to?'

Joining Addie in the doorway, I say, 'We're going to check out who screamed.'

Her eyes widen. 'There is a person who screamed?'

'Didn't you hear?' I ask, beginning to doubt myself.

She gestures to her earphones. 'My music was very loud,' she says.

Mouse is whining beside me, keen to start moving again, so I just nod and say, 'We need to get going. See you later.'

'Be careful,' she says, as we pass her on the doorstep, 'it will be dark in a very short time.'

As soon as we're in the courtyard, Mouse takes off, running through the gardens, glancing back from time to time to make sure I'm following. Despite our daily jogs, I can't keep up with him when he goes at full pace, but he stops occasionally, ensuring he's always in my sight.

I can hear Addie close behind me, her breathing loud and rhythmical like mine. We pass Tree Fern Glade, but this time I barely acknowledge the towering specimens of *Dicksonia antarctica*. I need to concentrate on the sudden downward incline in the path, marked with those ominous signs depicting a person falling off a cliff – images which do nothing to calm my adrenaline-enriched heart. I become aware of the sweat seeping down my back. The air has that thick, oppressive humidity that makes breathing difficult. I drag my thoughts from the physical and reflect on the scream. I was able to hear it from the bedroom, so I reckon we can't have much further to go.

Sure enough, I hear Mouse begin to bark from just ahead.

'Coming, boy!' I manage, between gasps. I can no longer separate out what is my body struggling with the terrain, and what pure and simple fear.

Glancing back, I see Addie has slowed slightly as we approach the eroding cliff. 'Be careful!' she shouts.

'Got it,' I call back.

I find Mouse standing at the edge of the steep drop I saw on Saturday, barking with a frenzy of concern.

I have to ignore all the signs warning of the eroding cliff. Someone is in trouble down there. I drop down on my belly and crawl, commando-style, to the edge. Looking down, at first I can make out only gorse bushes, their flowers gleaming an eerie yellow in the now-dimming light. My blood is pumping hard in my ears as I turn to Mouse.

'What can you see?' I ask him.

With a single bark, he begins to run down the sheer cliff side, sure-footed as a mountain goat. At the bottom, he makes his way straight to a spot among the spiky gorse and barks up at me. The sound echoes weirdly, bouncing off the cliff side.

And then, with the cold tensing of fear, I see it: a small patch of pink dandelion-seed fluff, surrounded by a bloom of dark red. Two flora that do not belong in this gorse-filled landscape.

19

Addie reaches the edge above me just as I'm starting to climb down the rocky face, feeling for hand- and footholds in the encroaching gloom.

'Steph, what are you doing? You need to come back up. It's not safe.'

'I have to get down there,' I say, panting a little as I stretch out a leg, feeling for a hold.

'Why?' asks Addie. 'What's down there?'

'I think it's Sonny.'

'Sonny?' After a brief pause, I hear a sharp intake of breath and she says, 'Do you mean she's fallen? Is she all right?'

'I don't know. I won't know more till I reach her.'

'I'm calling an ambulance. I think you should wait, rather than risk your own safety.'

'Don't worry – I'm making good progress, and it's not as high as it looks from above. I should be at the bottom shortly.'

As I say this, I glance down, taking in Mouse, a concerned guard overseeing my progress. I'd like to ask him to move, so that, if I slip, I can't fall on him. But there's no command I can think of to achieve this.

My hands are slippery, though whether from the hot air or the adrenaline, I can't say. Fortunately, I chose my trainers for their excellent grips, and they prove their worth on the rugged surface as I scramble down.

When I'm about six feet from the bottom, I jump, feeling a jarring pain in my right ankle as I land in what I intended to be a careful squat. Swearing loudly, I take deep breaths for a few seconds, until the pain eases. As soon as I've straightened up, Mouse nudges me over to Sonny's prostrate form. His sorrowful whine before I reach her tells me all I need to know. This doesn't stop me from feeling for a pulse and testing whether she's breathing. I attended a first-aid course when I first trained as a gardener, and I keep up to date. But, even without these skills, I would be able to tell that nobody with their head at that unnatural angle could still be alive.

At that moment, grief overcomes me. I sit down hard a few feet from Sonny's body with my legs out in front and fight to catch my breath. Mouse nudges his head into my lap for comfort, but I am unable to do more than rock forwards and backwards, one hand placed on his head, a wail climbing from my throat like a vine. Even in my state of semi-paralysis, I'm able to acknowledge that I am crying not just for Sonny but also for Ben, my missing ex-husband, and for the probability that he, too, is dead.

I have no idea how much time goes by before the grieving subsides. Wiping my eyes on the hem of my long t-shirt, I realise that night has almost finished closing its thick curtains around us. I need to take a look at the scene before the emergency services arrive.

Pushing myself to standing, I switch on my phone's torch and make a swift tour around Sonny's body. Her head's strange angle and the pool of dark blood in her pink hair both seem to be due to a large rock beside her. When I direct my torch at the rock, I can see blood on it. I take some pictures on my phone using the flash. When I glance at the screen, I see that there's a white glare to her skin and pale t-shirt, and the surroundings appear darker than they are. It's not ideal, but at least I'll have some record of the scene.

As I carry out my examination of the area, several questions occur to me:

What was Sonny doing at Coleton Fishacre? She isn't staying in the house, and she didn't join us for dinner.

How on earth did she fall from the cliff? Was it the result of an innocent stumble?

Or – and here my heart itself stumbles – was she pushed?

20

The sound of voices attracts my attention to the arrival of two paramedics, descending the slope by means of a rope and pulley, controlled from above by a colleague. After they've reached the bottom, they tug on the rope. It's retracted, and then lowered again, providing a stretcher.

One of the two on the ground approaches me. 'Are you all right?' she asks, as the other examines Sonny by the light of a strong torch.

'I'm fine, thanks. Please just see to Sonny.'

She's quiet for a moment, and I wonder if she's afraid to tell me the news. 'I know she's dead,' I say quietly. 'I just want her to be looked after.' A large tear falls from my cheek on to the back of my hand and I wipe it on my t-shirt.

'Of course,' she says. 'Don't worry – we'll make sure she's treated well. I'm so sorry for your loss.'

The other paramedic calls to her and she responds, 'Coming.' Turning back to me, she says, 'Let me get you attached to the rope so we can have you hauled up.' Mouse has appeared at my side, and she adds, 'and your dog.'

The controlled rope makes my return journey faster and less hazardous than the way down. The paramedic has managed to fix the rope system so that Mouse and I arrive at the top together.

After thanking the person in charge of the ropes, I turn to Addie. I'm surprised to see that a couple of others have joined her. Partially illuminated by the haphazard torches of their mobile phones, I make out Toby and Anil.

'Why did the others come out?' I ask her quietly.

'Apparently Koko saw Anil and told him about our search. Anil messaged Toby. They were all concerned.'

A voice comes, deep and commanding, with a strong Devon accent, and I turn to see a tall figure standing close by, holding a torch. 'Can I ask you again if you could all *please* return to the house?'

'Come on, everyone,' Addie calls, waving her phone light to rally the little group. 'The policeman wants us all to go inside.' As we start to walk towards the house, Addie turns to me. 'Steph, are you OK?'

I stop walking. 'I'm fine, thanks. I just can't believe Sonny . . .' My voice tails off, and Addie nods emphatically, her eyes huge in the torchlight.

'I know . . .' Her voice cracks. 'We'd met quite a few times, you know? She was a huge supporter of Coleton Fishacre. She'd become a friend.' Her voice breaks, and she clears her throat.

'I'm so sorry,' I say quietly, giving her hand a squeeze. 'She was amazing.' Although it's unfair, I feel a twinge of anger towards Sonny, for leaving the world a little less bright now she's gone. Running my gaze over the figures tramping down the slope ahead of us, I recommence walking and ask Addie, 'Where's Seb?'

'Oh!' she says, striding alongside me. 'He's staying in what used to be the maid's room, on the other side of the house, facing out to the fields. He won't have heard anything, and I don't think Toby messaged him.'

'What about Koko?' I ask. 'She saw us coming out. Why isn't she here?'

'I've no idea. I'll message her. She'll want to know about Sonny.' Her voice cracks on Sonny's name and I squeeze her hand again.

'I can't see Sarah,' I say, shining my light over the row of backs.

'I'm here,' says Toby's petite wife, peering from the far side of her husband's hulking frame.

'Sorry, darling,' says Toby.

'As I always say, you do make a better wall than a door,' she says. Her tone is light – gratingly so, given the circumstances – and I remember Toby saying on that first night how Sonny had vetoed her hire as a presenter. I wonder if she's happy that Sonny's dead. Perhaps new avenues will now open up to her.

'Come on, please,' comes the police officer's voice again.

'We're going as fast as we can, if you don't want another accident,' says Addie.

'Sorry, madam.'

As we walk, I shine my torch on Sarah's back, taking in her height and build. I try to imagine her pushing Sonny off the cliff edge. She's tiny – but so was Sonny. It wouldn't have taken much to see her tumble, just a sharp shove in the right direction . . .

A shiver runs down my spine.

21

Mouse has been trotting around the little group, like a good sheepdog keeping the flock together. When we reach the house, he comes to heel and I give him a pat as we wait to pass through the wooden door. He's been amazing. I don't want to think how long Sonny's body might have lain there, undiscovered, if it hadn't been for him.

After a brief consultation with Addie, the police officer has us assemble in the Saloon. Once inside the huge room, I run my eye over the gathering, all glancing about nervously like refugee children fresh off the train.

'You can sit down,' says the officer. 'I'm DC Rob Bridges. I appreciate it's late and you'd rather be in bed, but we won't keep you any longer than we have to.' Addressing Addie as we all take our seats, he says, 'Did you say some of the party are missing?'

'Koko Yamada,' she says. 'But I've messaged her, and she's coming down. There's also Seb Burroughs. I can go up to get him.'

'Please don't leave this room,' he says quickly. 'Do you have his phone number to call him?'

She nods and, taking out her phone, rings him. 'Hi, Seb. Please can you pull on some clothes and come to the Saloon as quickly as possible? The rest of us are down here already. I'm afraid something awful has happened.' His voice comes through the phone, but I can't hear his words. She responds, 'It will all be explained when you get here.' After hanging up, she tells the officer, 'He'll be down in a moment.'

'Thank you.'

Sarah, seated with Toby on the sofa opposite Mouse and me, says, 'Surely it was just a nasty accident? We don't all need to be detained like criminals.'

The detective constable regards her wearily. 'Mrs? Ms? Miss?'

'It's Ms Cartwright, Sarah.'

'I'm afraid it's far too soon to rule out the possibility of suspicious circumstances behind Ms Carden's death.'

She frowns. 'You mean, she might have been murdered?'

This question is greeted with a gasp by more than one member of our party.

As I look around the grand room again, with its expanse of windows – curtains as yet not drawn against the dark – I am aware of both the beauty of the setting and its isolated outlook. We gaze at one another with a sense of mistrust, and I realise I'm not the only one assessing who among us might be capable of murder.

The officer sighs and I feel sorry for him. This is a big group to manage on his own and I see now, in the bright lights of the Saloon, that he's younger than his build and deep voice had led me to believe. Tall and broad-shouldered but with an angry-looking spot on his sparsely bearded chin, he's probably only in his early twenties. His suit is a little short in the sleeves and legs, and his tie has been badly knotted. His hair is dishevelled at the crown and this, combined with dark shadows under his eyes, suggests he's either doing a long shift or he's been dragged out of bed.

Toby stands up. 'Can I pour us all a drink?' he asks.

The young officer shakes his head. 'Sarge asked me to keep you all sober.'

'It's a bit late for that!' says Toby, sitting back down with a laugh.

Addie shoots him a sharp frown. 'Show some respect. A woman has died. A woman whom many of us loved.'

'Sorry,' he mumbles, gazing at his lap.

At that moment, Koko enters, dressed in a black silk kimono over matching pyjamas. The gown billows behind her as she enters the room. Glancing at the detective constable, I see he's momentarily thrown by this ethereal vision.

After a beat, he clears his throat and says, 'Erm . . . can I take your name, please?'

'Koko Yamada,' she says, promptly turning her back on him and stalking over to Addie, who is now seated in an armchair near to the door. Taking Addie's hands, she says, 'Are you all right?'

'*I'm* all right. It's Steph who had to climb down a cliff and sit with a dead body until the paramedics arrived.'

Still holding Addie's hands, Koko turns towards me. 'You did all of that? You were very brave. Is there no chance that she is still . . . ?'

I'm starting to shake my head as the officer interrupts, 'I'm afraid the lady is definitely deceased, madam.'

'Ah,' says Koko. 'I was hoping . . .'

Addie says, 'I should have been clearer. I'm sorry.' Koko nods and releases Addie's hands, sinking into an armchair close by.

A knock on the open door announces another police officer, wearing a black trouser suit. Of medium height and lean build, she has glossy dark hair pulled back into a low ponytail.

'I'm so sorry for your loss,' she says. 'I'm Detective Sergeant Jasmine Bhatti. And you've met my DC, Rob.'

We all nod.

Sarah clears her throat. 'I still can't see why we're being kept here. I mean, Toby and I were in our bedroom! We can hardly have been in two places at once, can we?'

The DS eyes her without expression. 'We have yet to establish everyone's whereabouts at the time of Ms Carden's fall. In the meantime, I'm afraid we need to search everyone's rooms. Our forensics team has just arrived.'

Seb has appeared in the doorway while she's been talking. His sandy hair is sleep-ruffled and there's a stoop to his posture, as if he's supporting a great weight.

'Search everyone's rooms for what?' he asks, but his voice suggests less surprise or indignation than a long-suffering sense of, *Now what*? With a sigh, he says, 'I've just got here. Can someone fill me in on what's going on?'

The DS turns to face him. 'You are?'

'Seb Burroughs.' The DC notes this on his tablet as Seb steps further into the room and repeats his question to the DS. 'Can you tell me what's going on?'

While DS Bhatti explains the situation and Mouse snoozes beside me with his head in my lap, I take the opportunity to study our suspects and run through possible motives. I need to be careful that my mistrust of Sarah doesn't bias me against considering other possible culprits.

It's possible that Sonny's death was not a murder, but something tells me a practised gardener like her didn't just lose her footing. I remember the ease with which she got up from the ground when we had our first meeting. I wonder what she was doing in the gardens of Coleton Fishacre late in the evening.

The sergeant has stopped talking, so I ask Addie, 'Do you know what Sonny was doing here?'

She smiles sadly. 'She said she preferred the gardens when they were empty of visitors, and asked if she could come and go, after hours. I said yes, of course.'

Glancing around the room, I ask, 'Did everyone know that?'

'Know what?' asks Seb.

Before I can respond, Koko says, 'Yes. She informed me that I might see her around because she would be exploring the gardens after closing time.'

She has her hands folded neatly in her lap and is sitting very upright. I marvel at her self-possession in the wake of a murder. Then I remember that she returned to the house just after Sonny's fall. I try to calculate whether she'd have had time to push Sonny over the edge and race back. It seems unlikely, but I can't be sure.

Seb brings me back from my calculations. 'Her house isn't that far away and, like Addie said, she preferred it here when there weren't any visitors.'

In other words, it was common knowledge that Sonny was visiting the grounds in the evenings. That means anyone here might have tracked her down out there, with no witnesses . . .

At that moment, my eyes land again on Sarah, sitting opposite, who, with her arms folded and a slight lift to her brows, looks both impatient and . . . slightly smug. I remind myself once again that, whilst it's possible she's glad that Sonny's no longer on the scene, it doesn't necessarily mean that she's the one who took her out of it.

Her husband is now sitting with his head back, eyes closed. There is nothing to be read in Toby's posture, other than tiredness and probable overindulgence in wine before, during and after the meal. As I consider him, he emits a snore. I doubt that the killer would be able to fall asleep so easily. At least, I hope not.

My eyes drift back to Seb, who's just taken a seat in an armchair at the far end, near the piano. But, at that moment, I hear my name.

I catch DS Bhatti's eye. 'Sorry, I was miles away,' I tell her. Nudging Mouse gently from my lap, I stand up, but Mouse moves to follow. 'Where do you want me?'

'If you could come with me . . .'

Glancing at Mouse, I say, 'Stay here, boy, OK?'

He promptly stretches across the entire sofa and closes his eyes. I'm sure I shouldn't be letting him on the furniture, but he's earned some luxury. He must be shattered after our late-night exploits.

The detective leads me into the hall and two rooms along, to a library with a curved walnut veneer desk in front of a large bay window which reminds me of the circular tower I stayed in recently, at Ashford Manor in Derbyshire. Drawing the teal velvet curtains by means of a pull cord, she takes the seat behind the desk, and nods towards the padded leather chair opposite her.

'I am so sorry for your loss,' she says, once I've lowered myself on to the chair. Her manner is efficient but there's a kindness to her tone which makes me like her instantly.

She presses the red button on a small recording device on the desk. 'DS Bhatti,' she says into the machine, before looking at me. 'Would you please state your name for the recording?'

'Steph Williams.'

'Thank you. Now, you found the body, is that correct?'

'Yes. Well, my dog did.'

She nods. 'Please take me through what happened, from the start.'

I tell her about the distant scream, followed by Addie's accompanying Mouse and me to investigate.

'There was no one else at the scene when you arrived?'

'No.'

She nods, then glances down at her notebook, open in front of her. 'I understand that you climbed down to the body. Ms Carden had sustained a nasty head wound . . .'

I have a sudden, awful thought that she's going to try to pin this on me. If Sonny had been alive after the fall, it would have been in the killer's interests to get down there quickly and finish the job.

But she just says, 'It looks as though the wound was caused by the large rock beside her head. Did you have any other thoughts?'

I'm so nonplussed by her eliciting my opinion that I'm momentarily silent.

With a small smile, she says, 'Rob told me your name came up on our database, linked to another death. He put in a call, and the detective he spoke to in Derbyshire told him you'd been helpful with that case.'

'Oh! That must have been DS McLeod.' With a deep, calming breath, I push away my memories of what happened in Derbyshire. Closing my eyes, I bring back the awful sight of Sonny, lying beside the rock, blood dried in her hair, and her head at an impossible angle. Meeting the sergeant's considered gaze, I say, 'I agree with you. It looked like she'd fallen and hit her head on the rock, breaking her neck.'

She nods again. 'You didn't touch the body?'

'Actually, I did. I checked for signs of life.' I pull a face. 'Pretty pointless, I know, and I probably contaminated your crime scene.'

'It's never pointless. I've known people survive the most horrific injuries.'

I'd had her down as being in her early thirties, like me. But this nod to her experience has me reassess her age as closer to forty.

Meeting my eye, she says, 'If you were me, who would you talk to first?'

'Sarah Butcher,' I say at once.

She consults her notebook. 'I don't seem to have a Sarah Butcher . . .'

Names are important. I changed mine to distance myself from my ex-husband. Kicking myself for forgetting that Sarah does not share her husband's surname, I correct myself: 'Sarah Cartwright, Toby Butcher's wife.'

Narrowing her eyes, she taps the blunt end of her pen on the desk. 'That seems a bit of a remote connection . . . Ms Cartwright isn't even taking part in the competition, is she?'

'She's a producer on Sonny's TV show. Toby told me Sonny was standing down from the show, and Sarah has been wanting to move into presenting, but Sonny was blocking Sarah from replacing her.'

The narrowed eyes widen. 'Really?'

I nod. 'So there's no love lost there – at Sarah's end, at any rate, according to Toby.'

She makes a note. 'Right. Good tip. Thanks.'

'Also, I believe that Sarah might have poisoned another member of the group.'

She frowns. 'I'm sorry?'

'Delilah Deville is in hospital, recovering from digitalis poisoning. When I checked her drinks bottle, it contained foxglove leaves. And I saw Sarah coming out of Delilah's room the day before, when she was already suffering with symptoms. Sarah seems to feel quite threatened by Delilah – or by Toby's interest in her, at least.'

She looks sceptical. 'That doesn't sound like the most concrete evidence. Where is this drinks bottle now?'

'I'm not sure. The paramedics took it. I did report the poisoning, but the local police at Brixham said there wasn't enough to go on.'

She nods. 'I'll contact Brixham and see what they've got. Anyone else you have concerns about?'

I reflect for a moment, flicking through the contenders in my mind like a game of Who's Who?.

'Koko Yamada,' I say. 'She was coming into the house just as Addie, Mouse and I were leaving to investigate the scream.'

She consults her notes. 'This would be between nine fifteen and nine thirty?'

'I'd say it was around nine twenty.'

She makes another note and says, 'Do you have reason to believe Ms Yamada held a grudge against Ms Carden?'

I nod. 'Quite possibly. Koko's up for a job in the States and she said this competition was make or break on that front.' Bhatti raises an eyebrow. 'Also,' I continue, warming to my subject, 'Koko was worried Sonny was prejudicing the other judges against her.' While she makes more notes, I repeat my silent visual roll call before saying, 'I'd also look at Seb Burroughs.'

'The man who came down after everyone else?' When I nod, she says, 'Why him?'

'He's got a really bad temper. He yelled at me yesterday, for accidentally taking one of his plants. I mean, really yelled. And he wasn't thrilled with some of the feedback he received from Sonny. She suggested he change one quite big aspect of his design, but he was against it. Also, I don't think anyone saw him tonight from dinner – which he left early – until you called us all into the Saloon. He'd have had time to sneak back into the house while we were all distracted, and get cleaned up. What's more – and this might be relevant – his show garden build had been vandalised when he got to the site this morning.'

'Really?' She makes another note. 'I'll ask him about that.' She looks up. 'So, that's Seb Burroughs and Koko Yamada both with opportunity. Anyone else?'

'Anil Ahmad,' I say, after a moment's reflection. 'Sonny was quite critical of his design.'

'Really? What did she say about it?'

'Well, she told me it was flashy. But I think she just told him it was too ambitious.'

'That doesn't sound so bad.'

'Except that she was also a judge, so her opinion would have counted. And I get the impression Anil really wants this win.'

'Any idea why?'

I think back and say, 'There's a court case of some kind against his company. He didn't tell me any details. I think the case is overseas somewhere. He said they needed some positive publicity.'

'OK. I'll ask him.' She makes another note, then regards me shrewdly. 'You suspect foul play, don't you?'

'I do. I wish I didn't. It's just . . . Sonny wasn't unsteady on her feet. I can't see her stumbling and falling over the edge. Why would she even have stepped so close to an eroding cliff edge in a garden she knows well? I think someone pushed her.'

She consults her notes. 'From the timings you and Ms Adebayo have given, it would have been getting dark.'

'Barely. And apparently she knew the gardens in that area well. She must have known there was that drop just past the tree ferns. And there are warning signs.'

She nods. 'So, if it wasn't an accident, we're looking for whoever was with her. Do you know who she might have arranged to meet?'

I shake my head. 'Maybe it was a chance meeting.'

'It's possible, I suppose.' She looks unconvinced.

'So, what are you thinking?' I ask. 'Find out who she was meeting, find her killer?'

'Or,' she adds, 'if this person didn't push Ms Carden off the cliff, see if they can shed some light on her emotional state.' I stare at her. She can't really be suggesting Sonny might have killed herself. 'Don't look at me like that,' she says stiffly. 'We have to consider this from all angles. Anyone else?'

She's playing with her pen again, tapping it on the desk in a quiet rhythm. When I tell her that I can't think of anyone, she sets down the pen and says, 'Now, you need to tell me why I shouldn't suspect you.'

I meet her gaze. 'I was seen within moments of the scream being heard.'

'Rob spoke to some of the others outside, and we haven't found anyone who can corroborate your story of the scream.'

'That's strange.' I consider for a moment. 'I guess some of them may have been asleep. I know Addie didn't hear it, but she was walking through the dining room from the Loggia at the time. The fact that she was moving would have made it harder for her to hear above her own footsteps. Koko had earphones in, and said she was listening to loud music. Oh, and Addie told me that Seb's room is on the other side of the house. I don't know if that might also be true for Toby and Sarah.'

She passes me a business card. 'Please call me if you remember anything, or if anything occurs to you, however small.' She speaks into the recorder, 'Interview terminated,' and I get to my feet. 'Forensics have started on the rooms,' she says. 'You should be able to go to bed shortly. I'll have Rob let you know.'

'What are you hoping to find in the bedrooms?' I ask.

She regards me for a moment, as if trying to decide what to tell me. At last, she says, 'If there's been a struggle of some kind, there might be garments showing rips, or even spots of blood.'

'Oh, right.'

As I walk back to join the others, I can't help running through my own outfits, and whether I might have cut myself and bled on any of them, or torn them when I was fixing the trellis panels to the fence. Gardeners and pristine clothing do not generally go hand in hand.

Back in the Saloon, Addie is sitting quietly, gazing into space.

'Can't you go home?' I ask.

She shrugs. 'I don't like to leave everyone.'

'This isn't on you,' I say, crouching in front of her. 'You need to look after yourself. We're all grown-ups.'

'Speak for yourself,' comes Toby's booming voice.

'OK, everyone except Toby,' I amend, pleased to see a tiny smile tease the corners of Addie's lips.

She nods and addresses the room. 'I'll be in Delilah's room tonight. Don't hesitate to knock if you need me.'

Before leaving, she says quietly to me, 'I can't believe this has happened.'

'I know. Same here.' She squeezes my hand.

I take my seat beside Mouse, on the sofa opposite Sarah and Toby. The latter has closed his eyes again already. Sarah is watching something on her video camera.

I glance around. 'Where's Seb?'

The DC answers, 'Mr Burroughs has gone in for questioning with the sarge.'

I hadn't noticed DS Bhatti arriving for him, but I was probably talking to Addie at the time.

'I bet Seb did it,' mutters Sarah, without lifting her gaze from the viewing screen.

I wonder if she's trying to shift the blame. But Seb does strike me as someone who could be capable of violence when truly riled. I shiver as I remember his anger over the silver birch. Then I recall the fact that Sarah filmed the altercation.

I say, 'Sarah?' and wait until she meets my eye. 'One of my volunteers said you filmed Seb going off at me.'

She smiles but it's not a pleasant sight. I'm reminded of a crocodile. 'Yes,' she says in a languid drawl. 'That will make for some fantastic viewing. Can you imagine? *Love Island* eat your heart out. I'm thinking we'll call it *Gardeners Go Wild*.'

'I'd really appreciate it if you could delete it.'

'Now, why on earth would I do that?'

'Because it might present me in a bad light. I don't want potential clients to think I go around stealing from my peers.'

She sets the camera to one side and leans towards me. 'But that's exactly what you did, isn't it, Steph?'

'No. I thought the silver birch was a gift from the nursery.'

'So you say.' With that, she sits back and returns to her viewing. My nails are digging into my palms. I focus on relaxing my fists and calming my breathing. I will just have to get hold of the camera at some point and delete the footage.

Seb returns more quickly than I'd expected, and the DS asks Sarah to accompany her. When she rises, leaving the camera on her seat, I'm about to get up and swipe it. But the DS catches sight of it and says, 'Actually, can you bring the camera? We'll need to make a copy of the footage and go through it, in case there's anything useful.'

Sarah retrieves the camera and I'm left to stew.

Glancing around the room, I see Koko is still in a poised, upright position, but now has her eyes closed. I wonder if she might be performing deep breathing or meditation. Anil is on his phone, frowning as he types swiftly with his thumbs.

At that moment, a figure in a full protective suit comes to the door and DC Bridges strides over to speak to them. There's low murmuring, and then the figure disappears and the DC says, 'Ms Williams, you can go to bed. Forensics are done in your room. Sorry to have made you wait up.'

'What about me?' asks Anil as I get to my feet, but the DC shakes his head. 'Not till you've talked to DS Bhatti. Shouldn't be too long now.'

I wake poor Mouse, then the two of us bid the others goodnight before ascending the stairs to our room. He heads straight to his bed, where he curls up like a cat, tucks Mr Rabbit beneath his chin and promptly falls asleep.

I'm filthy from my cliff climb but I don't have the energy for a bath, so I change into a clean t-shirt, remove my shorts and crawl into bed, hoping that whoever has to wash the linen will forgive me.

Before drifting off, I consider messaging my brother and parents, to tell them about Sonny's death, so they hear it from me before the news hits the media.

But, when I check my watch, it's gone midnight and that particular message would make for an unfit lullaby.

22

I have troubled dreams in which I'm standing on the cliff edge over a cove, while my fellow designers slowly feed out a rope, lowering a comatose Sonny to the choppy waters below, where shark fins circle. As I shout for them to stop, Koko turns to me and says, 'You're not wearing *that*, are you?'

Looking down, I see I'm dressed in a long t-shirt made of pebbles. As soon as I'm aware of the stones, the garment becomes too heavy for movement, anchoring me to the spot. I'm faced with the dilemma of whether to remove the pebble top and attempt to rescue Sonny naked, or stand fixed to the spot as she's lowered to what I presume will be her death by either shark attack or drowning.

I'm saved the choice by waking, drenched in sweat despite the coolness of the room. Mouse is standing beside me, making anxious, questioning noises in his throat.

As I reach out a hand to stroke him, the events of the night before return with the force of a cricket bat to the skull: the distant scream; Mouse's urgent barking; the tricky climb down the slope; and the realisation that it was too late to save my heroine.

Sonny's dead. I reel as if discovering this fact for the first time, letting out a fresh sob. The three syllables march in my head, gaining momentum. *Son-ny's-dead; Son-ny's-dead; Son-ny's dead.* Breathing slowly until I've regained control, I reach for my phone and type the phrase in a message to my brother, which I delete immediately without sending. He has four children under ten. This is not something I can just drop on him with neither explanation nor preamble.

I need to find out what happened – for both Sonny's sake and my own.

I propel myself out of bed, grab my soap and towel and cross the landing to my bathroom, where I wash off the dirt in a shallow bath. My legs, torso and arms are covered in bruises and scrapes I hadn't noticed until now. After patting myself dry, I wrap my towel around me and return to my room, where I don a fresh pair of shorts and a white vest and apply arnica cream to the bruises.

As I pull on my trainers, I turn to Mouse and say, 'Shall we go for a walk, boy?'

He immediately brings me his blue lead.

'Good boy,' I say, as I attach it to his collar. 'Let's go and find Sonny's killer.'

He makes his rumble of agreement.

As soon as we reach the bottom of the stairs, I have a flashback to the previous night in the same spot, when I'd still been hoping we might be in time to help whoever had screamed. A tear falls, hitting my hand before dripping on to the pale carpet. I blink back further tears, taking a deep breath as we head for the front door and plunge out into the fine, misty morning.

Mouse and I walk, then jog, his tail wagging, as we travel towards Tree Fern Glade, relishing the earth's reassuring solidity beneath our feet. My bad dream slips from me like peas from a pod and I feel a sense of purpose as we reach the topmost point and begin the descent. I can't bring Sonny back, but I can help to bring her killer to account.

I stop abruptly just before the tree ferns, causing Mouse to look up at me curiously. Police tape has been stretched right across the path, at around waist height. I should have been prepared for this.

At that moment, a uniformed police officer steps out from the foliage and asks my name. The misty air lends to his outline an indeterminate quality, like viewing a newt through water. Only the chunky vowels of his local accent prove his solidity.

When I give my name, he says, 'Oh, right. DS Bhatti said to let you through.'

'Really?'

'Yeah. But I'm meant to keep an eye on you.' He pauses before adding, 'I couldn't tell if she was joking about that part.'

His honesty is disarming. 'I doubt she was joking,' I say, with a short laugh. 'Please do watch me, if only so I can't be accused of tampering with anything. Where is DS Bhatti this morning?'

He snorts. 'She's the sarge. She doesn't have to be up before midday.'

'What's that, Constable?' comes the unmistakable voice of the DS from behind me. I see the young man blanch.

'Morning, Sarge! Sorry. Didn't know you were there.'

'So I gathered.'

She lifts the tape and gestures for me to pass beneath it. Mouse keeps to heel as we slip beneath the raised cordon, followed by Bhatti and her detective constable, Rob, who's just arrived. He's carrying cups bearing the logo of a local coffee shop, Kingswear Coffee Company. The rich scent has me close to drooling.

'Would you like a coffee?' the DS asks me. I'm about to accept when I see the devastated look on her DC's face.

'Oh no, that's all right, thanks. I can get one at breakfast.' I ignore my taste buds, which are almost reaching out for the cup of their own accord.

The sergeant glances down at Mouse. 'This is the dog that found the body?'

'That's right. This is Mouse.'

She nods. 'OK. Just don't let it off the lead.'

'I won't.'

'Forensics already did a sweep up here last night, but I wanted to make sure we didn't miss anything in the dark,' she tells me.

Glancing down into the valley, I see that the scene of death looks less menacing in daylight. The gorse bushes take on a more benign appearance, as if last night they had been dressed for Halloween.

I murmur to Mouse, 'See anything, boy?'

He whines, then tugs on the leash. I let him lead me to a wild rose, where I have to hold him back from plunging in head-first. 'Whoa, boy! If there's any rosebush-exploring to be done, that'll be my job. Stay.'

I peer into the bush. There's something white inside. My heart begins to race as I prepare to reach for it.

At that moment, Bhatti arrives at my side. 'Found something?'

'Mouse has. I don't know what it is.'

Bhatti calls to Rob, who comes over wearing thick gloves. With his eyes screwed tightly shut as if this can protect him from the thorns, he reaches into the bush, drawing out a square of white fabric.

'It looks like a pocket,' I say.

'It does,' says Bhatti. 'Right, bag that up, Rob, and get it over to the lab.'

I try to remember what Sonny was wearing when I found her lying on the ground.

Addressing the sergeant, I say, 'Sonny was wearing a white top when we found her, wasn't she?'

'It was certainly pale.'

'So, if the pocket was torn off, someone was definitely here with her. It's looking more and more like a fight,' I say.

'Or perhaps they tried to stop her from falling, by grabbing her clothing.'

I hadn't thought of that.

While she and the DC continue to explore the area, I notice that several of the rose's stems have been broken. 'Look,' I call to them, and they come over.

I point out the damage, and the DS says to her DC, 'Take some shots of this, would you, Rob? And if you look just to the right, you'll see that the grass has been flattened beyond it.' Keeping my distance, I squint at the spot she gestured to. Glancing at me, she says, 'Quite a large area has been flattened. It's my guess that two people were standing here.'

We move out of the way to allow Rob to move in and take pictures.

As we wait, I ask her, 'Did anything turn up in the room searches?'

'There was nothing. Or, more accurately, there were a number of torn items of clothing. But all of it looked like the typical wear and tear we'd expect with your trade as gardeners. None of it fitted with what we believe happened here.'

'And the poisoning . . . ?'

'Rob's going to talk to Brixham station today. Please don't say anything to Ms Cartwright in the meantime, about your theory.'

I nearly tell her that it's more than a theory – but is it? What court of law would uphold my testimony against Sarah's? The officer I spoke to at the local station was right: there is no tangible proof. Even if they conducted fingerprint analysis on the bottle, I'd bet anything that my own fingerprints would appear at least as prolifically as Sarah's. I sigh and watch DC Rob Bridges at work. He's very thorough, taking pictures from every angle.

When he's finished, DS Bhatti addresses me once more.

'That's gone a lot more quickly with the help of you and your dog. Many thanks for that. Rob and I will stay a while longer, in case we've missed anything. Later, we're going to go through the footage from Sarah Cartwright's filming at Poplars Farm. You should get to your breakfast.'

Before Mouse and I take our leave, the sergeant pats his head and tells him he's a clever boy, and Rob feeds him a treat.

After that, we manage a short jog around some of the other pathways, arriving back at the courtyard pleasantly out of breath (on my part) and feeling more prepared to face the day ahead. My brain and body are both always better for exercise.

I'm about to open the front door when I see Koko arriving out of the corner of my eye. I stop to greet her.

'Hi, Koko.'

'Good morning, Steph.'

I notice she has something behind her back and try to remember if she appeared to be hiding anything when Addie and I encountered her on the doorstep last night. I can't remember seeing anything, but I was preoccupied.

'Koko, can I ask you something?' She nods, but looks wary as I continue, 'What were you doing last night, when we saw you coming back into the house?'

With a sigh and a quick glance around, she draws her hands from behind her back to show me a collection of small plastic bags. She opens one and allows me to peer inside.

I frown as it seems she is showing me some twigs. But then I understand. 'Wait. Are these cuttings?'

She nods and whispers, 'Mainly root cuttings. Also, there are some small seedlings.'

'You mean you've been stealing from the garden?'

She shrugs her slim shoulders. 'I would not call this stealing. Can anything that grows in nature really belong to a human being?'

I laugh. 'I'm not sure that would hold up as defence in a court of law.'

She smiles but doesn't speak, so I say, 'This is what you were doing last night, gathering specimens?'

'Yes. I returned just before it would become too dark to see the roots in the soil. I did not know about Sonny's fall, or I would have gone to try to help.'

'OK. But you have to tell Addie about those cuttings. I'm sure she'd have let you take them if you'd asked.'

'Ah, but if I do not ask, she cannot forbid it.'

I can't argue with her logic, even if I'm not happy with her ethical stance.

We part ways in the hall. After taking Mouse up to our room, I have a wash and pull on my uniform of denim shorts and t-shirt.

When I reach the table on the Loggia, I see that everyone else is there.

I fill my thermos and a cup at the coffee machine, then take the end seat at the table.

'Any update on Delilah?' I ask.

'Yes,' says Addie with a weak smile. 'She's made a recovery. They're keeping her in a bit longer for monitoring, but they don't believe there's any permanent damage.'

'Oh, thank god,' I say.

As I lift my cup to take a sip of coffee, Seb says, 'You sure you want to drink that?'

'Why not?'

'Well, according to you, we've now had one attempted murder and one actual murder.'

'Who told you that?' I ask.

He shrugs. 'We all know there were foxglove leaves in Delilah's drink. Don't *you* think someone put them there?'

Glancing at the faces around the table, I see several look unnerved; frightened even. I take a deliberate sip before answering. 'Delilah was targeted,' I say. 'The poison was in her personal drinks container. And Sonny's killer didn't use the same method.'

'Delilah's illness was an accident,' says Addie firmly. 'The police at Brixham confirmed it.'

Keen to move the conversation on, I say, 'Addie, I'm sure you've gone over this with everyone else before I got here, but are we going to carry on with our builds? I mean, is the competition going ahead?'

Addie nods. 'I had a chat first thing with our trustees, and I've notified the other judges and the sponsor. They're all devastated, of course. But they're in agreement that we should continue, out of respect for Sonny, and for what she would want. She was a firm believer in the show going on.'

She surveys the assembled party. 'Can I have your attention for a moment, please?'

My phone buzzes in my pocket but I leave it for now, as Addie starts to address us about the need to be wary of the press.

'As Sonny is . . . *was* so well known, the police believe there will be a lot of media interest.'

'What should we say, if we are approached?' asks Seb.

'Just tell them you've nothing for them, and send them to me if they become troublesome,' she says. 'You can inform them that Detective Sergeant Bhatti will be holding a police conference later.'

Koko is looking alarmed. 'Troublesome? What is it that these reporters might do, exactly?'

Addie gives her a reassuring smile. 'I only mean that they might become rather pushy, trying to persuade you to tell them things about the case. As it's an ongoing investigation, the police have stressed that we will be in legal trouble if we share information.'

'Oh!' says Koko. 'Pushy people.' She shrugs. 'This kind of person I can deal with.'

Toby says brightly, 'Right! Shall we get on and build these show gardens, like Sonny wanted?'

'Good plan, mate,' says Anil, before helping himself to a pastry from the basket.

'I'm still going to win, you know,' says Toby, as he gets to his feet and slides his chair neatly into place.

'You're bloody not!' says Anil, through a mouthful of pain au chocolat.

After breakfast, I collect Mouse from our room and we head downstairs. It seems strange to be following this already familiar routine when Sonny is dead and Delilah is still in hospital. We're early, so we take a quick walk up to Scout Point before heading down to board the minibus.

Mike is waiting for us at the back of the bus. He and Mouse share an enthusiastic greeting, then Mouse sits beside him and I take a seat in the row in front.

Stroking Mouse, Mike says softly, 'I wanted to check you were all right. It seems like you're having to deal with a lot right now. I'm so sorry you and this guy were the ones who found the body last night, especially after what happened yesterday morning with Delilah.'

'Thank you,' I say, unable to think of anything to add.

He nods and rubs his face. His normally neatly trimmed beard is untended, and his hair is dishevelled. I wonder how much sleep he got last night.

'I've been wondering if they're all linked,' he says. 'You know – maybe the same person or people who tampered with Delilah's water bottle also destroyed Seb's garden and hurt Sonny.'

I meet his eye. 'If so, you realise you're basically accusing Sarah of murder?'

He looks around quickly, but Sarah has taken the Volvo as normal, and Toby is at the front of the bus, well out of earshot, especially against the noise from the old engine.

'I know you think Sarah put those leaves in Delilah's bottle,' he says. 'But is there any chance you made a mistake? I hate to think anyone here could have done such awful things.'

'Sarah has means and motive, as they say on the detective shows. She's definitely jealous of Toby's attentions to Delilah. But yes, it's possible she was in Delilah's room for some other reason entirely. She might have been looking for proof that Delilah was sleeping with Toby.'

It occurs to me that, in sharing my theories, I have been trusting Mike implicitly. Might I be wrong to do so? But looking into his frank, open gaze, I'm sure he's incapable of harming anyone.

'What?' he asks, in response to my stare.

'I was just thinking that you're easy to be around. And you're good in an emergency – I was so grateful for your help with Delilah yesterday.'

He smiles. 'Right back at you.'

Our eye contact lasts for longer than necessary. When I feel heat begin to suffuse my cheeks, I say, 'Anyway . . .'

'Anyway.' Although his tone is no-nonsense, his voice is slightly croaky.

I speak quickly, to hide both our blushes. 'Remember Toby said that Sarah is possessive of him around other women.'

'I forgot about that,' he says quietly. 'I think I blanked it because it came too close to cradle-snatching for my liking. It's what my teenage daughter would refer to as the "ick factor".'

As I file away his being a dad for later, I say, 'I feel the same way.'

He pulls a face. 'I remember you said you thought Toby was just paternal towards Delilah?' When I nod, he continues, 'That's good. But it also means Delilah might have been poisoned for no good reason.'

I arch a brow. 'As opposed to being poisoned for a really good reason?'

'Sorry! No! I just meant . . .'

I let him squirm for a moment before touching his shoulder and saying, 'It's OK. I know what you meant.'

He takes a deep breath. 'If it was Sarah, do you think she was trying to kill Delilah?'

'I honestly don't know. I haven't confronted her, because the police said there wasn't enough to go on. Working on gardening shows, she would have picked up knowledge about common poisonous plants like foxgloves and delphiniums, but she'd be unlikely to have any idea how much damage they could do. She might have thought a small number of foxglove leaves in the drinks bottle would only make Delilah a bit sick, so she'd have to bow out of the competition but would recover quickly.'

'That makes sense. I can't see her – or anyone here – as a cold-blooded killer.'

I decide not to point out that, the way I see it, one of our number pushed Sonny to her death. We don't speak for the rest of the short journey, lapsing into a thoughtful silence. I remember the notification sound from my phone during breakfast and pull it out of my pocket, to find a message from Mum. It simply says:

Thank you.

With a small smile, I tuck my phone away. At least she and Dad appear to have made up.

23

When we reach the car park, I hear Seb, sitting a few rows ahead, exclaim at something I can't see at first. But then the bus inches further through the gates, and I get a view of the car park.

The place is packed with reporters wielding microphones and notepads. There's even a mobile broadcasting unit.

'Shit,' says Mike, getting to his feet and striding to the front of the minibus. I release Mouse from his seat belt and give him a stroke.

'Don't worry. It's just humans being humans,' I tell him softly.

As soon as Addie has parked, she and Mike get down from the bus, doing their best to fend off the swarm of reporters while the rest of us disembark.

One journalist manages to catch me by the elbow as I'm attempting to slip through unnoticed. A skinny white man with big brown eyes behind thick glasses, he coughs before stepping so close, I can feel his breath on my ear. Mouse grumbles a warning and I'm ready to push the man away, until his words unsettle me.

'Sonny Carden – she was murdered, wasn't she?' he says, in a whisper like the wind through dry reeds. 'Pushed from that cliff. Who was it, d'you reckon? One of the men here? Jealous rival to husband Paul's affections?'

I stand, frozen for a moment, until Mouse has had enough and starts barking, and Mike steps in and elbows the man aside. I nearly tell Mike that I can look after myself – but, in this instance, I must admit that I'm glad of his help.

'Thanks,' I say. But even as I'm speaking, another journalist reaches me, plunging her microphone into the air between us. 'Steph Williams, isn't it?'

'I've got nothing to say to you . . .' I begin.

But she pushes on. 'What can you tell me about Jamie?' she asks, naming a young man from my recent placement at Ashford Manor in Derbyshire.

And, for a moment, I have trouble catching my breath. But Mouse, sensing my panic, begins to snarl and she backs off in alarm. He and I duck and weave through the remaining throng until we get to the little gate and the safety of the show gardens.

Chaplin is waiting with Toby beside Toby's plot. As we send the dogs off to play, Toby says, 'That was a bit much, wasn't it?'

'It really was.'

He peers towards the car park. 'It looks like Mike and Addie have got them under control now. Hopefully they'll bugger off.'

'I doubt it.' Glancing at his garden, I see that the trench for the stream is now ready for its stainless-steel chute, and most of the fence is covered in mirrored surfaces.

'You've done a lot,' I say.

'What do you think?'

'It's certainly looking reflective.'

He smiles. 'I know it's a bit disjointed at the moment. It'll come together once the plants are in.'

'Good luck. I'd better get back to mine.'

With a wave, I continue along the verge towards my plot, passing Seb's recovered garden, where I'm glad to see no sign that he is reinstating the decking, and then Koko's plot, where she is finally placing pots containing grasses and perennial plants. She's already deeply focused on her task, so I say nothing as I walk by, arriving at my plot.

But this space can't be mine. The spiral path has already been filled with bark chippings. Backing out, I check rather stupidly for my name on the post at the front. But there it is: 'Steph Williams, "The Journey"', on the laminated sheet.

'Where are you going? Are you all right?' asks Gertrude.

I lift the brim of my cap and rub my forehead. 'I just . . . How did this happen?'

I see now that Jay and Alex are with her. They all begin to laugh.

'Come here,' says Gertrude softly. As I walk towards her, she takes both of my hands in hers. 'I am so, so sorry for what you've been through. We all are.' Jay and Alex nod.

'But this,' I say, gesturing to the beautifully filled path. 'How? I don't understand.'

Looking towards Alex and Jay, Gertrude says, 'Can you give us five minutes, kiddos?' They nod and slouch away, and she continues, 'I thought that you might be busy all morning, you know, with the police? So, Alex, Jay and I had a chat first thing, and we agreed it would be good if you could come back to find the next big job already done and dusted.'

'That's brilliant,' I tell her, close to tears. 'Thank you so much.'

Waving away my gratitude, she shoots me a concerned look. 'So, how are you doing? I mean, I heard that you were the one that found the body?'

News travels fast, I think. With a sigh, I say, 'It's been pretty awful, and I haven't really come to terms with it yet . . .' Feeling my eyes well up again, I stop talking.

'I'm not surprised,' she says. 'You must be in shock. We were all stunned when we heard. I mean, how on earth did she manage to fall off the cliff like that? Isn't that area of the garden full of warning signs?'

'It is, yes. I don't really know what happened.'

She sighs, tugging on one of her plaits. 'Of course you don't. I didn't mean to interrogate you.' She pauses before saying slowly, 'Do you know, I'm just remembering, I saw Sonny and that Sarah woman having a right old barney.'

'Sarah, the videographer?' I check, in case she's talking about one of the volunteers.

'That's right. I forgot to tell you, in all the excitement about the digger being on its way. But they were really going at it.'

I frown. 'When was this?'

She screws up her eyes in thought. When she opens them, she says,

'It must have been Sunday, because Sonny was here already, waiting to do her visits. You remember how she did them in the morning?' When I nod, she continues, 'She'd been chatting to me, but then she walked off towards the car park, and Sarah came leaping at the poor woman, screaming and shouting. I ended up trying to get between them. Fortunately, you all arrived at that moment in the minibus, and Sarah backed off.'

'Did you hear what the argument was about?' I ask.

She shakes her head. 'But Sarah was blazing like anything. I thought she was going to slap Sonny or something. That's why I stepped in.'

I fish out DS Bhatti's card and pass it to Gertrude. 'Can you give this detective a call? She'll want to know about the argument.'

Gertrude nods gravely. 'I'll do it in a moment.' She goes quiet, then says softly, 'Sonny was a wonderful woman.'

I suddenly remember Gertrude's conversation with her. 'Oh, no! You were going to take part in her summer school!'

She shrugs. 'I think there are more important things than whether or not I get to enjoy a few weeks of horticultural shenanigans, don't you?'

'Let me know if there's anything I can offer that might make some amends.'

She smiles, gesturing around her. 'You don't think you might be doing it already?'

'Well, the offer stands, if you think of anything else.' I walk over to the pathway. 'It looks like all the bark is in.'

'About two more barrows and we're done,' she says, with a grin.

'That's amazing. You've all done brilliantly. Thanks so much,' I say, aware I'm repeating myself.

She beams. 'Just our little gift to you, to say thank you for letting us be part of Team Steph.'

At that moment, Alex and Jay reappear, each pushing a wheelbarrow full to the brim with bark chippings. Gertrude directs them to a couple of spots where the path is sparse, and they proceed to top them up.

I'm busy thanking them when Mattie turns up, canvas holdall slung over her shoulder. 'It just took me ten minutes to get through the bloody gate,' she says. 'Did you know there's a tonne of journalists out there?'

I exchange a look of concern with Gertrude.

'What? What is it?' asks Mattie.

'I'm afraid it's bad: Sonny is dead,' I say, as gently as I can.

She drops the holdall. 'What? Are you serious?'

'Not the kind of thing we'd joke about, I'm afraid,' says Gertrude.

I take out my phone and search the headlines. Sure enough, Sonny's death is already among them.

'Here,' I say, passing my phone to the artist. 'But the police have asked us all not to discuss it, so I'm really sorry but I won't be able to answer your questions, even though I'm sure you'll have plenty.'

She reads the brief lines announcing Sonny's death and passes my phone back, her previously bright, open face as closed as a daisy before the rain.

'Well, that's shite,' she says.

'I know.'

My head jerks as a voice comes from close by, reminding me of the presence of Alex and Jay. 'We've finished the path.'

Turning to face them, I manage a smile. 'That's fantastic. Thank you both so much.' I run my eye around the beautiful dark curve of my garden's spine. 'It looks perfect.'

They both grin, which transforms their faces. It lasts only a second, making me wish I'd caught it on camera.

'What's next?' asks Alex.

'Planting!' I say, feeling my heavy heart lighten at the prospect of filling the plot with living colour and shape. Sonny would have loved seeing the plants go in. I decide that every act of placing a plant in the soil will be a deed of remembrance.

We spend the next few hours – with a couple of breaks for coffee and lunch – deep in the blissful act of planting. It's hot work, but I'm delighted with everyone's enthusiasm for the task. We start by positioning the large feature shrubs, moving each one by increments in every direction, until we're all happy with its placement. Then, we take turns to dig the hole and bury the plant in its pot.

We break again just before three o'clock, when Addie comes round to tell us that the remaining two judges have arrived and are waiting in the refreshments field to say a few words to the competitors.

I start to walk along the grass verge, gathering the others as I go. Mouse runs to join me, and I'm glad of his solid, reassuring presence. We walk in silence.

24

Frank and Gillie are standing by the table when we reach the refreshments field, and they gesture for us to sit on the benches.

As soon as we're seated, Frank clears his throat.

'We just wanted to say that we're very proud of you all for continuing with your builds, in the light of . . . after . . . in . . .' He breaks down, shaking with sobs, and Gillie steps in, her soft voice full of empathy.

'Frank and I considered Sonny a close friend. She was always game. It didn't matter how successful she became with her nursery, her onscreen appearances and her design business, she always had time for her fans, her students, her peers and her clients. She will be sorely missed by so very, very many. And, as Frank said, Sonny would be deeply proud of you all for forging on. Addie agrees with us that it is, without a doubt, what she would have wanted.'

My own eyes have clouded over. Addie, sitting quietly beside me, squeezes my hand. Glancing around, I see that Sarah is filming. I wonder if she has permission; it seems such a private, intimate moment.

Gillie suggests we hold two minutes' silence, after which we all head back to our gardens. While Mattie works on, intent on her colourful world, Jay, Alex, Gertrude and I take stock of the work still to do.

'It's nearly four thirty and we've got loads of the big things to plant still,' says Alex.

I find it quite refreshing to work with people who don't worry

165

about using horticultural terms. 'That's true,' I say. 'But we can do that tomorrow. I'm sure between us we can get the big things planted.'

Jay, who rarely speaks – to me, at any rate – nods and says, 'Do me and Alex get to fill the pond?'

'Of course, if you'd like! We'll leave it till the day before the judging, though. I don't want it getting full of soil and leaves.'

Jay nods but then says, 'If you're having a boggy bit, you need to be careful the soil from that doesn't get in the main pond.'

'That's a very good point. I'll entrust that to you and Alex, as you're both so good at the technical side.'

We smile at one another until Jay breaks eye contact and retreats behind their long hair. It was a precious exchange while it lasted.

Gertrude says goodbye to Mattie and gives me a big hug before starting for the car park. 'Oh!' she says, turning back, 'don't forget to cut loose.' I find myself smiling in spite of the heaviness weighing on me.

After my co-workers have departed, I walk to the grass verge and admire how much the garden is already coming together. It always surprises me how quickly a bare spot can be transformed into living art.

I walk my new spiral path to the back, where Mattie is still working away with her paints. I stand close enough for her to spot me, without intruding on her space.

Catching sight of me, she picks up her phone to turn off her music before removing her headphones. 'Hiya. What did the judges have to say?'

'Just that Sonny would want us to carry on with our builds,' I say.

She nods and steps away from her creation. 'What do you think? It's nearly done.'

I'm in awe of how the paint has added another layer – figuratively as well as literally – to her mural. Blinking back tears, I say, 'Bloody hell, Mattie, it's amazing.'

She nods. 'I'm pretty pleased with it, to be honest.'

My eye falls on a new detail and I move in closer to where two tiny figures are seated on a miniature bench with their backs to us. One of them has a shock of white hair, the other pink hair as fluffy as dandelion seeds. It's clear that they are Sonny and her husband, Paul. They have their arms around one another and, even from the back, look utterly content. A bird is perched on the gate above them, a weird and wonderful beast of blues and purples, with a spiral crest of pink feathers and a calm, understanding look on its face.

Mattie points to the bird. 'That's my own take on the bird of peace,' she says. 'Why should doves get all the credit?'

Below the bench are the words, *In loving memory of SC. May all your seeds germinate and all your plants bloom.*

My eyes fill yet again. Mattie says, 'Ah, no, I didn't mean to upset you. Come here.'

She holds out her arms and I accept the hug, managing to sob out, 'You didn't upset me. It's beautiful. Sonny would have loved it. We'll have to make sure Paul sees it.'

'Sonny was one of a kind, wasn't she?' she says, still holding me.

I nod awkwardly against her shoulder. 'She really was.'

By the time Mouse and I have climbed aboard the minibus along with the other designers, I've forgotten about the reporters. The car park gate has been kept closed since this morning, after Addie successfully ejected them and placed a member of the National Trust staff in a high-vis vest there to vet all visitors.

But the gate monitor has now gone home and it falls to Mike to let the minibus pass out of Poplars Farm and through the throng of press still loitering on the other side. Poor Mike ends up waving to Addie to go on without him. We all turn to look back and glimpse a surge towards Mike and then his face, pale and anxious, in the midst of a sea of microphones. I hope he will be all right.

'Never leave a man behind,' calls Toby, but Addie ignores him.

The journey passes largely in silence. When we arrive back at Coleton Fishacre and disembark, Addie is standing at the foot of the minibus steps. She seems distracted.

'Are you OK, apart from the obvious?' I ask her.

'I have to go back for Mike,' she says. 'I've just tried ringing him, but he didn't answer. He doesn't always have a signal at the farm, which means he also won't be able to call for a cab to get back here.'

I feel the lure of a cool bath receding as I make up my mind. 'I tell you what, I'll just go up for my keys and I'll take the van to fetch him.' Mouse barks once on hearing one of his favourite words. 'You want to come in the van, boy?' He rumbles his agreement.

Addie squeezes my hand. 'Thank you. Now, be careful. Don't talk to any of the reporters.'

I raise an eyebrow. 'Can I take sweets from strangers?'

'Oh, dear, do I sound like a mum?'

I smile. 'Only in the best way.'

Leaving Mouse waiting in the shade, I run up to our room and back down with the key to the van. When I open his door he leaps in and I put on his seat belt. I've left the vehicle parked beneath a large hornbeam, so it's not quite as hot as it might otherwise be. He sits very upright for the short journey, proud of his conveyance. I suppose he doesn't have any concept of what a banger the old van really is. I, meanwhile, am just relieved it started without fuss.

I'm also reassured to see Mike still in one piece as I pull up to the gate at Poplars Farm. Catching several journalists clocking me, I wind down the window and shout, 'Mike! Get in!' Within seconds, he's scrambled into the back seat and I'm screeching away like we've just pulled off a heist.

'You rescued me,' he says as he straps himself in. 'I couldn't get a signal to call a taxi. I thought they were going to eat me alive out there.'

'Well, Mouse thought it would be a bit mean to abandon you to the sharks.'

Mouse lets out a single bark, though whether to signify agreement or as a reaction to my naming one of his favourite animals, it's hard to say.

'Is your car back at Coleton Fishacre?' I ask.

'Yeah. Thanks so much for this.'

I laugh. 'You can stop thanking me now.'

As we reach the long country lane that leads to the house, I say, 'Why aren't there any reporters over here?'

'I think Addie got on to the police, and they put out a release stating any reporters found on site would be charged with contaminating a crime scene, or something.' He pauses before saying, 'Or it might have been trespass. Anyway, it seems to have worked.'

'Thank god.'

'Indeed.'

I pull up the old van beneath the hornbeam and turn off the engine, and we all climb down.

'Thanks again,' says Mike. I roll my eyes and he says, 'Well, I'm sorry, but I was brought up to be polite.'

He's standing so close that I can't help breathing in his scent. He smells of pine and something else – mint, maybe? I'm impressed that he smells so good after a whole day of working in the heat.

'Excuse me,' he says, 'did you just sniff me?' He has one eyebrow raised and a smile twitching at the corners of his lips.

I jump back, feeling my cheeks flush. 'No, I . . . I mean . . .' With a deep breath, I decide to take a risk. Meeting his gaze, I say, 'You smell good.'

Mike's smile deepens and he leans forward and places a kiss on my lips. I lean into it, closing my eyes and focusing on the sensation of his soft, warm lips, tasting the slight salt tang behind the pine and mint.

After a moment, he peels away. 'I've been wanting to do that for days,' he says.

And then he unlocks the door of his vintage Mini, climbs in and drives away, leaving me standing in the car park, experiencing more emotions than I know how to process.

25

Toby and Sarah arrive last to dinner, when we're standing with our drinks in the dining room. He's holding his phone and they seem to be discussing something on it.

'Have you all seen this?' he asks, holding up his screen. We gather round to read the headline:

Celebrity gardener believed to have been pushed to her death

'Well, we knew that,' says Seb.

Toby clears his throat and reads on: "'Celebrity gardener Sonny Carden's fatal fall from a cliff on Monday night is believed to have been murder. Sonny, 78, was the much-loved presenter of such long-running television shows as *Down to Earth* and *Sonny in the Garden*. Her body was found yesterday at the foot of cliffs in the National Trust property of Coleton Fishacre, formerly home to the wealthy D'Oyly Carte family. A statement from DS Jasmine Bhatti of Devon Police confirmed Ms Carden's death is being treated as suspicious. A number of individuals believed to have been the gardener's protégés are under investigation.'"

'It goes on,' he says glumly. 'It names Sonny's poor husband, Paul, the artist.'

'Poor sod,' says Seb, and we all nod.

'Does it name any of us?' asks Anil.

'It names everyone,' says Sarah. 'Including me, and I'm not even in the bloody competition.'

'Shit,' says Seb, and Anil puts his head in his hands for a moment.

'Do you want me to read on?' asks Toby.

'No,' says Addie firmly. 'That's quite enough fiction for one evening. I hope you all know better than to let the newspapers get to you. One thing I will share is what Sonny used to claim when a journalist ran a less-than-flattering story about her: all publicity is good publicity. Now, let's top up our glasses and go out to the Loggia for our meal.'

Dinner is a honeydew melon starter, followed by a delicious pasta dish, featuring roasted vegetables and a creamy sauce, served with French beans and crispy bread rolls to mop up the sauce.

Despite the good food, there's a brittle atmosphere.

'Where are we up to with the police?' Toby asks.

We all look to Addie, but she catches my eye. 'Will you take this?' When I nod, she addresses the others: 'Steph is helping the police, so she knows more than I do.'

Sarah pipes up, 'Is that "helping the police" as in, you're their main suspect?'

'No,' snaps Addie, before I can respond. 'Steph is their main witness, as she found Sonny's body.'

I address the group: 'I'm afraid I don't have anything new to share with you.' I hope they can't tell that I'm holding back information. I'm not about to tell them that Mouse found a torn-off pocket.

As I tear off a piece of my roll and mop up some sauce, Seb says, 'So does that mean we're all in the clear? They told me not to leave the area.'

'No one is to leave the area,' says Addie.

Toby says, 'We're all going to be sticking around anyway until the builds are finished, aren't we?'

There's a murmur of consensus.

I say, 'If anyone has any information, you can come to me or call DS Bhatti. Did you all get her card?' Everyone nods.

'If you're not the main suspect, what is your involvement?' asks Sarah, narrowing her eyes. 'Last time I checked, you weren't a police detective.'

I meet her gaze. 'I've just been unfortunate enough to be involved in a couple of other investigations, so DS Bhatti knows she can trust me.'

'So, what?' says Sarah. 'You're immediately off the hook, and we're all still on it?'

'Yes,' I say, with a bright smile. 'I'm actually the murderer, but I've managed to con the police into believing I'm innocent.' I rub my hands together.

She makes a scoffing sound but the others laugh – and, thankfully, the conversation moves on.

I look around the table, taking in Toby's flushed cheeks as he reaches for the wine bottle, Addie's sad smile, Koko's upright wariness and Anil's banter, as if he's afraid of letting the conversation move on to anything serious. Seb is wearing a frown, but that's not unusual for him. Every now and then, my thoughts flick back to that moment outside with Mike, and I feel my cheeks flush.

At last, unable to cope with the tension both in my head and among the party, I address Seb. 'It looks like you're making good progress on restoring your garden.'

He smiles unexpectedly, pushing a hand through his mop of blond hair. 'The volunteers have been amazing. I never thought we'd get back on track so fast.'

'That's great,' says Addie, 'I'm so pleased. And the cameras should deter any repeat performance by our vandal. I did tell the police, as well, and they said they'd keep an eye out when they're passing.'

'To be honest,' says Seb, 'I think whoever wrecked it might've done me a favour.'

'How'd you work that one out?' asks Anil.

'Sonny said my deck was clashing with the surroundings. I wasn't going to listen, 'cos it had taken me so much work to assemble. But now it's been torn to shreds,' he shrugs, 'feels like I might as well use the opportunity to put something else there, you know?'

No one says anything for a moment, and I wonder if they're all thinking the same as me: that his garden will definitely be better without the deck. After a moment, I say cautiously, 'I thought the pebbles and undulating landscape were wonderful and seemed almost authentic. I guess it's true that the deck didn't quite fit – to my mind, anyway. It was a bit . . . artificial.'

I hold my breath, tensing for an outburst, but he just says, 'Really? You see, my vision was a garden on the edge of the Yorkshire Moors.'

'I get that. What are you thinking of putting in place of the deck?'

'I'm not sure yet. I'm going to do some 3-D modelling tonight, see what comes up.'

'I'm wondering . . .' I say slowly, 'could you use something less structured as the base for the seating area?'

He reflects for a moment, then says, 'Like what . . . grass maybe? Or slate chippings?'

'Yeah – either of those sounds good.' We exchange a smile, and the others murmur their approval. Then I take a deep breath and turn to Sarah. 'How's filming going?' I ask her.

She shoots me a bright smile. 'Pretty good. I've got some moments I'm really looking forward to sharing with you all.' I remember I still haven't got hold of the camera to delete the row with Seb. Perhaps if Sarah sets it up for us to view, I might be able to get close enough to wipe that scene.

Koko, who has a vegetable stir fry in coconut sauce and is eating it delicately with what looks like her dessert fork, says, 'I've been wondering: do you think the same person who hurt Sonny might have vandalised Seb's garden?'

'No, I don't,' says Addie. 'And please don't forget that the police have not ruled out an accident as far as Sonny's death is concerned.'

'So, who did trash my build?' asks Seb, sitting back in his chair.

'I believe it was just local vandals,' says Addie.

'I don't buy it,' says Anil. 'I mean, Seb's plot isn't even the first or second one, is it? It's the fourth one along. No, sorry, mate, but I reckon someone was gunning for you.'

The rest of us tense for the explosion, but again Seb nods calmly. 'Yeah, I thought the same. I appreciate your honesty.'

'So, who do you think that you may have upset?' asks Koko.

Seb shrugs. 'Pretty much everyone.'

When we see a smile creep across his face, we all begin to laugh, relieved both at Seb's reaction and to have an excuse to let go.

Once the laughter has died down, Addie says, 'I hope nobody here has spoken to the press about the vandalism. The police have, of course, been informed but, whilst that behaviour was reprehensible, it is certainly not on a par with what happened to Sonny.'

Sonny's name sends me straight back to the cliff edge. I wonder who was out there with her. Scanning my fellow competitors one by one, I reflect once again on Seb's anger over her criticism of his design. My eye falls on Sarah, cheeks flushed from the wine, red curls tumbling about her face. From what I've witnessed, there are complex emotions behind that sweet appearance. I wouldn't like to get on her bad side – the way Sonny did, according to Gertrude. My gaze travels to Sarah's husband, but all I see is bonhomie. Moving on to Anil, who's joking with Toby, I wonder how much he would do to save face and retain his company.

I remember the white pocket lying in the rosebush. And then I have a thought which sends me hurrying from the table and up to my room, not even tasting the delicious-looking vegan lemon mousse that has been set before me.

What if the pocket Mouse found doesn't belong to Sonny? What if it belongs to her killer?

26

Up in the bedroom, Mouse greets me as if he hasn't seen me in weeks.

'I thought you'd be asleep,' I tell him, crouching to stroke him. 'Do you want to watch sharks with David Attenborough?'

When he rumbles his assent, I set up the programme on my laptop on the dressing table and he sits in front of it, watching avidly with Mr Rabbit at his feet.

I, meanwhile, perch on the bed with my phone, scrolling through last night's photographs of Sonny's body among the gorse bushes.

DS Bhatti and I were right: Sonny was wearing white. But she was wearing a white t-shirt, not a shirt with buttons. As I zoom in on her t-shirt, there is no suggestion that there was ever a tailored pocket on this casual garment. My heart rate speeds up as I absorb this implication.

I have a sudden film reel in my head, of Sonny scrabbling at her assailant as she starts to fall backwards. Her hand seizes hold of the other person's shirt. But it has landed on the pocket, which tears uselessly away beneath her fingers. Or perhaps it comes off in her assailant's hand as they tug her fingers from their clothing, desperate not to be dragged down with her. And then Sonny falls, with a scream so loud and haunting that it can be heard by a keen-eared dog and his average-eared human all the way back at the house.

I dig out Bhatti's card and send her a message:

Shirt pocket not Sonny's but murderer's.

I wait a few minutes, but receive no response, so I videocall Danny.

He answers promptly, but with the camera off. 'Hi sis. Can't talk at the moment. Sorry, it's bath time.'

'Yours or someone else's?'

'The wee little man,' he says, in an approximation of a Scottish accent so poor, I grimace.

'Never again, Dan. Promise me,' I say.

'Och, it warn't that bad, lassie.'

I hang up quickly and type:

Call me when you're done. And please, please, if you love me, spare the people of Scotland (and my ears) any further attempt at a Scots accent.

A few minutes later, I receive a series of memes from him, depicting men in kilts, some of them playing bagpipes.

When, after another twenty minutes' wait, there's still nothing from him or the sergeant, I decide to seek out Sarah. Leaving Mouse with his sharks, I go back downstairs to find that the others have retired to the Saloon for post-dinner drinks.

Sarah looks surprised when I approach her. 'Steph? What is it?'

'Did you film us at dinner on Monday night? I can't remember.'

'No, I haven't done any filming in the house yet. The light's not right, so Wild Path are sending over some kit to light it.'

'Ah.'

'Is it important?' she asks. When I nod, she whispers, 'For how Sonny died?'

I hesitate, unsure how much I should say. I settle on, 'Maybe.'

Her eyes grow wide. 'What did you want to know?'

'I'm interested in what everyone was wearing.'

'Why didn't you say? Come with me.' Toby is deep in conversation with Anil about building frameworks – though whether that means scaffolding or something else, I have no idea. They're clearly enjoying the technical detail. Sarah touches her husband on the shoulder to get his attention and says, 'I'm just showing Steph something. I won't be long.'

He nods and smiles, then returns to expounding on his topic.

Sarah leads me up the staircase to their room, which turns out to be on the far side of mine, at the end of the passage. We must be directly above the Saloon, so I shouldn't be as surprised as I am by the room's size and grandeur. Like the Saloon, it boasts windows on all sides, offering spectacular views. Despite my mission, I'm distracted by the lovely space. I take in the bat screen at the central window, the curved ceiling which matches the curved corridor elsewhere, and the pretty dressing table.

Sarah notices my awe and smiles.

'Lovely, isn't it? It was Lady Dorothy and Rupert's room until the couple broke up. You know their son Michael died in a car crash, and it pretty much signalled the end of their marriage?' I nod and she says, 'Turns out money really isn't everything.'

I catch her eye and we exchange a sad smile. And, for a moment, I forget my misgivings about her.

She takes a camera case down from a bookshelf and sits on the bed, removing a digital stills camera and turning it on before passing it to me. 'Scroll through,' she says. 'I'm pretty sure I got everyone.'

'Great,' I whisper, aware of Chaplin slumbering in his bed by the window.

'You don't need to whisper. That dog will sleep through anything. Glad we didn't get him to be a guard dog.'

'I didn't even notice you taking these,' I say, as I start to scroll.

'The sign of a good photographer,' she says smugly.

I don't respond. I'm too busy examining the images of our party from the run-up to Sonny's death.

Toby was wearing his traditional Hawaiian-print shirt. Addie was in her orange and yellow print dress. Koko was in another tailored shorts suit, this time in brown linen. Sarah is missing from the photos, of course, but I remember that she wore a cap-sleeve summer dress in green gingham.

There are three people in white, and one of them is me – though I'm in the halterneck dress. That leaves Anil and Seb, both wearing white tailored shirts with breast pockets.

I sit down on the padded stool at the dressing table.

Glancing at Sarah, I see her eyes are narrowed again as she watches me. 'Anything you'd care to share?'

'No. It's nothing, really. Just a hunch. Probably won't amount to anything.' Smiling at her, I say, 'Please could you send these over to me?'

'You're not some undercover detective, are you? Only you're beginning to sound like one.' She pauses before adding wistfully, 'That would make a great story for my documentary.'

'Sorry, no. Just helping the police, like I said at dinner.' I throw her a bright smile while handing her my card with my phone number and email address.

With a huff, she grudgingly agrees to send me the photographs.

I've just closed her bedroom door and am crossing the landing back to mine when my phone rings.

I step quickly inside. Mouse has moved right up to the laptop, and is offering his own commentary on the sharks. He glances at me then returns to his viewing.

Clicking the green button on my phone, I say, 'DS Bhatti, hi.'

'Hello. Thank you for making contact.'

'I've got it down to two.'

'I'm sorry . . . ?'

'The list of suspects. I've come across new evidence and I've got it down to two.'

'I'd be very interested to hear what you've found. Would you be able to come in to the station to give an official statement?'

'Sure.'

And so it is that I find myself driving to Torquay with Mouse just after nine o'clock at night, as the sky is beginning to darken and the lights along the roads are coming on.

27

Mouse is very excited to make a new friend in the police station. Fortunately, the man behind the desk seems equally delighted with Mouse. He even rustles up some treats from a drawer.

When DC Rob Bridges comes through a door at the back to call me in to interview, Mouse is happy to stay behind with his new friend.

'Cupboard love,' comments the DC as he leads me to an interview room.

'And don't I know it.'

Detective Sergeant Bhatti is waiting for me in the room, a laptop open in front of her on the chipped melamine table. 'Ms Williams, thanks for coming out. I know it's getting late. Rob, you can stay.'

'Sarge,' he says, taking the chair beside her. She gestures for me to sit opposite, in an ugly orange plastic chair.

Once I'm seated, she clicks something on the laptop and says, 'Beginning recording.' She passes the laptop to her DC and sits forward.

'So, what do you have for us?' she asks.

'That pocket didn't come off Sonny's clothing . . .'

'Ms Carden was wearing a t-shirt rather than a formal shirt,' says Bhatti. 'In fact, it was pale pink, it just looked white in the dark. Which means the pocket we found must have come from her murderer's clothing.'

'You do believe she was murdered then, that it wasn't suicide.'

'I've always believed that,' she says. 'But – come on, Rob, you know this . . .'

179

'It's important not to let first impressions govern process,' he says, clearly reciting a lesson she's taught him.

She nods, turning back to me. 'So, what have you got?'

'Only two people were wearing white shirts with breast pockets at dinner yesterday.' I explain how, thanks to Sarah's photographs, I was able to narrow down the suspects to two men in the party.

DS Bhatti shoots me a sharp look. 'This is the same Sarah – Cartwright – that you believe administered poison to Ms Deville?'

'Er, yes. And Gertrude Jones also rang you on Tuesday, to tell you she'd seen Sarah arguing with Sonny?'

She nods. 'You didn't tell Ms Cartwright why you wanted to see the images?'

'No, but she guessed it had something to do with Sonny's murder.'

With a sigh and a nod, she says, 'I suppose it can't be helped. Do you have the photographs?'

I'm about to say no when my phone pings with an email from Sarah. I download the images and offer my phone to DS Bhatti, who swipes through, examining them, before handing it to her DC.

'Can you fill in the details on the spreadsheet?' she asks him. He nods and sets to work as she continues speaking. 'Right, so that's two men, Seb Burroughs and Anil Ahmad, both of them wearing white tailored shirts with breast pockets last night, the night that Sonny Carden was found dead.'

Unsure if a response is required, I say, 'That's right.'

The DC hands the phone back to me, saying, 'Can you email those over, please?'

He tells me the email address and I send the photos over. I hear the ping as they arrive in the laptop's inbox.

'This is great stuff,' says Bhatti. 'I hope it goes without saying that you mustn't say anything back at the house that might lead the suspects to know we're investigating them.'

'Of course. What will you do next?'

'Rob and I will have another search in the rooms of Mr Ahmad and Mr Burroughs, to see if anything was missed by the forensics team.' She looks at her colleague. 'I think button-up shirts were found in both of these men's rooms?' He nods and she continues,

'But forensics didn't find any torn white shirts. Of course, they didn't know they were looking specifically for a white shirt with a pocket missing. It may be that the garment wasn't badly damaged when the pocket came off. It's definitely worth another look.'

I say, 'We leave on the minibus for Poplars Farm at eight forty-five, so the place should be clear from then until shortly after five.'

She glances at Rob, who nods and inputs the information.

Sensing that the interview is coming to a close, I say, 'Did you find anything out about Delilah's poisoning?'

DS Bhatti looks to her DC. 'Rob, will you take this?'

He scrolls on the laptop, then reads from the screen: 'Ms Deville is fully conscious and has made a full recovery. This means we're not looking at a second murder. Also, Brixham said the evidence was contaminated.' He looks at me. 'Apparently, there were too many fingerprints on Ms Deville's bottle. It looked like half the medical team had handled it, for starters.'

DS Bhatti addresses me, 'Do you have reason to believe the two cases are linked?'

'Not so far.'

'It is a bit of a coincidence, though, isn't it?' She turns to her DC. 'Two potential attempted murders within less than twenty-four hours. What do you think, Rob?'

'It's worth looking at them contiguously, Sarge.'

'Yes, that's what I think. Great word, by the way.'

They both laugh, as if at some in-joke. I wait, but nobody explains.

She turns back to me. 'In the meantime, it might be wise for you to practise extra caution around the others at the house. In particular, avoid being alone with Mr Burroughs or Mr Ahmad, in case they pick up that you suspect them. The same goes for Ms Cartwright.' She stands. 'Right. It's getting late and I'm sure you want to get to bed. You've been a great help, Ms Williams. We appreciate you taking time out to talk to us again.' She shakes my hand.

Rob gets to his feet and I take this as my cue to leave, but a thought strikes me as I reach the door. Turning to face the DS, I say, 'Did you find out who vandalised Seb's garden?'

'It's one thing after another with you gardeners, isn't it?' she says. 'More drama than my local am-dram group.' She looks at her DC. 'Rob? Anything?'

He shrugs. 'I spoke to Ms Adebayo, but she thinks he'd angered someone, quite likely outside the group. She's had cameras installed, so it shouldn't happen again.'

'We're normally pretty nice people,' I tell them. 'Can I ask: are you going to put a stop to the competition?'

The DS shakes her head. 'I don't have reason to believe anyone else is at risk, so that won't be necessary at this stage.'

Back in the lobby, I thank the desk clerk for looking after Mouse. Then I say, 'Come on, boy.'

Mouse surveys me for a moment, clearly weighing up the relative fun of staying with this new friend – who has a bag full of treats – versus coming with me.

'Don't you want to see Mr Rabbit?' I ask him.

He barks once at this, and trots eagerly out of the station at my heel.

Half an hour later, I'm parking the van and thinking longingly about my bed when my phone rings with a video call. Seeing it's Danny, I answer, saying, 'Hold on: let me get up to the room.'

As soon as we're safely inside, with the door locked, I say, 'Are you all OK?'

'We're fine. It's you I'm worried about. Karen just showed me a headline about Sonny. Are you all right?'

Tears fill my eyes at his concern. 'I'm all right,' I say quietly. 'Mouse found her body.'

'Oh, sis.' We're quiet for a moment, and I fish for a tissue in my pocket and wipe my eyes. Mouse has gone to bed, and I watch him turning around until he's comfortable, with Mr Rabbit and his lead under his chin.

At last, Danny says, 'Did she really fall off a cliff?'

I sink down on to the bed. 'Actually, it looks like she was pushed.'

'Good god. But who on earth would push her? I mean, she was *Sonny*.'

'I know. Worst thing is, it's someone here.'

'What? Are you safe?'

'So long as I don't tell them I know.'

'Why haven't they been arrested?'

'We've got it down to two men. The police are going to do another search of their rooms tomorrow.'

'I don't like the sound of that "we".'

I can't help a small smile. 'Sorry, Danny. I'm helping the police but only with information.'

'Just this once, couldn't you think about your poor brother's heart?'

'I will be very careful. I promise.'

He sighs. 'Trouble certainly does follow you around, sis.'

'Don't say that!'

'Sorry.'

'You're right, though.'

We sit in silence for a moment, until he says, 'Listen, if you're OK, I could do with getting some sleep while Stevie's down. He's still doing six hours straight, which is amazing, but I'm zonked.'

'I understand. You go.'

'I'll stay on the call if you need me.'

I smile at his sweet concern. 'I'm fine. Off you go. You certainly need your beauty sleep.'

'Ow! Uncalled for!' he complains, but he's laughing as he ends the call.

My phone rings again moments later, while I'm washing my face. I dry it quickly and answer the call when I see it's Mum.

'Louise, are you all right?'

'I take it you've heard about Sonny.'

'Your dad and I saw it on the news just now. What on earth happened?'

I fill her in on the bare minimum.

'I think you should come home,' she says.

I haven't lived in the Peterborough house since I was sixteen. 'Come on, Mum. That's not necessary. I'm fine.'

'You're fine now, but someone pushed *Sonny Carden* off a cliff.' She makes it sound as though Sonny would be harder to push than a mere mortal such as I.

'You forget that I can look after myself.'

'Hold on. Your dad wants a word.'

Dad comes on the line and says, 'You stay right where you are, love.'

I hear Mum in the background saying, 'Oh, Nigel', but I can tell the fight has gone from her voice.

'Thanks, Dad. How are things? Are you forgiven?'

'More or less,' he says cheerfully. 'But I learned my lesson.'

'Well, that's the important part.'

We finish the call soon after, and I climb into bed. I'm so tired, my normally active brain doesn't even have the energy to conjure up strange dreams.

28

Unusually, I can't face a run when I wake the next morning, so Mouse and I settle on taking another turn in the garden. At least I know he'll get plenty of exercise at the farm later with Chaplin.

When I arrive on the Loggia for breakfast, I find the others in a surprisingly chatty frame of mind, with talk of plant deliveries and what tasks remain to be done.

Addie says, 'Mike's done an amazing job with some of the volunteers. It looks like they'll get Delilah's garden finished in advance of the deadline.'

Her mention of Mike sends me right back to that kiss in the car park. When someone says my name, I jerk. 'Yes? What?'

Everyone laughs. Koko says, 'I was just asking if you would like another cup of coffee.'

'Oh! Yes, please.'

'Steph never says no to coffee,' says Anil.

'True,' I say.

I watch him for a moment and then turn my gaze to Seb. But we're all wearing the same slightly glazed, wrung-out look from four days of building and planting in scorching heat, with a poisoning and a murder thrown into the mix. It's hard to tell if either man might be carrying the additional burden of the murder itself.

I reassure myself with the reminder that DS Bhatti and Rob are going to conduct a search of the two men's rooms while we're out today. Hopefully they will come up with conclusive evidence, in the form of a white shirt missing one pocket.

I finish breakfast, then fetch Mouse, and we board the minibus, which is thankfully quite cool. Mike's already on board, and he catches my eye and smiles in a way that has my stomach doing things it hasn't done in a while. I remind myself that romance can wait until Sonny's murder has been solved.

I'd forgotten about the press who might be awaiting us at Poplars Farm. I'm clearly not the only one – there's a collective groan when we pull in through the gates and see a few journalists and photographers still milling about the car park. But they seem to have lost some of their urgency, as if they know we're not going to give them any leads. The woman who knew my identity yesterday tries to question me about Sonny. 'I hear you found the body, Ms Williams,' she shouts, but Toby blocks her from me physically, proving his worth as the 'wall', as his wife likes to describe him, and we all make it through the gate to the gardens without incident.

Sarah has arrived early and is already filming. She trains the camera on Toby and me, as we walk side by side with the dogs. It doesn't seem like fascinating content to me, but perhaps Mouse will gain a following.

She stops at Toby's plot with him, and we release the dogs before I continue along the grass verge, checking out the other plots. There hasn't been any fresh vandalism, so either the surveillance cameras are doing their job or the vandal was a one-hit wonder. I suppose the digger is no longer on site, meaning a repeat performance would be a lot more work.

Gertrude greets me with her usual wide-beam enthusiasm and we begin to line up the next shrubs for planting, consulting my plans along the way. By the time Alex and Jay arrive half an hour later, we're ready to start positioning and digging. I feel lucky to be able to rely on such a committed team.

With all that's going on at Coleton Fishacre and even here, at the farm, it's a treat to be able to plunge back into the world of plants. I can see my own excitement mirrored in Gertrude's face as the garden's primary features slot into position.

A couple of hours later, Alex says in a doleful tone, 'I can't believe we're nearly done with all the big things.'

'Well, I can't believe just yesterday you were worrying we'd never get them all in,' I say, and they reward me with a small smile. 'Anyway, this is where the fun really starts. The small plants will go in much more quickly, so we'll see whole flower beds come together within a couple of hours.'

We plant the final two shrubs – a third button bush and another *Buddleja* 'Golden Glow' – within the next twenty minutes.

Seeing it's nearly eleven, I suggest a break. Gertrude and I head to the oak tree with the thermos, while Alex and Jay go for ice lollies in the refreshments field.

'How are you doing?' Gertrude asks me, staring into her mug as if it might contain wisdom rather than strong caffeine.

'Glad to have the garden to focus on.'

She nods and takes a sip from her mug. 'Did you see that most of the papers now are saying that Sonny was pushed?' She shudders. 'It's such an awful thought.'

'It really is.'

We meet one another's gaze. She looks so sad, I'm about to move over to give her a hug when she says, 'Ooh! That Ryan I like has agreed to help to show people around your garden during the flower show.'

'Oh, that's great. Thanks for that.'

She gives me a cheeky grin. 'I didn't ask him for you.'

I laugh. 'Well, in that case, I hope it works out for you.'

'Me, too. He's lush. And he only lives twenty minutes from me. And he has a whippet called Tom. I love a whippet.'

'He sounds perfect.' I don't tell her about my kiss with Mike; I don't know yet what it means.

She and I exchange a smile before heading back to the plot.

As soon as I've demonstrated to Alex and Jay how to soak plants in their pots, they devise an entire system of soaking and planting, typical of the orderly approach they've demonstrated in the jobs they've carried out so far.

We work largely in silence, but with absolute efficiency. Alex and Jay each take charge of several buckets in which they soak the plants. During these preparations, Gertrude and I busy ourselves with digging the holes. The plants are then brought to us several at a time. The ground is parched, and I emphasise the importance of properly 'puddling in' each plant. This is done by Alex or Jay, using a watering can. I reckon some big corporations could learn efficiency measures from these two.

By the time we stop for the day, it's ten to five and we've made a huge inroad into the planting, including several large groups of pinky-purple *Echinacea purpurea* among lime-green *Euphorbia characias* subsp. *wulfenii*.

The curved bed closest to the pond is shaded by one of the fabulously weird button bushes, together with a *Callistemon Laevis*, also known as the bottlebrush tree, and a corkscrew hazel. Here, I intend to keep the soil damp, to provide a home for the violet-speckled toad lilies, which I've interspersed with ferns in the form of the dramatic purple and pink *Athyrium niponicum* 'Ursula Red', and *Dodecatheon tetrandrum* 'Red Wings' with its delicately inside-out purple flowers. Although the Dodecatheon would, by nature, flower earlier in the year than the toad lilies, the nursery has again done me proud. I cross my fingers and hope once again that the judges won't look unfavourably on my playing with the natural order of things.

29

On the journey back to Coleton Fishacre, my thoughts travel from my glorious garden-in-progress to the police search. I wonder if DS Bhatti found the incriminating white shirt in one of the bedrooms. It's frustrating being a civilian, without access to the police databases. I take my phone out and send a message to the DS:

Did anything turn up in S or A's room?

I suppose, at worst, I'll have my answer when – or if – someone is arrested. But surely the police would have come to the farm if they had found incriminating evidence.

When we arrive at the house, Mike – who was near the front of the bus during the journey, talking to Addie – is waiting. 'You up for another guided tour?' he asks as I step down with Mouse.

I shake my head. 'I'm sorry. I'm done in. And there's so much going on . . .'

He nods, but I see a flash of disappointment in his eyes before he smiles. 'Of course. No worries.'

'Another time,' I say, hoping he can tell how much I mean it.

Up in our room, while Mouse wolfs down his dinner and settles for a nap, I take a cooling bath. Then I don a pair of cream linen wide-leg trousers for a change, pairing them with a bright pink racer-back vest. Finally, I pull my hair up into a ponytail on top of my head and slip my feet into a pair of tan sandals.

The house seems quieter than usual as I descend the stairs, and I find I'm the first to arrive in the dining room. There are open bottles of wine on the table, and I help myself to a glass of red.

I'm just examining an oil painting of a rain-drenched French street on one wall when Seb and Anil walk into the room together, chatting about their builds. A surge of adrenaline instantly kicks my heart into a higher gear at finding myself alone with both of the prime suspects.

As I turn to greet them with a smile – which I hope looks convincing – Anil tells Seb, 'It's all finally coming together, so I should get finished on time.' He holds up his crossed fingers.

Seb nods. 'I can't believe how quickly mine's been rebuilt. I'm not being funny, but I was about to jack it all in after I saw it on Monday. I'm glad I stayed, though.' They busy themselves pouring drinks before Anil turns and acknowledges me.

'Steph, hi. How's your build coming on?'

'Pretty good, thanks.'

'Yours is mainly plants though, isn't it? Not a lot of hard landscaping or structure?'

I bristle at this barely disguised criticism. 'There are ways of providing structure that don't involve expensive kit like cranes and scaffolding.'

He laughs. 'Ooh, touched a nerve there, did I?'

'Have you actually seen my garden?'

He shakes his head. 'I'll be sure to look tomorrow, though. Do you want to see mine?'

'What? You mean you'd allow me behind the wizard's curtain?'

His face suggests that he's noted the *Wizard of Oz* jibe about dazzling with special effects, and isn't best pleased. I chide myself for poking what might turn out to be the bear.

'Of course,' he says, good-naturedly. 'It's a bit late now for you to start hiring expensive kit and copying me, isn't it? You know, you could come up tonight after dinner, if you fancy it?'

As I stand, weighing up playing it safe versus satisfying my curiosity, I say, 'What a shame Sonny won't see our finished gardens.' I watch their faces closely, but neither gives anything away.

Seb says, 'Yeah. I'd have liked her to see I got rid of the deck after all.'

'It's made a big difference,' says Anil. 'I like the slate.'

'Thanks.'

Koko enters. Pouring herself a glass of water at the drinks table, she says, 'What have I been missing?'

'Only Anil offering to show me his build,' I tell her.

She seems unsurprised. 'Oh, yes. He showed it to me yesterday. It is a very enterprising design, which I appreciated very much.'

'There you go,' says Anil. '"Very enterprising design". Not too ambitious now, am I?'

So he has held on to that criticism from Sonny.

As Koko has had a private viewing and come out unscathed, I make up my mind. 'I'd love to see your build, Anil. Thank you.'

He nods and smiles, and I relax. The prospect of viewing the hitherto concealed garden is rather exciting.

The others enter and Toby breaks my train of thought, booming, 'Evening all,' as he walks to the drinks table and pours two glasses of wine. Passing one to his wife, he glances around, holding up the bottles. 'Anyone else?'

Once we all have our drinks, we walk out to the Loggia, where a cool sea breeze brings with it the mingled scents of honeysuckle and jasmine with a light sprinkling of sea salt.

As Toby keeps up his usual chatter, breaking off occasionally to reply to some good-natured teasing from Anil, I find my gaze wandering between Seb and Anil. Could one of these men really have killed Sonny? I close my eyes briefly and Sonny's body, inert and broken, swims into my mind, closely followed by Delilah's pale form.

Opening my eyes, I address Addie, 'I don't suppose you've had another update about Delilah?'

'Oh my goodness! I can't believe I forgot,' she says. 'They think she'll be able to come out tomorrow.'

The table's occupants send up a cheer for this one piece of good news, and several glasses are recharged. I watch Sarah closely. She shuts her eyes for a moment and rests her head against the chair back, her entire being suffused with relief.

When she opens her eyes, she catches me watching her. There's a fraction of a second when a bolt of understanding passes between us. I know that she poisoned Delilah. And she now knows that I know.

The atmosphere changes as the drink takes effect, so that Anil, Seb, Sarah and Toby become increasingly rowdy while Koko, Addie and I look on. I have stuck to water since that initial glass of red, so that I can be the driver for our outing later. As I watch Anil putting away the white wine, I'm sure I made the right decision.

At the end of the meal, Anil pushes his chair back and looks at me. 'Ready for our jaunt? We need to go now, while it's still light.'

I glance at my watch and see it's gone eight o'clock already. 'Let me just check on Mouse and I'll be right with you.'

I run upstairs, making up my mind as I go. Keen though I am to visit Anil's garden and see my competition for the gold medal, I will not go alone. Mouse stirs as I approach and I crouch and say quietly, 'Hey, boy, fancy another trip in the van?'

He's awake at once, placing Mr Rabbit carefully in the dog bed and picking up his lead.

'Good boy!'

I grab a sweater and the key to the van and we head out.

Anil is waiting in the car park, standing beside a red classic Porsche that until now has been covered in a cloth.

I can't help the whistle that escapes my lips. 'This is yours?'

'I've just hired her for a couple of weeks. She's a beauty though, isn't she?'

'It really is,' I say, patting the bonnet. 'But we're going in my banger.'

Anil surveys my old van with evident misgivings. 'Are you sure this thing even runs?'

'Oh, it runs,' I say, crossing my fingers that the engine won't let me down. 'Come on, get in.'

I walk around to the driver's side and unlock the doors. He opens the passenger door. 'Oh god, there's dog hair all over the seat!'

'That's Mouse's seat,' I say. 'You can go in the back if you prefer.'

'Yeah, that might be better.'

As Mouse jumps into the front, I open the back and enjoy Anil's body language as he climbs in and makes his way past the dirty tools and wheelbarrow to the seat behind Mouse, his arms close to his sides, like a child walking through a nettle patch.

I shut the back and walk around to strap Mouse into his seat.

The short drive feels longer than usual with the creak and grumble of my old motor as it rattles its way to Poplars Farm. I catch sight of Anil in the rear-view mirror, sitting very upright and tense. I'm caught between wanting to laugh and feeling slightly embarrassed at the state of my vehicle. The old van always seems shabbier when we have a passenger.

At least the journalists have vacated the scene when we reach the farm. I climb down to open the gate, then drive us into the car park. As I pull up and turn off the engine, I have a momentary twinge of doubt about the wisdom of coming here with Anil to visit his garden. But I have Mouse with me, and I am more than a little curious to see the costly creation before the grand reveal.

Anil practically skips over to his plot, barely giving me time for another glance at Delilah's garden, which is nearly finished, thanks to Mike's diligent attentions with his team of volunteers. The groups of foxgloves take on a slightly sinister air in the light of her recent digitalis poisoning. But the garden is otherwise a delight, filled with woodland scent and colour.

'Come on,' says Anil, already vanishing behind his screen. 'We don't have much daylight left.'

I follow, keen to see if I agree with Sonny's assessment of his design as flashy. 'You know,' I call to him, 'part of me wants you to keep the screen up for the flower show. It makes for a really dramatic entrance, having to go around it.'

He laughs and points up. That's when I see why he needed cranes and scaffolding. His plot is largely taken up by an enormous sheet of fibreglass, designed to look like the facade of a tall house, with other buildings behind. He starts climbing a metal staircase, reminiscent of a fire escape, and I move to follow, but Mouse stops at the bottom, sniffing hard at a patch of earth. He refuses to budge.

'All right, boy,' I say, unclipping his lead. 'I'll see you in a bit.'

Anil has already started up the stairs, so I follow him to the top. And then we're standing on a roof, surrounded by plants. It's so realistic, I blink as if I might be imagining it.

'Not bad, huh?' he asks me.

'Really good,' I say, in awe. 'Magical, in fact.'

'And Sonny said I was being too ambitious . . .' he says.

'She really bothered you with that comment, didn't she?'

'You'd think I'd never built a show garden before.'

'I suppose she was worried about the shorter than usual time frame.'

He shrugs. 'I may not have time to finish what I'd planned for the ground area, but up here's the important part and it's nearly done.'

'Have you thought about accessibility?' I ask.

'Oh yeah, 'cos a bark path is really friendly to wheelchair users, isn't it?' he says with a laugh.

I hold up my hands. 'That's a fair cop. I thought you hadn't seen my build.'

'I saw it when it was just the path and the empty pond.'

'Oh, right. The pond's still empty, actually. We're leaving that till last.'

Mouse appears at the top of the stairs as I'm examining the features. Whatever Sonny's misgivings about Anil's design, I have to admit I'm charmed.

'I can't believe you have a chimney!' I say, examining what turns out to be real brickwork.

'Cheers. It took a lot of planning, because of the support structure. That's a real chimney, obviously.'

'Right,' I say, but I'm distracted now by Mouse, who has something dangling from his mouth. While Anil walks around the space, offering a running commentary on the different elements of his rooftop garden, Mouse comes towards me and drops the object at my feet.

It is covered in soil and resembles nothing so much as a large, filthy rag. But I know without examining it exactly what Mouse has found. It's the item of clothing the police were looking for in Seb and Anil's rooms. It's a white shirt with the breast pocket missing. This is the proof that Anil killed Sonny.

Feeling suddenly dizzy, I reel away from the edge and pull out my phone. I type a quick message to DS Bhatti:

Help. With the killer at Poplars.

I push my phone back into my pocket as Anil says, 'Don't go too near the edge. I haven't got the railings in yet. We don't need another fall, or people'll think this competition is jinxed or something.' He laughs and I join in, hoping I sound genuine. Luckily, he seems not to pick up on my sudden fear. My blood is pumping loudly in my ears and I'm breathing too quickly.

'We need to get back,' I say. 'It'll be dark soon.' My voice quavers, but he doesn't notice.

'Sure,' he says. 'Let me just show you . . .' He suddenly stops talking. 'What have you got there?' he asks Mouse.

Mouse bares his teeth as Anil walks towards us. The dirty garment is still in a heap at our feet.

'Give me that,' Anil says, moving towards a growling Mouse. 'Can you get him to back off? What's he got?'

'I think he's found an old rag.'

There's a long pause and I'm sure Anil is going to spin me a yarn. Sure enough, he says, 'Where did he find it? Only I lost a t-shirt a couple of days ago. I took it off in the heat and couldn't find it later.'

'Oh, maybe that's it,' I say, trying to sound casual. 'It must have got buried when the scaffolding went up.'

'Can I have it, boy?' Anil says, advancing closer. 'Tell him it's OK, would you?'

I'm torn between keeping us safe and retaining the evidence.

'It's not going to be wearable any more,' I say. 'Could you let him keep it?'

'I'm sure it'll wash out,' says Anil. 'It's a favourite.' He bends to pick it up but Mouse barks and he snatches his hand back. 'For fuck's sake. Can't you call him off?'

When I don't respond, he stares at me. Mouse keeps up a low growl beside me.

Then Anil's face goes hard. 'You know what it is, don't you?'

He's so close, I can smell the alcohol on his breath. I take a step back before remembering where I am. Glancing behind me, I see I'm about ten centimetres from the edge. It would be so easy for him to do the same to me as he did to Sonny. One hard push, and I'd fall. It's not as high as the cliff, but it's high enough to break every bone in my body. I need to keep him talking, to give time for DS Bhatti to see my message and get over here. Or at least for me to come up with an escape plan.

'What is it?' I ask. 'What did my dog dig up?'

'Like I said, you know what it is. And you obviously know why it's important.' His voice softens to a wheedle. 'Sonny's gone – you can't bring her back. But if this comes out, it'll destroy me, my company, my partner, everything we've spent years building up. Please, Steph, hand over the shirt.'

Even though I already know he's the killer, there's still something shocking in hearing him confess so easily. But he's said it and there's no going back. And he's not going to want to let me go now I know the truth.

'I'm sure it was an accident,' I say quickly. 'You didn't mean to push her. I know you didn't mean to kill Sonny.'

He steps closer still, blocking my way to the staircase. He has a look of panic on his face that has me holding my breath. Because Anil is feeling cornered. And cornered animals always attack.

I send a wish into the ether: *Please let DS Bhatti have picked up my message. Please let her be close.*

He takes a step back and I let out my breath.

Running a hand through his hair, he gazes past me, into the oncoming darkness.

'I didn't mean it,' he says, and his voice breaks. After taking a moment to steady himself, he continues, 'I only went out there to talk to her. But she wouldn't listen. I kept telling her to shut up and listen but she just kept talking and talking, she wouldn't let me finish. I had to explain why the win was so important. We've lost so much business already, in Dubai and the States, and it's only a matter of time before word reaches here about the lawsuit.' He starts rocking backwards and forwards. I suddenly realise how much he's been carrying, how much of a toll it's taken to put on a front that everything was fine.

'I just needed her to hear that I knew some stuff about her, you know?'

I try again to move forward, away from the edge, but he doesn't budge.

'What sort of stuff?' I ask, playing for time.

'About her brother's kids, that kind of thing. Nothing too bad, you know? I'm not a monster. I just needed her to hear me out. But she just kept saying she didn't want to hear it. She wouldn't listen.'

'Had you arranged to meet her there?'

'No, but I'd bumped into her at the tree ferns on Saturday night, and she'd said it was her favourite part of the gardens, so I knew if I waited there on Monday after dinner, she'd turn up.' His eyes turn pleading as he says, 'I had to talk to her. It's just, she'd been making it sound like I wasn't going to win, and I really need the win. My partner's been putting all this pressure on me to bring in new business.'

'How did she fall?' I ask softly, not sure I want to hear his response.

'I only shoved her when she wouldn't listen. It was just this one shove. I mean, I'd already pushed her towards that area, as a kind of warning, you know?'

I nod, fighting an urge to unleash my anger – to scream in his face like a banshee. I take a deep breath, telling myself, *You are on the edge of a rooftop. Do nothing to provoke an attack. Remember Mouse needs you.*

Oblivious to my rage, Anil continues, 'So, like I said, I'd just pushed her on a bit, towards those signs, the ones warning about the cliff?'

His voice goes up in a question so I nod to show I know the signs. But it's getting dark, and I'm not sure he can see me. Weirdly, I feel safer, now I can't make out the details on his face. It helps that I can still feel and hear Mouse's reassuring presence beside me, intent and focused, growling a caution.

Anil continues in the gloaming, 'So I'm there, going, "Just shut the fuck up and listen to me", but she just keeps saying, "Anil, let me go. We can talk about this later". And I'm going, "You need to listen to me *now*", but she won't hear me out.'

I feel sick at the thought of Sonny's terror in those moments, as she pleaded with Anil to let her go.

'So, what?' I ask. 'You pushed her again?' I'd rather block my ears than hear the rest, but Mouse and I need time.

'It was only this one shove,' he says. 'Because she just won't shut up, you know? And I'm thinking, if she falls, then at least she'll maybe listen to me afterwards. Anyway, she doesn't fall straight away, she's hanging on to my shirt pocket, and she's going to take me with her.'

I become aware that tears are spilling on to my cheeks, and I'm finding it hard to catch my breath. I focus on slowing my breathing and then, in as calm a voice as I can muster, I say, 'So, you ripped the pocket off to save yourself.'

He starts to cry and his crying turns into a long whine of distress. He bends forward slightly, one hand on his chest, as if in pain.

At that moment, with my back to the edge, I hear rather than see the cars that pull into the car park.

'What? Who's that?' he says, straightening. I turn my head and glimpse blue lights flashing. 'What did you do?' he hisses. His voice is filled with fury and loathing.

I sense rather than see his lunge towards me, and manage to sidestep at the last second. At the same time, Mouse goes for him. I hear the scream and then the thud as Anil falls over the edge and hits the ground. I have a moment of panic, unsure if Mouse went with him. And then my brave, loyal dog licks my hand.

'Good boy,' I tell him. 'Very good boy.'

30

DS Bhatti meets us with a torch at the foot of the metal staircase.

'Are you all right?' she asks.

My legs are wobbly and she puts out a hand to steady me. 'Yeah,' I say. 'Got a bit hairy for a minute there. Is Anil . . . is he . . . ?'

'He's unconscious. We won't know the extent of his injuries till he's been examined at the hospital. There's an ambulance on the way.'

She crouches and addresses Mouse, 'Can I have that, please, boy?' I've forgotten all about the shirt but Mouse hasn't: he's picked it up and brought it down. I see it now, in the beam from her torch.

'Give,' I say, and Mouse lets her take it from his jaws.

'Is this what I think it is?' she asks.

'Yes. Mouse dug it up in Anil's plot. You'll see the hole at the foot of the staircase.'

At that moment, my teeth start to chatter and she calls, 'Rob!' Her DC runs over. 'Find a blanket for Ms Williams, will you, and an evidence bag for this shirt?' She holds it up.

He shines his torch on the grimy item. 'We've got it?'

'We've got it,' she says.

'I'll fetch a bag now, Sarge.'

'Can you also see about a guard for Mr Ahmad for the hospital?'

'Will do.'

'Thanks, Rob. Prioritise the blanket and the evidence bag.'

He runs off towards the cars.

'Come on,' says Bhatti, 'we might as well go after him. Can you make it?' She puts her arm through mine and I lean on her.

'Thanks,' I say through chattering teeth. 'Am I under arrest?'

She laughs. 'What am I arresting you for?'

'Well, because you don't know I didn't push Anil over the edge.'

'Actually, we know very well that you did not. I was near the steps when he went over. I witnessed your brave dog defending you.'

'Well, I'm responsible for Mouse's behaviour, and he went for Anil . . .'

'Your dog saved your life. He deserves a medal, not to have his owner in prison.'

I burst into tears, and Mouse, walking silently beside me, licks my fingers. I stroke his soft head.

The area is lit partially by the headlights from the cars in the car park and partly by officers milling about, carrying torches. I see Rob reappear, holding a blanket.

'Come on,' says DS Bhatti gently, taking it from him and draping it around my shoulders. 'Let's get you home.'

We reach the car park.

'My van . . .' I say.

She says, 'You're in no fit state to drive tonight. We'll get a uniformed officer to drive you back to the house. Rob can arrange for someone to deliver your van separately.'

She opens a door in the back of one of the police cars. I give her the van key as I wait for Mouse to jump in, then I climb in after him. 'Thank you,' I say to her.

'No, thank you. You helped us catch a killer. I'll need to take a full statement from you tomorrow, so don't leave the area.'

Before she shuts the door, she says, 'You've got an impressive dog there. If the two of you ever fancy joining the police . . .'

'We won't, but thanks for the thought.'

'Fair enough.' She leans in and says in a more serious tone, 'Take care of yourselves, won't you? You've been through an ordeal.' She starts to shut the door, then stops. 'One more thing: at some point I'm going to want to know what you were thinking, travelling alone to a remote spot with a potential murderer.'

'Yeah,' I say. 'I'm kind of wondering that myself.'

The uniformed officer who drives us back to Coleton Fishacre doesn't speak, giving me time to get my jumble of thoughts into some kind of order. I summarise the events like plot points:

Anil killed Sonny.

Anil fell but is not dead.

Mouse saved my life. Again.

The officer opens the car door for us before I've even realised we've arrived at Coleton Fishacre. Mouse and I climb out and I leave the blanket on the seat and thank the officer for the lift before crossing the circular courtyard to the front door. At least my teeth have stopped chattering.

There's still a light on in the hall and the door is opened by Addie.

'Steph, where have you been? Where's Anil? The two of you were gone so long, I've been worried. You weren't answering your phones. Did something happen?'

I haven't even thought about my phone since messaging Bhatti.

'Do you want to go into the Saloon?' I ask her. 'I have bad news.'

She ushers me into the large room, where we both take seats near the door, she in a chair and me on a sofa, with Mouse beside me, his head in my lap.

She surveys me, dread writ large on her expressive face. 'Don't tell me there's been another accident. Is it Anil? I can't deal with any more.'

I take a deep breath and tell her, 'Anil killed Sonny.'

She stares at me. 'Anil? Are you sure?'

'I'm sure.'

'What happened? Are you all right?'

I stroke Mouse's ears as I tell her everything. By the end, my teeth are chatting again.

'Hold on.' She grabs a throw from the arm of another sofa and drapes it around me. 'I'll fetch you some tea.' She disappears from the room.

I sit, cuddling Mouse, my mind a refreshing blank, until Addie returns, bearing two mugs instead of the usual dainty cups. She passes one to me. 'It's full of sugar, for the shock.'

'Thanks,' I say, sipping and instantly wincing as the cloying sweetness hits my tongue.

'What else can I get you?' she asks.

'To be honest, I just want to take this up to bed.'

She nods. 'Hug first?'

I put down my mug and she puts her arms around me. It feels good to have positive human contact after my awful encounter with Anil.

As if reading my thoughts, she says, 'I should never have let you go alone with Anil.'

'Hey,' I say, 'it's not your fault. We didn't know he was the killer. Anyway, last time I checked, I was a grown woman.' Mouse pokes his head into the middle of our cuddle. 'Anyway, this one would never have let Anil hurt me.'

'You have a wonderful dog there.'

'I really do.'

31

Despite the traumatic events of the night, I sleep deeply. But, when I wake at the usual time, the events of the last few days come flooding back. First, I remember Anil on his rooftop, showing no remorse as he owns up to murder. And then I recall Sonny's inert body, lying among the gorse. I groan, causing Mouse to come running from his bed to lick my hand.

Keen to reset my own body and mind, I set off with him promptly for our run and we really let loose, stretching our legs on the slopes between Coleton Fishacre and the beach. I'm dreading having to tell the others about Anil, but I've promised myself this little bit of time to celebrate my loyal, courageous dog.

I've brought a towel and I join him in charging at the foamy waves, then dashing back out as the waves retaliate. We have a wonderful time, with the fulmars screeching over our heads and seals bobbing like buoys in the distance.

Back at Coleton Fishacre, after I've washed and dressed, I walk out to the Loggia and find everybody already there. Just as I'm steeling myself to tell them the news, Toby gets up from the table and offers me a hug, which I accept.

'What was that for?'

'Oh, only for catching Sonny's killer,' he says.

The others get to their feet and gather around me by the coffee machine, patting me on my shoulders and back.

I catch Addie's eye. 'I take it you told them?'

She nods. 'I hope that was all right. I thought it would save you from having to revisit . . . you know.'

I nod. 'I appreciate that. I can't say I was looking forward to it.'

'Sit down,' says Seb. 'I'll get you a coffee. I can fill your thermos, too.'

I pass him the flask. 'Thank you.'

The others take their seats and I sit in the nearest vacant seat, facing the views. From my companions' faces, I can see they're all bursting to ask me questions.

Koko sips from her cup before saying, 'I cannot believe I went up there with him the day before.'

'Steph doesn't want to talk about it,' says Sarah.

But I say to Koko, 'You weren't in any danger. It would have been fine for me, too – except that Mouse found a piece of evidence. That's when Anil turned, because he knew he was in trouble.'

'What evidence?' asks Sarah.

'I'm not sure how much I'm allowed to share. I've still got to give my statement to the police.'

Seb brings my cup of coffee, placing the thermos at my feet, and I smile my thanks as he returns to his chair.

'I have some good news,' says Addie. 'Delilah is being released from hospital today.'

'Thank god for that,' says Sarah.

'Really?' says Toby. 'I thought you didn't like her.'

'I can't stand her,' says his wife.

'But you didn't mean to make her so ill that she lost consciousness, did you?' I say.

She scowls at me. 'What are you talking about?'

My hands are shaking and I set down my cup. 'I'm talking about you, putting foxglove leaves in Delilah's drinks bottle.'

There's a collective gasp, and Toby says, 'Now, hold on.'

I lean forward. 'You told me yourself, Toby, that Sarah's been jealous of Delilah for years. And I saw her coming out of Delilah's room the day before she was taken to hospital.'

'Now, now,' says Addie.

But I address Sarah: 'You work on gardening programmes, so I imagine you've heard warnings about foxgloves. But you got the dosage wrong, didn't you?'

She's about to argue again. But then the fight goes out of her and she simply nods.

With a frown, Koko says, 'Delilah can be quite an annoying lady, but I do not understand why you would dislike her so much as to poison her.'

'Have you seen her?' says Sarah. 'She's ridiculously gorgeous – all long legs, shiny hair and flawless skin. When Toby used to work with her, he talked about her non-stop. He was smitten. I couldn't believe it when she turned up here. Anyway, Steph's right,' she says, with a resigned sigh. 'I didn't mean to make Delilah seriously ill. I only wanted to send her home from the competition, and away from my husband.'

Toby looks as if he's been smacked. Staring at her, he says, 'Smitten? With Delilah? Darling, I'm smitten with *you*. You must know I'd never look at another woman.'

'Also,' says Koko casually, spreading margarine on a bread roll, 'you do know that Delilah is a lesbian? She is going to marry her long-term girlfriend early next year.' She bites into her roll.

'Of course she is!' says Sarah. She shoves back her chair, so that it scrapes on the wooden flooring, then she stomps into the house.

With an apologetic look at the rest of us, Toby gets to his feet and hurries after her.

32

Mouse and I walk out to the van after breakfast in time to see Sarah and Toby's Volvo leaving the car park. I hope that, like us, they're on their way to a police station.

We make the half-hour trip to Torquay with the windows open to a salty breeze, reminding us of our earlier outing to the beach.

Inside Torquay Police Station, there's a surreal moment when DS Bhatti leads me through an office filled with police officers and admin staff, and they all get to their feet and clap.

'I hope you know they're applauding the dog,' she says with a smile as heat flushes my cheeks.

'That's all right, then,' I say. 'He deserves it.' Mouse knows it, too, stopping to be petted by several of his admirers en route.

As soon as we're seated in the interview room, Rob comes striding in. He bends to whisper something to his sergeant. She looks at me.

'Rob says there's been a confession on the poisoning case.'

'Oh good!'

She looks surprised. 'You mean, you didn't know about this?'

'No, I did. I mean, Sarah confessed to us all at breakfast. I just wasn't sure she was going to turn herself in.'

'Apparently, she just called in at Brixham Police Station.'

'Right. So, what happens next?'

'That's down to Ms Deville.' She glances at her DC. 'Sit down, Rob.' He sits and busies himself with the laptop.

I frown. 'You mean, Sarah might not be charged?'

'We're waiting to see if Ms Deville wants to press charges. You'd be surprised how many victims choose not to, often against our advice. I find it abstruse.' She says this last with a quick glance towards her junior colleague.

'It's anathema to me,' says Rob.

They both laugh.

With a sigh, I ask, 'What has Delilah said?'

Consulting the laptop, Rob says, 'Ms Deville has been released from hospital this morning, and we have reason to believe she will be making an appearance shortly at Poplars Farm.' He glances at me. 'We've not had a chance to speak to her yet.'

'You can go over there and talk to her, Rob,' says Bhatti.

'Right, Sarge. Will do.'

'Now,' says the sergeant, turning her attention back to me, 'I believe you have a statement to give us.'

Nearly two hours later, I'm pulling in at Poplars Farm car park, where, thankfully, there's not a journalist in sight. Word must not have got out yet about Anil's arrest.

Mouse and I walk through the gate to the gardens, where he is greeted immediately by an enthusiastic Chaplin. I wonder if that means Toby has come straight here from the station. I let Mouse off the lead and the two run off to play while I turn my attention to Delilah, who was unconscious the last time I saw her. She is now seated on a bench that surrounds the trunk of her tree. A book in her hands, her back resting against the bark, she is thankfully a far cry from the pale, prostrate form the paramedics bore away.

Seeing me watching, she waves and moves to stand up. 'Steph! Hi!'

'Don't get up,' I call, but she ignores me, using one hand to push herself to standing. I walk to meet her and she throws her arms around me and plants a kiss on my cheek.

'What was that for?' I ask her.

'That's for saving my life. If you hadn't told them it was digitalis poisoning, I might have died.'

'I'm sure they'd have worked it out.'

But she shakes her head. 'I found out that they'd been planning to treat me for heatstroke until you told them it was digitalis. I can't believe Sarah had it in for me like that. I mean, I knew she didn't like me much, but still . . .'

'It does seem quite extreme,' I agree, helping her back to her seat before joining her on the bench. 'But it was clear she didn't know enough about dosages. She was only trying to make you a bit sick, to send you home and keep you out of Toby's way.'

'Oh well,' says Delilah, 'if she only wanted to make me *a bit* sick . . .'

I hold up my hands. 'I know . . . Anyway, how are you feeling?' I study her. She still has shadows under her eyes, and her cheeks are slightly sunken, her frame more spare than I remember.

'Sooo much better!' she beams. 'I think now I'm just weak from barely eating while I was ill.'

'Did you know Sarah has turned herself in?'

She nods. 'I just had a call from the police. They want to know if I'm going to press charges against her. What do you think I should do?'

'I think you should. Otherwise, she might do it to someone else.'

She considers this, then shakes her head. 'I don't *think* so. Apparently, she's showing remorse. I'm quite tempted to leave it. I mean, Toby's a good friend – or used to be – and I'm not sure I want to get caught up in a legal case when I've got a wedding to plan.'

'Well, it's up to you,' I say.

She smacks her forehead. 'I can't believe I'm sitting here going on about me after what you've been through.'

'That's all right. You've been out of the loop.'

Her eyes fill suddenly with tears. 'I really liked Sonny.'

'Me, too.' I look away, not wanting to start crying myself.

'Anil didn't hurt you, did he?'

'No. He tried to, but Mouse didn't let him.'

She looks horrified. 'Oh my god.' She shudders. 'I'm really shocked at Anil. I thought he was a bit arrogant, but I never thought he'd hurt someone.'

'Same here. Except I didn't even think he was especially arrogant. He was obviously desperate.'

She pulls a face. 'You know, it's not a very nice feeling, to think that someone could hate you like that.'

I realise her mind has reverted to her own situation, which makes sense. She's had little else to think about in hospital.

'Sarah doesn't hate you. She just thought you were after her husband.'

For a moment, her mouth becomes an 'o' of surprise. Then she says, 'Are you sure?' When I nod, she says, 'Doesn't she know I'm a lesbian?'

'She does now. Koko told her.'

'I like Koko,' she pronounces. 'She says what she thinks. Talking of which.' She waves an arm at her garden. 'What do you think?'

'It's beautiful,' I say.

'Do you think I've cheated, not doing the work myself?' she asks quietly, with a look of concern.

'Absolutely not. For a start, you were sabotaged, and also, this entire garden is from your designs.'

She nods, looking reassured. 'I can't believe how Mike and the volunteers did all of this for me. I'm going to spend the whole day here, enjoying my very own slice of woodland.' I give her a hug and leave her to it.

When I pass by later, she's lying on her back on the ground beneath her tree, her eyes closed in sleep, her hair spread out around her, looking like a fairy creature of the woods.

33

By the end of Friday, all of the gardens except Anil's are complete. It turned out that Chaplin was there with Toby, who had been allowed to continue, the rationale being that he clearly hadn't known about the poisoning. Although there's no denying that his mirrored landscape is a feat of reflective brilliance, I can't decide if it's spectacular or a gimmick too far. His wife doesn't make an appearance.

When I ask about her, he says, 'She's taking some time to herself.' I don't press him for more information. As far as I'm concerned, she's had a very lucky escape, as Delilah has decided not to pursue a court case.

Seb's portion of moorland is lovely, but I'm not convinced it qualifies as a garden, despite the seating area, created from the more sympathetic slate chippings. In contrast, Koko's design is exquisite. She has created a prairie-style garden, with undulations of tufted grasses including stipas and *Miscanthus sinensis* 'zebrinus' growing alongside clumps of pale-flowered perennials, such as the white, airy *Gaura lindheimeri* and pastel-pink achilleas. Abstract sculptures punctuate the low-growing mounds of *Stachys byzantina* 'Silver Carpet'. I stop to stare at one point, when she's putting in the last few plants, and she looks up from her planting.

'What do you think?' she asks.

'It's spectacular,' I say. There's a warm sea breeze, which runs its fingers through the delicate stems of the perennials and grasses, causing an effect like the rippling of water. I find myself disagreeing with Sonny's opinion that it needs a single focal point.

In my own garden, now that the mural is complete, I've closed the remaining gap on the back fence using some reserved trellis and five passionflowers. Alex and Jay have kept their promise of filling the pond and there is now a still, clear surface, offering changing reflections depending on where you stand. Mattie's trompe l'oeil reflects artfully, so that her painting is not only a trick in itself, but is also a reflection of itself. As Alex succinctly puts it, 'I like it. But it does my head in.' If I wanted to sum up my creation, I think this would make the perfect quote.

Back at the house that evening, I run my cool bath, adding salts to soothe my aching muscles. I climb in and am soon lost in my thoughts. So much has happened in less than a week. I keep picturing poor Sonny, frightened and stranded on that cliff edge, and how Anil gave her the shove that ended her life.

With a shudder, I pull my thoughts away from her death and focus instead on recalling her warmth and encouragement as my mentor – and how I've dedicated every plant to her memory. In spite of the heatwave, the infighting, the poisoning and the murder, I have built a garden that I'm proud of. I'm sure Sonny would have been proud of me, too. Crossing all my fingers and toes, I wonder if there's a chance I might win.

34

My brother Danny brings his two oldest kids, Alice and Frankie, to the opening of the Coleton Fishacre Flower Show. Although I won't be doing any gardening today, I have donned the tool belt chosen by Alice for my Christmas present. I am also now wearing an official flower show t-shirt. Addie sweetly presents each of the kids with a t-shirt of their own, which they pull on immediately and wear with great pride, despite the fact that the garments are designed for adults, and hang down past their knees.

We start by going around the stalls that have been set up in the field at Coleton Fishacre. There are plant nurseries galore in attendance, and I wish – as I always do when surrounded by beautiful plants – that I had a garden of my own. *One of these days*, I promise myself, thinking of my bank balance, which has been looking a lot healthier recently.

We're at the show before the crowds, and the kids enjoy running from stall to stall, making friends with the stallholders.

Then, to Alice and Frankie's delight, we board the minibus, which will provide a shuttle service to the show gardens at Poplars Farm throughout the show. Unlike the rusty orange banger employed during the run-up, this is a shiny model, supplied by a local taxi firm. It even has air conditioning.

When we reach the farm, I lead them past the show gardens to the oak tree, where a small platform has been set up for the announcement of the winners.

Addie gets up first and welcomes everyone to the inaugural Coleton Fishacre Flower Show, before introducing the judges of the garden design competition, Frank and Gillie, along with Paul, Sonny's husband.

The small crowd of designers with their families, along with volunteers and a few journalists, falls silent as these three take the stage. Glancing around, I see Seb with a woman and child, plus Delilah with her arm around another young woman. As soon as Addie stepped down from the stage, she was flanked by a pair of teenagers who must be her children. She catches my eye and we exchange a smile.

'Could the designers come to the front?' asks Paul, and I step forward with my fellow competitors. We join hands and nod encouragement to one another as Paul smiles down at us.

'It's my honour to be here today, in my late wife's stead. And I don't need Sonny to be here to know what she would say to you. She would tell you how proud she is of every one of you, for building a spectacular garden in such limited time and space.' He has hit the nail on the head, and we all laugh. 'And she would also say,' he continues, '"Come on, Paul, no one wants to hear you waffling on!"' We laugh again.

He glances at Frank and Gillie, on either side of him. 'I've been told that these two had a very tough time choosing the winners, but I have the easy bit. It is my pleasure to announce that the Coleton Fishacre Gold goes to . . .' he pauses for dramatic tension, and I hold my breath, '. . . Koko Yamada for her exquisite, painterly planting in "Meet Me on the Prairie". The crowd erupts in cheers and applause as Koko steps up to receive her medal and certificate. I'm surprised to find that I don't feel envy. Her garden is, indeed, exquisite.

After Koko has posed for her picture, Paul continues, 'And now for the silver.' There's another long pause before he announces, 'This one goes to Steph Williams for her innovative design and visitor experience in "The Journey".' Although Delilah and Seb have let go of my hands so I can collect my prize, I stand frozen, sure I've misheard. 'Come on, Steph,' says Paul. Delilah pushes me gently forward, and I step on to the stage, where Paul gives me a hug and whispers, 'You and your amazing garden were Sonny's favourite.' There are tears in my eyes as I smile for my photograph before receiving a hug from Gillie and a handshake from Frank.

After I've stepped down, the kids run over with Danny to hug me before we listen to the final announcement: Delilah wins bronze for 'Into the Woods', and she's clearly thrilled. Glancing around, I see that Toby and Seb are shaking hands and clapping each other on the back in commiseration.

I leave my family to walk over. 'You OK with the verdict?' I ask them.

Toby shrugs. 'My garden's already sold to Channings Wood men's prison, though god knows what the prisoners'll make of it. Heigh-ho. It's all money in the pocket, plus some decent publicity.'

'Oh, that sounds good!' I say. 'How about you, Seb?' I'm expecting a gloomy response, but he smiles and gestures towards the woman and girl I saw him with earlier, who are standing close by.

'It's all good. Jan says I don't have to move out . . . I won't have to leave her and Millie.'

I squeeze his arm. 'Oh, that's great news.'

He beams and nods towards Delilah. 'And it's all thanks to her.'

I frown. 'What are you talking about?'

'Didn't you hear?' When I shake my head, he says, 'Delilah's the one that wrecked my garden, with the digger you hired. Apparently, her dad was a bit of a sod in her childhood, and she's had a thing ever since about men who bully women.' He meets my eye. 'You were the one being bullied – you know, over the tree you took?'

When I blanch, he says, 'It's all OK! When Delilah told me why she'd done it, I realised it was time to make a change. So I've signed up to anger management classes, and Jan says I can stay so long as I keep up with them.'

I don't have time to absorb all of this, as Alice and Frankie have reappeared and are dragging me by the hands. Laughing, I give in and let them pull me towards the gardens.

We start at the opposite end, with Delilah's woodland plot, where we smell the bluebells and admire the big tree before moving on to Anil's garden, which has been blocked off with metal fencing.

214

Alice asks, 'Is this the garden by the man that killed Paul's wife?'

I raise an eyebrow at my brother before answering, but he shrugs to show he has no idea how she knows about this. 'Yes,' I tell Alice, 'he didn't have time to finish before he was arrested, so it's not safe. You can see pictures on the fence here, though.' Glancing at Frankie, I ask, 'Shall I pick you up?'

Frankie shakes his head. 'I don't think I'd like a garden by a murudderer.' No one corrects his pronunciation. I, for one, am hoping it's a word he won't need to use very often.

We move on to Toby's garden, where the kids run around, oohing and aahing over their reflections in the myriad shiny surfaces. Toby is now in situ, polishing one of the mirrors, and he laughs at the children's enthusiasm.

'Did you show them the pictures of the rooftop?' he asks. Lowering his voice, he checks, 'Is that too close to the bone?'

I shake my head. 'It doesn't seem real that I was up there, to be honest. By the way, do you know who copied his garden years ago, so that he insisted on keeping that screen up?'

He flushes and I stare at him. 'Wait! Was it you?'

He screws his eyes shut. 'If I admit it, will you promise never to mention it again?'

'Er . . . maybe.'

Opening his eyes, he says ruefully, 'Not my finest hour.'

'Oh my god, Toby!'

The children run past us, out of the garden, and I join Danny in racing after them, to Seb's garden, where we pay only a cursory visit to the slice of Yorkshire moor, with Danny quickly intercepting Frankie as he prepares to wade into the stream.

At the next plot along, Alice pronounces Koko's miniature prairie 'pretty but not very exciting', and Frankie dismisses it as, 'a bit messy'.

Koko shakes her head when I try to apologise. 'It is not a garden for children. I understand this.'

Finally, we reach my garden. Gertrude is already there, hanging out with a fellow volunteer. With short grey hair, a stocky physique and a face full of mischief, he can only be the 'young man' she told me about.

'Ryan?' I ask.

His eyes grow wide. 'How did you know?'

Gertrude puts a finger to her lips, so I just laugh, shake his hand and introduce my family to the pair of them.

Alice and Frankie immediately insist on walking the spiral path to the middle and back . . . repeatedly. Danny and I, meanwhile, walk it once before sinking gratefully on to the bench on the far side of the dew pond, with our backs to the mural. I remove my cap to wipe my forehead.

'It's so hot,' I say, replacing my cap and fanning my face with the flower show brochure.

'You should have put in some shade,' says Danny. 'Like Delilah's tree.'

'I know. I should have incorporated a canopy or something.' I laugh. 'Though I'd have needed sponsorship money, because it would have had to be custom-made, in the shape of a spiral.'

'It's a lovely garden,' says Danny. 'You've done great.' He gestures to the twisted stems of the corkscrew rush, standing in big clumps at the edges of my pond. 'You've got some weird and wonderful stuff going on. It's kind of eerie, with the strange carved seats and the ornate mirror.'

I grin. 'That's what I was going for!'

He turns to examine the mural. 'And that's awesome.'

'I know. Mattie did me proud. Oh – and I was interviewed yesterday by the production company Sarah works for, Wild Path Productions, so I'll be on the TV show they're making.'

'That's great!' he says, giving me another hug before meeting my eye. 'I saw they've made a little memorial to Sonny. Did you want a quick look?'

I shake my head. 'I had a look yesterday. It's lovely, but I don't need to see it again.'

'OK. In that case, did I see a sign for ice cream?'

He calls the kids and we walk to the next field, where the refreshments table has been transformed into an ice-cream stall. I sink with relief on to a bench and tuck into a 99 cone.

Frankie gets distracted from his own ice cream by the arrival of Mouse, leading Mike by the leash.

'Thanks for minding him,' I say, as Mouse runs first to me and then to the kids for cuddles.

'Oh, he's been a very good man,' says Mike in a doggy voice, making Alice and Frankie laugh.

'He's being Mouse!' says Frankie, slapping his legs with glee.

Mike joins us. 'Did you see the memorial?' he asks quietly.

I nod. 'It's a nice gesture.'

At that moment, Frankie complains loudly, 'I'm still too hot.'

'Me, too,' says Alice.

'We're all too hot,' says their father. 'Time to take Mouse to the beach? We can cool down in the sea.'

'Yayyy! Seaside!' shout Alice and Frankie, jumping up and down.

As we walk towards the car park, the children running ahead with an excited Mouse, Danny says quietly, 'How are you feeling about meeting your birth mother in a few days?'

'Nervous, excited and scared,' I say.

He squeezes my hand. 'She's going to love you.'

'That's what Mum said. I'm just hoping Verity didn't have a bad reason for giving me up. You know, like she knew I was going to be a gardener and she hates plants.'

'That'll definitely be it,' he deadpans. He shouts suddenly, 'Alice! Frankie! Stop when you reach the gate!'

'We know!' Alice shouts back. 'We're not babies!'

Danny says, 'I have to go. But we'll drop Mouse back in time for tea.'

'Thanks.'

'And congrats. I'm proud of you.'

He kisses me on the cheek, then strides after his kids, who are waiting impatiently beside the gate to the car park.

I check my watch. It's nearly ten. And, if the number of vehicles poised to pour through the main gate is anything to go by, it looks like Addie and Sonny were right: all publicity really is good publicity.

Strolling back to my garden, I take a seat in a folding chair with its own parasol on the grass verge opposite, and await my first visitors. Gertrude and Ryan are holding hands, and she shoots me a wink. I'm glad to see that the situation has worked out for her.

I'm messaging my parents about my silver medal when the main gate is opened, the visitors' car park starts to fill and hordes of people begin streaming through the little gate to the show gardens. I am kept busy all day answering questions about the plants – my toad lilies, with their violet spots, are especially popular – along with who created the trompe l'oeil, how I went about designing and building my spiral, who made the furniture, et cetera, et cetera.

Around lunchtime, Addie comes over. 'Congratulations,' she says, and we share another hug.

'Thanks so much. For everything.'

'You're very welcome.' Turning, she nods towards Mike, who is busy talking to some visitors near Seb's garden.

'He really likes you,' she says quietly.

'And I really like him,' I say.

'Good,' she says, squeezing my hand to let me know how pleased she is. Gesturing to the hordes, she says, 'Sonny would have loved this.'

35

Three days later, my intricately planned and developed garden has been entirely dismantled. It's curious how upsetting I find this, given that it was always the intention. It brings home to me how much worse it was for Seb, when his partially built garden was wrecked by Delilah.

Hope and her husband have been back to reclaim their plants, and Mattie has returned with two helpers to remove her trompe l'oeil, cutting it from the fence with Addie's permission.

'What will you do with it?' I ask.

'I'm going to give it to Sonny's husband, Paul.'

I blink back tears at this lovely gesture, and give her a hug.

By mid-afternoon, the furniture maker has collected her benches and mirror, and I, along with Gertrude, Alex and Jay have returned the bark chippings to the car park, for collection by the company that supplied them.

There is only the pond remaining, which I leave, knowing the farmer has promised to deal with it. He did talk about possibly keeping it as a miniature reservoir, to be connected to his overflow ditches. In this time of unprecedented heat, it's hard to imagine the overflow ditches ever being full again, and I have to remind myself that the heatwave can't last forever.

On our final morning, Mike meets Mouse and me at the house before breakfast and accompanies us on our run to the beach. It's a fine, clear morning, and he falls into an easy rhythm with us. When we reach the sea, Mouse is delighted to have another friend to play with, daring Mike to chase him into the waves. Mike acquiesces, of course.

Mike has brought a thermos of fresh coffee to the beach and, after a while, he and I sit and drink it while Mouse amuses himself by biting the waves as they come rolling in. As Mike puts it, 'The ocean doesn't stand a chance.'

While we're sitting, we find ourselves going over all the events that have happened in less than two weeks.

Mike says, 'I feel so bad about Sonny. If we hadn't invited her to be a mentor . . .'

I squeeze his hand. 'I know. But it's not your fault.'

He sighs. 'It was such a horrible way to die. I'm so sorry that you had to be the one to find her.'

I meet his gaze. 'As my family will tell you, these things tend to follow me around.'

'So, I'm going to meet your family . . . ?' He meets my eyes with a smile and the mood changes. I lean in to kiss him, but a large black dog chooses that moment to shake water all over us.

'Hey!' Mike says to Mouse. 'I thought you liked me.'

'Oh, didn't you know? Shaking water on you is a sign of his devotion.'

'And what about you?'

'Not shaking water on you is a sign of mine.'

He laughs.

'Time to go back?' I suggest. Even the towels are soaked through.

Back at the house, Mike joins us for breakfast and then helps me to load the van. We hug, kiss and promise to get together again soon. As I see him in my rear-view mirror, standing waving, I know we will.

Finally, I strap Mouse into the van's passenger seat with Mr Rabbit, and we set off to London, to meet my birth mother.

36

Verity is waiting for me on the prearranged bench in the London park.

She stands up as I approach, smiling warmly. 'Hello, Steph. I am Verity.' She has a Caribbean accent – Jamaican, I think. She holds out a hand, which I shake. It feels warm and somehow both familiar and strange at the same time. Curious to think that this stranger is responsible for my existence.

'Shall we walk or just sit?' she asks.

'Can we walk?' She nods.

We stroll along the walkway. It's late June, and the well-tended park boasts beautiful borders packed with delphiniums, phlox, hardy geraniums and vibrant perennial poppies.

'You must have a lot of questions,' she says.

I nod. Words are failing me right now. Part of me would like to turn and run. This is too big, too much.

I glance at the woman beside me. She's tall, like me, and wears her hair naturally, in long twists that trail down her back. She has an orange and pink skirt and blouse in an African wax print and her lips and toenails are painted a matching shade of pink. Her look is bold and joyful.

I suddenly wish I'd made more effort with my own clothing. I'm in an oversized black t-shirt with cut-off jeans. The only bright colour is a lime-green sun visor, pulled over my curls.

'I didn't want to leave you,' she says abruptly, gesturing to a bench. We sit, turning to face one another, and she takes one of my hands in both of hers. 'I had to go back home,' she says. 'My father was very sick, and my mother had already passed. There was no one else to look after him. His illness was infectious, and I couldn't risk you catching it. But I didn't know how long I'd be gone.

'I left you in the care of your father, John, and his mother, Denise. It was very hard to do, and I should have known it was a bad idea.' Her voice turns scornful as she continues, 'He was way too busy partying to take care of a baby, and Denise didn't like that he'd had a baby with a black woman. She was a true racist, that woman – she really hated me and she had stopped her son from marrying me, even after I was pregnant. I had hoped, because you were light-skinned, that she would still care for you. That was a big mistake.'

I stare at her. 'What happened?'

'I came back for you after my father passed, of course, but Denise told me you'd been given up for adoption. All those months I'd been away, every time I rang that awful woman told me you were doing fine – when really she'd given you away like . . . a sack of potatoes or an unwanted present.' She sounds more sad than angry, but I suppose she's had a long time to process it all.

'So, why didn't you get me back?'

'You had been legally adopted. I had no recourse. I went to one lawyer after another, but they all said the same thing – the adoption was watertight. Apparently, my ex had made up some story about how I had run away back to Jamaica, abandoning my child.'

'My father didn't want me, then,' I say dully.

She squeezes my hand. 'I'm sorry, sweetheart; I wish I could tell you a different story. That man was a useless layabout and I was a young, foolhardy girl, fresh off the plane, and ready to be swept up by the first man in England to smile at me.'

'What was it like, coming here?' I ask.

She shakes her head. 'Now, that is a whole other story.' She gestures for us to walk again, and we get to our feet.

'I'm sorry about your parents,' I say, as we stroll through an avenue of lime trees.

'And I'm sorry I can't offer you grandparents,' she says.

'I've been wondering something,' I say. 'What took you so long to register on the database?'

'Oh! I didn't even know it was a thing until quite recently, when my friend Petra told me about it. But I was concerned. You already had parents, and it might be confusing for you to have me turn up, all of a sudden. So, even when I found out about registering on that database, I hesitated for a while. It was my husband, Winston, who convinced me.'

'You got married?'

She nods. 'To a very nice man. You know what they say: once bitten, twice shy. I wasn't going to fall for another useless man.'

Her reference to an unfortunate partner makes me think of Ben. I wonder if he's still alive somewhere.

We reach the end of the walkway, where I've left Mouse tied to a tree. He's snoozing beneath a huge rhododendron, Mr Rabbit tucked between his paws.

'Is this your dog?'

I nod. 'This is Mouse.'

At the sound of his name, he wakes up and stretches. I untie him and Verity strokes him. He licks her hand.

'You're a lovely boy, aren't you?'

'He's also saved my life more than once.'

Her eyes grow wide. 'Really?' She looks confused. 'But I thought you were a gardener?'

'I am. But that's a story for another time.'

'There will be another time? I shall look forward to that,' says my birth mother with a smile.

Epilogue

After my meeting with Verity, I still have a week before I'm due to start my next project.

In the meantime, Mouse and I go to stay at my brother and Karen's for a few days, to look after the kids while their parents take a much-needed break.

On the second night, when I've just finished reading all the bedtime stories, and have collapsed on the sofa with a glass of wine, an email comes through on my phone.

The account name is vaguely familiar and I click to read the message.

> Hi. You may remember me. I was at school with your ex, Ben. I saw you on TV with your show garden, and realised this is your new name, so I found you through your website.
>
> I'm sorry but I didn't know who else to contact.
>
> I know where Ben is and I think he might have done something terrible.
>
> Please can you contact me?
>
> Sandeep Chopra

My hand is shaking as I set down my wine glass and begin to type a response.

Acknowledgements

The Gardener Mysteries series owes its existence to a team of wonderful, hard-working people. I would especially like to thank my fabulous agent, Jenny Todd at The Literary Office, for her support, encouragement, dedication, invaluable advice and enduring sense of humour.

My publisher, Embla Books, was incredibly supportive at a time when perimenopausal fatigue made it difficult for me to work, and I am very grateful. Jane Snelgrove, Editor at Large, has been especially patient throughout the many evolutions of this novel.

Huge thanks are due also to Emma Wilson and Melanie Hayes at Embla, who oversee proceedings with energy and enthusiasm, and to the rest of the brilliant Embla team: Vishani Perera, Danielle Clahar-Raymond, Katie Williams, and anyone I've missed!

Thanks, too, to my fabulous copy editor, Jenny Page, and proofreader, Dushi Horti, who were thorough and thoughtful and spotted plenty of embarrassing continuity errors!

Thank you to Lisa Horton for designing another gorgeous cover.

Many thanks are due also to the following people:

Belinda Smith at the National Trust in Devon, for suggesting the gorgeous Coleton Fishacre as the location for *Murder in Bloom*, and for her patience, persistence, enthusiasm and kindness. James Grainger, Head Gardener at Coleton Fishacre, for his beautiful photos of the plants, advice on seasonal interest in the gardens, and for kindly, patiently and always good-humouredly answering my many questions, including, 'What would be a good spot from which to push someone to their death?' Claire Sainsbury, Gardener at Coleton Fishacre and kind advisor. Lauren Hutchinson for additional help and advice, and all the lovely Coleton Fishacre staff who gave me such a friendly welcome when I visited.

Other Experts and Advisors

All mistakes are entirely my own, but there would be many more if it weren't for the expertise of the following people:

> Detective Inspector Scott Kingsnorth, valuable and generous reader and advisor.
> Christina Erskine, garden designer, thoughtful reader/critic and lovely sister-in-law! Find her at The Urban Hedgerow (www.urbanhedgerow.co.uk).
> Fred Gillam, aka Fred the Forager, who generously shared his knowledge about foxglove (digitalis) poisoning. Find Fred at: thewildsideoflife.co.uk.
> Richard Hucker, bioanalytical scientist and forensic toxicology analyst (retired), for putting far more effort and time than I deserved into providing additional advice, especially around paramedic equipment.
> The Horticulture Team at the Chelsea Physic Garden, plus Sally, the friendly volunteer who responded to my email.
> Pardeep Jagpal of the National Poisons Information Service (NPIS), who kindly took time out of a busy schedule to answer my layperson's questions about the treatment for poison(s).
> Thanks to Beth Walton-Cole for reading the early pages, and advising on sensitivity issues. Deb Carden (another

lovely sister-in-law!), for happily sharing her surname with Sonny and not even objecting when her namesake met a rocky end. And finally: Gavin Sargent. You know why.

Bibliography

Enormous thanks are also due to the writers of the following books:

Poisonous Plants in Great Britain by Frederick Gillam (2022, Wooden Books).

Poisonous, Noxious and Suspected Plants of our Fields and Woods by Anne Pratt (SPCK).

Coleton Fishacre: a souvenir guide by Jo Moore, available from the National Trust shop.

A Note from the Author

Murder in Bloom is set in and around the stunning Arts and Crafts house of Coleton Fishacre in Devon, once home to the D'Oyly Carte family and now owned and managed by the National Trust. I have taken some liberties with this glorious location, especially with the site and description of the cliff edge – and my invention of a gorse-filled valley at its base.

About the Author

Rosie Sandler lives in Essex, UK, where she writes novels, poetry and short stories. She loves dressmaking and wearing colourful outfits, which often leads to joyful encounters with strangers. A garden lover, Rosie has been developing her own garden, creating a series of vibrant perennial borders within separate 'rooms'. She dreams that she and her husband will one day live beside a lake. Or at least a big puddle. Rosie is co-author of the Agatha Oddly trilogy of children's detective novels.

About Embla Books

Embla Books is a digital-first publisher of standout commercial adult fiction. Passionate about storytelling, the team at Embla publish books that will make you 'laugh, love, look over your shoulder and lose sleep'. Launched by Bonnier Books UK in 2021, the imprint is named after the first woman from the creation myth in Norse mythology, who was carved by the gods from a tree trunk found on the seashore – an image of the kind of creative work and crafting that writers do, and a symbol of how stories shape our lives.

Find out about some of our other books and stay in touch:

X, Facebook, Instagram: @emblabooks
Newsletter: https://bit.ly/emblanewsletter